UHTRED
THE BOLD

By

H A Culley

Book one about the Earls of Northumbria

Published by

Orchard House Publishing

First Kindle Edition 2019

Text copyright © 2019 H A Culley

The author asserts the moral right under the Copyright, Designs and Patents Act 1988 to be identified as the author of this work.

This novel is a work of fiction. The names, characters and events portrayed in it, which sticking as closely to the recorded history of the time and featuring a number of historical figures, are largely the product of the author's imagination.

It is sold subject to the condition that it shall not by way of trade or otherwise be lent, resold, hired out or otherwise circulated without the author or the publisher's prior consent, electronically or in any form of binding or cover other than the form in which it is published and without this condition being imposed on any subsequent purchaser or owner.

Replication or distribution of any part is strictly prohibited without the written permission of the copyright holder.

All Rights Reserved

TABLE OF CONTENTS

Author's Note

This book is set in a period when Northumbria encompassed a large part of Northern England – a very much larger area that present day Northumberland. In addition to that county Bernicia covered the Borders Region and Lothian in Scotland and County Durham, Tyne and Wear and Cleveland in England. Deira, the southern part of Northumbria, corresponded roughly to Yorkshire.

In the last book of the series '*The Kings of Northumbria*' I said in the historical note that Uhtred the Bold died at the Battle of Carham and, indeed, several sources reflect this account of his death. However, further research on my part leads me to believe that Uhtred was killed some months before the battle by Thurbrand the Hold on the orders of King Cnut (or Canute).   As a blood feud evidently followed his murder this makes it the more likely of the two accounts of Uhtred's death. Therefore this is the version I have followed in this novel.

One source states that Uhtred was summoned to meet Cnut in the hall of a local thane at a place called Wiheal, though it is impossible to identify the pace with any certainty. He and his forty warriors were disarmed and divested of their armour before entering the hall. Once inside and unable to see clearly in the dark interior after the brightness outside, he and his men were set upon by Thurbrand the Hold in front of Cnut and slaughtered to a man.

Why Cnut would have selected an obscure hall, if he did, is unclear. I am also puzzled by his presence. Uhtred was influential and powerful; surely he would have wanted to distance himself from his murder. I have preferred to have Uhtred go down fighting after being ambushed en route to Gainsborough, Cnut's interim base. It also allows me to have two of his men escape to tell the tale and identify the killers.

In past books about the Anglo-Saxon period I have used the ancient names for places, where known, to add authenticity to the story. However several reviewers have said that this is confusing, especially when the reader has also had to cope with the unfamiliar names of the characters. I have therefore used the modern names for places with two notable exceptions. I have retained the Anglo-Saxon name for Bambrough – Bebbanburg as that will be very familiar to readers who like this period, and I have used the old name for Yorkshire - Deira. As this would have been divided up into a number of administrative shires at this time to call it Yorkshire would be confusing.

I have also used Aldred instead of Ealdred for Uhtred's eldest son. This is to save confusion when so many characters have names beginning Ea.

Since the demise of the Kingdom of Northumbria it had been split in two, the Danes ruling the old Saxon Kingdom of Diera, centred on York, in the south and the hereditary lords of Bebbanberg governing Bernicia (including Lothian) in the north.

At the time that this novel begins Northumbria, or what remained of the ancient northern kingdom, was divided into two; Deira in the south centred on York; and Bernicia between the River Tees and the Firth of Forth. Although absorbed by Bernicia in the seventh century, the northern region of Bernicia between the River Tweed and the Firth of Forth was still known as Lothian.

The inhabitants of Lothian were descended from the Goddodin, a tribe of Britons who had more in common with the Welsh and the people of Strathclyde than they did with their conquerors – the Angles from Bernicia. Over the centuries the three peoples of what had become Alba – the Picts, the Britons of Strathclyde and the Scots of Dalraida – had united. However, to save confusion I have used the modern name of Scotland and used the name Scots for the inhabitants. For some time before the start of this novel the Scots had sought to make Lothian part of their kingdom.

Although the first King of the English, Æthelstan, had subjugated the Danes of Yorvik – the Danish name for York – and brought them under his rule, they had retained their Viking identity and their relationship with a king who lived in Wessex was a fragile one. Since Æthelstan's time the differences between the Danes and the Angles – the inhabitants of Deira before the time of the Danelaw – had been somewhat eroded by the passing of the years, inter-marriage and conversion to Christianity; nevertheless Deira stood out as a largely Danish ghetto in the midst of an Anglo-Saxon England. Although people of Danish descent lived in other parts of England, notably in northern Mercia, they were very much in the minority.

Thus in the late tenth century Bernicia was surrounded by potential enemies: the Scots to the North, the Danes to the South and the Scandinavian raiders from across the North Sea, the Northern Isles and from Ireland.

List of Characters

In order of appearance, historical characters are shown in bold:

Waltheof - Earl of Bernicia, Uhtred's father
Æthelred – King of England
Uhtred – Waltheof's elder son, later nicknamed the Bold *(the narrator of the story)*
Ælfhelm – Earl of Deira
Kenric – One of Uhtred's companions, later Thane of Carham
Borg – A Norse boy, body servant to Uhtred, later one of his household warriors
Ulfric – One of Waltheof's household warriors, later Thane of Norham
Olaf Tryggvason – A Norse leader, later King of Norway
Kenneth III - King of Scots
Ælfleda – Waltheof's wife and Uhtred's mother
Eadwulf – Uhtred's brother, later nicknamed Cudel (cuttlefish – an invertebrate) presumably because he lacked backbone
Osmond - Ealdorman of Edinburgh, one of the three shires of Lothian
Malcolm - Nicknamed Forranach (the destroyer), King Kenneth's cousin and successor
Drest – Malcolm's cousin and Kenneth's champion
Leland – Captain of Waltheof's household warriors, later Uhred's captain

Aldhun – Bishop of Lindisfarne, later Bishop of Durham

Ecgfrida – Aldhun's daughter, later Uhtred's first wife

Cædmon – Uhtred's body servant after Borg

Aldred – Uhtred's eldest son

Leofwine - Ealdorman of Durham

Ealdwulf – Archbishop of York prior to 1002

Sicga – Thane of Ayton

Hacca – Osmond's son, later Ealdorman of Edinburgh

Angus – Malcolm's illegitimate son, sometime Ealdorman of Edinburgh

Owain ap Dyfnwal – Nicknamed the Bald; King of Strathclyde

Gosric - Ealdorman of Selkirkshire in Lothian

Iuwine – Ealdorman of Berwickshire in Lothian

Swefred – Thane of Dunbar

Giric – Kenneth's son, later co-king with his father

Sweyn Forkbeard - King of Denmark, later King of England

Eric Håkonsson – Jarl of Lade and ruler of Norway under Sweyn Forkbeard, later Earl of Deira

Sigurd the Stout – The Norse Jarl of Orkney who also ruled over the Shetland Isles, much of the Hebrides as well as Caithness and Sutherland on the Scottish mainland

Wulfstan Lupus – Archbishop of York from 1002 and Bishop of Worcester

Uuen – Uhtred's body servant after Cædmon's death

Edmund Ironside – Son of King Æthelred, later King of England

Horsa – Captain of Bebbanburg fortress under Uhtred

Styr – Wealthy Danish noble living in Deira

Sige – Styr's daughter; Uhtred's second wife

Thurbrand - Uhtred's killer. In this novel I have portrayed him as Styr's son

Osric – Captain of Uhtred's household warriors after Leland

Eadulf – Uhtred and Sige's son

Thorkell the Tall – Danish jarl, later Earl of East Anglia

Cnut – Sweyn Forkbeard's elder son, later King of England, Denmark and Norway

Eirik – A Norse boy, body servant to Uhtred's sons

Ælfgifu – Uhtred's third wife. Daughter of King Æthelred and Emma of Normandy

Ealdgyth – Uhtred's daughter, later married Maldred of Dunbar, brother of King Duncan of Scotland

Wictred – One of Uhred's housecarls

Ælfflæd - Uhtred's posthumous daughter, later wife of Siward, Earl of Northumbria

Chapter One – Invasion

June 985

'Lord, the Danes are raiding north of the Tyne,' the breathless messenger panted as soon as he'd been shown into the hall at Bebbanburg.

Waltheof, Earl of Bernicia, looked up startled from the table where he'd been discussing likely crop yields and taxation with his steward. Viking raids had all but died out during the rule of King Edgar but the last few decades had been more turbulent ones for England.

The present king, Æthelred, nicknamed the ill-advised, was widely suspected of murdering his half-brother, King Edward the Martyr. That, coupled with his weak and corrupt rule, had brought the kingdom close to breaking asunder. The Norse and the Danes had taken full advantage of the situation; not just the raiders living in the Viking homelands, but also some of the Danes living in Deira.

'Are these raiders from the south or from overseas?' Waltheof asked, not so much because he wanted to know, but to buy himself some time to think.

'The villagers which have fled into the hills say that they arrived in fifty longships, lord.'

Waltheof hoped that fifty was a wild exaggeration. Each ship would be carrying between thirty and sixty men and between two and three thousand warriors would be a vast host; nearly as many as the original

Great Heathen Army which had devastated the country over a century ago. Now the Danes had settled and had been incorporated into Anglo-Saxon England, but bands of young warriors brought up on the sagas of Ivor the Boneless and the other sons of Ragnar Lodbrok still occasionally came raiding. However, these tended to be small bands of less than a hundred. This sounded much more serious.

'Will you call out the fyrd, father?' I asked from the corner where I had been playing dice with two of my friends.

'Even if all the freemen and trained warriors from all over Bernicia answered my call to muster, we would be lucky to raise more than two thousand, Uhtred,' my father replied. 'No, we need help from Deira to defeat this army.'

Deira was the name given to the kingdom based on York which had originally been settled by Angles, the same people who had settled Bernicia. Saint Oswald had combined the two into the Kingdom of Northumbria over three hundred years ago but it had been split apart again when the Danes came and conquered most of Northern England. Only the land between the River Tyne and the Firth of Forth had escaped relatively unscathed. This was Bernicia, which my ancestors had fought to keep as an independent realm.

When the old Anglo-Saxon kingdoms had been united under the rule of King Edgar's grandfather, Æthelstan, he had made my great-grandfather Earl of Bernicia and the family had continued to govern the far north east of England ever since. Now it seemed that our rule was about to be challenged.

Older and wiser heads might worry about the future but I was fourteen and newly classed as a warrior. I saw this as a change to win fame and glory and didn't think what the implications of such a large army of invaders might be. However, my hunger for renown would have to remain unquenched for a while.

'Uhtred, take half a dozen men and ride to York. Implore Earl Ælfhelm to raise his fyrd and make haste to come to our aid. Perhaps we can trap this Viking host between us.'

'Yes, father.'

Waltheof frowned and I realised that I should have called him lord. He was entrusting me with this task as one of his warriors, not as his son.

I took my two dice-playing friends, Feran and Kenric, both sons of thanes, and four of the household warriors with me. It was late in the day but the weather was fair and, being mid-June, the days were long. We rode into Alnwick at dusk that day and spent the night in the hall of the local ealdorman. We left just after first light, heading south west to Hexham where I planned to stay the night at the abbey. I intended to cross the Tyne there and then make our way to Durham and thence down the old Roman road to York.

That way I expected to avoid the Viking army, who I assumed would still be in the vicinity of Jarrow. I was wrong as it turned out.

We were lucky with the weather. The first day had been sunny and, although dark clouds scudded in from the west on the next day, no rain fell. However, I wasn't so optimistic as to believe that we would complete our journey in the dry. It might be the middle of summer but it had been a mainly wet one so far and everyone was concerned about a poor harvest.

Being overcast, the day was muggy and I sweated in my byrnie, a coat of chain mail which protected my torso and upper arms. Under that I wore a leather jerkin and a linen under tunic. I was tempted to take my mail off, but that would have been foolish in the circumstances. The only concession to comfort I allowed was to sling our shields across our backs and ride bareheaded, hanging our helmets from our saddles and wearing our leather coifs pushed back. Not only was that more comfortable but it allowed us to hear better, something that proved invaluable.

I became aware of the proximity of Vikings when I heard voices as we rode along a track through the woods on the north bank of the River Tyne. Whoever was chatting away wasn't trying to hide their presence and we had time to urge our horses into the undergrowth beside the track before they came into sight.

'They're not Danes,' Ulfric, one of my father's household warriors, whispered in my ear as we cautiously watched them emerge around a bend from behind the cover of a hawthorn bush and the overhanding branches of an oak tree.

Ulfric's father had married a Dane and he'd been brought up bilingual.

'It's similar though – perhaps Norse?'

I wondered what on earth Norsemen were doing in Northumbria. They lived in Ireland and in the Orkneys. Oh, there had been some who had settled in York and the surrounding province of Deira in the time of the Danelaw, but the latter had now been absorbed into the Danish population and there weren't enough living in the Orkneys to put together such a large army as had been reported.

They could be Irish Norsemen, of course. There were enough of them in Dublin and the surrounding countryside, but that didn't make sense either. If they had landed in force it would have been in the west and they would be making their way east, not the other way around. I shook my head to dispel such speculation and concentrated on the immediate situation.

There were ten of them, presumably a scouting party returning from Hexham to report to the main body. Scouts normally ranged up to ten miles ahead of the army so the implication was that the latter were a lot closer than I had assumed. They were riding two abreast and paying scant attention to their surroundings. Just as I thought that they would pass our hiding place without noticing us, Feran's mare whinnied as she caught the smell of a stallion amongst the Norse horses.

The Norse and the Danes used horses to ride from place to place but they weren't trained to fight on horseback; neither were most Saxons, but one of my ancestors had decided that using cavalry to attack the enemy had its advantages and ever since then the permanent warriors of Bebbanburg had been taught to be ride and fight mounted.

We had pulled up our coifs, tied our helmets on our heads and brought our shields around to protect our left side as a matter of course as soon as we'd hidden amongst the trees. Now I drew my sword whilst the others did likewise or else took a firm grip on the battle-axes that hung from their saddles.

I didn't need to give the order to charge. As soon as Feran's mare alerted the Norse to our presence we erupted out of the undergrowth whilst the enemy were still looking startled. I picked on the warrior nearest to me, a giant of a man with a bushy brown beard into which he'd tied a selection of finger bones and wearing a byrnie and a helmet with a fixed visor with small eyeholes.

I'd always been taught to look my opponent in the eye but this man's eyes were hidden in the shadows behind his helmet. He raised his axe and aimed at my head. However, his horse was panicking and trying to pull away from me. Not only was the man not used to fighting on horseback, his horse had been stolen from a farmer and was more used to a sedate ride to market pulling a cart than combat.

The Viking brought his axe down, but the blow was mistimed and his horse moved away from the snapping teeth of my stallion at the crucial moment. His wild swing not only missed me, but the momentum of the axe nearly caused him to tumble out of the saddle. He ended up bent double. Whilst

19

he attempted to straighten up, I brought the edge of my blade down on his exposed neck and half cut his head from his body.

Leaving him, I quickly looked around and saw that Kenric was being engaged by two Norsemen, one of whom had been unhorsed and was trying to pull my friend out of his saddle as Kenric fended off the attack from the second warrior, who was still mounted.

I kicked my heels into my horse's sides and he leapt forward, knocking the Viking on foot to the ground. I thrust my sword into the neck of the other man and he fell from his horse as his life blood spurted everywhere.

Suddenly it was all over. The others had disposed of six of Vikings but the seventh was galloping away to the east as fast as he could. If he got away he would alert the main host to our presence and we would be hunted down. I kicked my horse into a gallop and chased after the lone survivor.

He had a two hundred yard start on me but I was mounted on a tall stallion who had been fed well. The small farm horse ridden by my quarry was no match for mine and I began to overhaul him. I had my sword ready to thrust into his back as soon as I came close enough when suddenly the Viking's horse stumbled. The beast's foreleg had caught a fallen branch lying across the track. Its rider shot over his horse's head and lay on the ground winded and unable to move. The horse stood still for a moment and then went to crop grass by the side of the track.

I dismounted and was about to thrust my sword through the Viking's neck when I saw that he was just

20

a boy, perhaps a year younger than me. He glared at me and spat his defiance as he struggled to pull his dagger from the sheath hanging from his belt. I put the tip of my sword at his neck and told him to lie still. Evidently it was close enough to the Norse phrase for him to grasp its meaning, or else my meaning was clear, and he stopped moving.

'Hvad hedder du?'

I glanced round and saw that Ulfric had caught me up, closely followed by the rest.

'Borg,' the boy replied warily, from which I assumed that Ulfric had asked him his name in Danish.

'Tell him that I will spare his life if he answers my questions, but if he doesn't I will kill him after cutting off his manhood.'

Ulfric looked at me strangely but I knew that, being newly pubescent myself, that it was the one threat that was likely to frighten him enough to make him talk.

The boy didn't immediately grasp what Ulfric was saying. Norse and Danish were similar but evidently there were some differences. However, Ulfric soon got his message across and the boy instinctively put his hands in front of his groin.

It took a little while but half an hour later I had learned that his father had been a minor jarl who had led the scouting party. I suspected that he'd been the man with the bushy beard who I'd killed as he was better dressed than the rest. To my surprise Borg said that they didn't come from Ireland or the Orkneys, but from Norway itself.

'Our leader is Olaf Tryggvason, the great-grandson of Harald Fairhair,' Borg told them after he'd been allowed to get back to his feet and had been disarmed.

I knew a little of the history of Norway and Denmark. I seemed to recall that Harald Fairhair was the first king of a united Norway, but his grandson had lost his throne to Harald Bluetooth, King of Denmark.

'Olaf allied himself with Otto, the Holy Roman Emperor, against Harald Bluetooth. He had hoped that Otto would help him to regain the throne of Norway, but the emperor betrayed Olaf when Bluetooth converted to Christianity and we were forced to flee across the sea.'

'And land here in Northumbria,' I concluded grimly. 'Does Olaf intent to stay or just raid?'

'We are forced to seek new lands. We heard that the area north of the Danish enclave of York were sparsely populated and would be easy to conquer,' Borg replied. 'Your puny forces won't be able to stand against two thousand Norse Vikings,' he went on to claim with a triumphant smile.

I sucked my teeth. The combined force of fyrd and professional warriors in Bernicia could probably match Olaf's army in numbers, but not in quality. The Norse would be armoured and well-armed for the most part; the fyrd were freemen armed with scythes, pitchforks and a few swords and spears. Most didn't have helmets, let alone any form of armour. The total number of my father's thanes and household warriors, who were similarly armed and trained as the Norse were, was six hundred at most.

'If this Olaf wants land, why is he heading west instead of north?' I asked.

'He has heard that there is much plunder at Hexham. After we've sacked the place, we'll head north.'

'Not south, where the land is more fertile and prosperous?'

'No,' Borg shook his head vehemently. 'We do not wish to fight the Danes; besides, my father said that he had reached an agreement with Earl Ælfhelm that he won't interfere, provided we don't stray south of the Tyne valley.'

It made sense. Ælfhelm was a Saxon but many of his thanes were of Danish extraction. He'd been appointed by King Æthelred, but he was dependent on the Danes if he wanted to keep his earldom. It was clear to me now that my mission to seek aid from York was doomed to failure.

The Earl of Cumbria was not likely to come to our assistance either. His preoccupation was with the Irish Norse, who raided his coastline, and the Strathclyde Britons. They had already conquered the northern part of Cumbria and had laid claim to the rest of it, down as far as the River Mersey.

However, if Olaf intended to move north, it was possible that this would alarm Kenneth, King of Scots, enough for him to help us. Of course, it was a dangerous tactic. The northern part of Bernicia, known as Lothian, had become a bone of contention between our family and the Scots ever since a previous king of ours had agreed to cede Lothian to the Scots in return for their king's oath of allegiance as his vassal.

Their king had died soon afterwards and his successor had reneged on the agreement, denying subservience to England. Consequently one of my forebears had driven the Scots back north again.

To seek aid from the Scots was therefore a risk but one I thought worth taking. Kenneth faced trouble at home from three rival claimants for his throne, all descended from previous Kings of Scots, so he was in no position to try and take Lothian from us. Given the current circumstances, it was more likely that he'd prefer us as peaceful neighbours rather than a few thousand warlike Norsemen. That was my hope at least.

'What do you want to do with this piece of scum,' Feran asked, bringing me back to the present.

My friend was ashamed of his failure to keep his horse quiet whilst we were hiding in the trees and he was in a bad mood in consequence.

'I suggest I slit his throat,' he suggested with an unpleasant smirk.

'No, I promised him his life. No man makes me an oath breaker,' I warned my friend.

Feran sulked like a spoilt child at my reprimand and I wondered for a moment why I had chosen him to be one of my companions. However, now was not the time to ponder about his qualities, or lack of them.

'Ulfric, Translate please. Tell Borg that I offer him a choice. I will set him free but I will blind him and cut out his tongue first. That way he won't be able to betray our presence, not until we are far away at any rate. Alternatively, he can swear on his father's honour and whatever gods he believes in not to run away or betray me. In which case he can remain whole and become my servant.'

'He says that he would rather die than become a thrall.'

'A thrall?' I asked.

'A slave.'

'He will be my bondsman but I promise not to mistreat him. I'll only beat him if he deserves it.'

Borg gave me a wary look after Ulfric had explained. I suspected that thralls were treated worse than dogs by the Norse; I had certainly heard that the Danes of Deira did so.

'He says that, provided he is treated with respect, then he will serve you.'

'Get him to swear.'

After Borg had given me his oath we returned to the rest of his scouting party and dug rough graves for them in the trees. Borg reverentially took his father's sword and closed his hand around the hilt before covering him with earth.

'Now he will go to Valhalla,' he explained to Ulfric.

The rest of the armour, weapons and other valuable possessions were loaded onto the Vikings' horses and I gave my new body servant the worst of the nags to ride. I believed that he could be trusted after giving me his word but I wasn't taking any chances. He wouldn't get far on that sorry excuse for a horse. Besides, the rest thought I was mad to trust

Borg and giving the boy the worst mount mollified them somewhat.

We rode at a canter to Hexham to warn the bishop and the local thane about the approaching Viking horde and then we took the road north into Redesdale. After spending the night at Otterburn we continued up the broad valley to the pass through the Cheviot Hills that divided Bernicia from Lothian. The rain, which had been threatening for the past day or so, had started to come down in torrents. At least it would keep those with any sense indoors. The fewer who knew of our passing the better.

We were soaked and chilled to the bone by the time we saw a settlement loom out of the deluge that had reduced visibility to a hundred yards or so. I had never been in this part of the world, despite the fact that it was in my father's earldom, but I thought that the place was probably Jedburgh. I knew that Bishop Ecgred of Lindisfarne, the island just across the bay from my home at Bebbanburg, had converted the population to Christianity and founded a church there a hundred and fifty years ago, so we made for the small stone building with a tower located between the main street and the river known as the Jed Water.

The sight of a group of well-armed men was enough to drive those few who had braved the downpour back inside and I had a feeling that it wouldn't be long before we were challenged by the town watch.

I dismounted outside the church and looked around. There were two stone buildings, one either side of the church itself. I guessed one was the priest's house, though it seemed rather grander that the residences of most poor priests. The other building had me puzzled. It was two storey and too long to be a house.

A man in a brown robe came to the door of the house. By the silver crucifix hanging from a chain around his neck I surmised that he must be the priest but he looked to be more richly dressed than I was expecting. Most priests wore a wooden cross, not an elaborate silver one. Then I noticed the five or six men dressed in homespun robes who had come to the door of the other building to gawp at us.

Then it clicked. The original church must had developed into a monastery, albeit a small one, over the last century or so.

'Father Abbot?' I asked tentatively, approaching the man in the doorway of the house, whilst shaking my cloak to get the worst of the water off.

'Alas, I am but a humble prior, my son' he replied with a smile. 'Our abbot lives in Melrose.'

It was then that I recalled that the blessed Saint Cuthbert had been a monk at Melrose. The monastery there had been founded hundreds of years ago, around the time that my distant ancestor, Catinus, had become the first of the non-royal lords of Bebbanburg.

'We seek shelter for the night, Father Prior. I am Uhtred, son of Earl Waltheof.'

'We are honoured, lord,' the prior said as his expression changed from one of polite enquiry to one of panic. 'We had no warning of your coming and we have little to offer you in the way of a feast.'

I smiled. 'We would be grateful for somewhere out of the rain to spend the night and a fire to dry our clothes. Anything you can provide in the way of food would be appreciated. I expect no feast; indeed I can only apologise for imposing ourselves on you. However, we would like to get out of this rain.'

'Of course, lord. Apologies. Come in, come in. Brother Marcus, roust out the ostler to take the horses up to the livery stables and prepare pallets for Lord Uhtred's men.'

'Thank you, Father Prior. Ulfric, tell Borg to come with me. He can spend the evening getting the rust off my helmet and byrnie.'

~~~

The next morning the rain had stopped and everywhere steamed gently as the growing heat of the sun dried everything out. I had hoped that the prior might have known where King Kenneth was, but Jedburgh was too far south to take much interest in what happened in Scotland. Before leaving I warned him about the Viking Army and suggested that he and the townspeople should take refuge in the countryside as the town lay on their likely route north.

We reached Melrose mid-morning and at last found out where the King of Scots could be found. The abbot was something of a gossip and liked to question travellers to find out what was happening in the wider world. Not only had he already heard about the Vikings in the Tyne Valley. But he also knew where Kenneth was at the moment.

I had hoped that he would be at Dunfermline just across the Firth of Forth from our fortress at Edinburgh. However, it seemed that he was much further north at St. John's Town of Perth at the western end of the Firth of Tay.

It would probably take four days for us to ride there, and we would have to hire a boat to take us and our horses across the Firth of Forth. Alternatively, we could travel via the bridge over the River Forth at Stirling, but that would add another two days to our journey. I really needed to get to see King Kenneth as quickly as possible if we were to have any chance of combining our forces before it was too late.

It was Kenric who suggested that it would be a lot quicker, and less dangerous as we wouldn't have to ride through Scottish territory, if we returned to Bebbanburg and took a ship north to the Tay.

Dusk was drawing a veil over the land as we crested the last rise and rode down to the village of Bebbanburg. We reached the gates to the fortress but found them shut for the night. Inevitably the hiatus of getting them opened again brought my father to the gate tower.

'Why are you back so quickly, boy? You can't possibly have been to York and back; and what's that Dane doing with you?' he bellowed down to me.

'He's not a Dane he's Norse,' I called back. 'Open the gates father and I will tell you all that I have learnt in your hall. It is unseemly to yell at each other out here for all the world to hear.'

'Don't be impudent, Uhtred. You're not too old for me to beat you,' he roared back.

'I'd like to see you try,' I muttered under my breath.

Both of us were strong willed and, although I'm sure he loved me in his own way, we were constantly at loggerheads these days.

A quarter of an hour later I sat down between him and my mother, the lady Ælfleda, at the high table. I had left Borg to see to my horse and, divested myself of my byrnie and clothes, had a servant rub the worst of the dirt and sweat from my body with a wet cloth before dressing in a fresh tunic and leggings.

'Well, why are you back?' he barked at me before my bottom had even reached the chair.

'Husband, let the boy eat. I'm sure his news can wait for a minute or two more,' my mother said soothingly.

My father grunted and allowed me to take a drink of ale and a mouthful of bread and cheese before prompting me with an impatient 'well?'

'There are two thousand Norse warriors led by Olaf Tryggvason in the Tyne valley. By now they will have sacked Hexham and probably be headed north for Jedburgh. I managed to warn both places in time for them to evacuate everyone but the bad news is that they are here to settle.'

My father sat digesting these unwelcome tidings for a minute or two before he spoke again.

'And you know this how?'

'We ran into a scouting party and killed them all but one boy who we took prisoner. He's the son of a jarl and, after a certain amount of persuasion, he talked.'

'He's the Dane you brought with you?'

'Norse, yes.'

'Pah. He probably spun you a pack of lies to save his own skin.'

I shook my head vehemently.

'No, I don't think so. Everything he said rang true. He even explained what had driven Olaf and his men into exile from Norway.'

'Why didn't you do as I told you and continue to York? If this tale is true, we need Ælfhelm's help even more if this isn't just a raid.'

'Because Olaf has made a pact with Ælfhelm. He'll stay north of the Tyne if the Danes of Deira remain neutral.'

'And I suppose that this Norse boy told you this as well?'

'Ask Ulfric if you don't believe me!' I responded with some heat. I was getting tired of my father's sceptical attitude.

'Mind your manners, boy!'

He glared at me and I had the sense to resume eating with my eyes on my food whilst he calmed down.

'Why did you come back here?' he asked eventually and in a more reasonable tone. 'You could have sent as messenger whilst you shadowed the Vikings.'

'Because it doesn't matter where they go and what they do if we don't have the forces to defeat them,' I explained in as reasonable a tone as I could manage. 'My proposal is that I sail north to the head of the Firth of Tay, to St. John's Town of Perth, where King Kenneth is at the moment. It's in his interest to defeat these invaders too.'

'Yes, I can see that the Scots wouldn't want Vikings on their southern border,' he mused. 'Especially as they aren't likely to stop there. I need to sleep on this,'

He didn't say anything else for the rest of the meal and I chatted to my mother and my nine year old brother, Eadwulf, who wanted to know all about the fight with the Norse patrol.

As my father got up to leave he turned to me and said something that was totally unexpected.

'You seem to have done well, Uhtred. But I think I'd better go and see Kenneth myself. You take charge of the muster and get everyone to move up to Falkirk. It will be easier for the Scots to join us there and for us to intercept the Norse army, using it as a base. Send Ulfric and five others to monitor the movements of the enemy so that we know where they are when the time comes.'

I was staggered that my father was effectively putting me in command of the Bernician army. For a moment I was suspicious. After all I was only fourteen and I would have expected him to put one of the ealdormen in command, but I was so pleased that I quickly forgot my concerns.

Then another thought flitted across my mind. Without Ulfric, I had no one who could translate my instructions to Borg. It seemed that we would have to learn each other's language if he was to be of any use to me.

Chapter Two – The Muster at Falkirk

August 985

As I rode along the south bank of the Firth of Forth the sun was sinking in the west and its dying rays blinded me. As dusk turned into night I could just make out the myriad points of light twinkling ahead of me that had to be the camp fires of my father's army. We were now entering the westernmost area of Lothian, some fifteen miles from the Scottish stronghold of Stirling.

The land to the west of the cliff on which Stirling stood was a boggy plain with the apt name of Drip Moss. To the west, and north of the River Forth, lay the Kingdom of Strathclyde.

Strathclyde also claimed the area south of the river as far as the beginning of the estuary – the Firth of Forth. Where exactly the river ended and the forth began had been a matter of dispute for hundreds of years and the border had moved back and forth over that time.

In recent times the westernmost point of Lothian had been taken as the mouth of the River Carron. A little way upstream a wooden bridge crossed the Carron and several centuries ago a king of Northumbria had built a small fort there to defend the bridge. A settlement had grown up to the east of the fort and now it had expanded into a sizeable town called Falkirk, named after the multi-coloured stones which had been used to build the Church.

The army of Bernicia was mustering around the town and, judging by the number of campfires, it probably numbered about a thousand so far. I suspected that this was mainly the thanes, household warriors and fyrd of Lothian. The contingents from Bernicia proper had much further to come. My escort and I had taken three days to get there but the rest of our men would be coming on foot and that would take perhaps three times as long.

I was too weary to do much that night except eat the food that Borg had prepared and sink into a deep sleep. I awoke the next morning to the sound of rain pelting down on the roof of my leather tent.

Shortly after dawn Borg brought me a bowl of pottage for my breakfast. He scowled at me and went to get clean, dry clothes out of an oiled leather sack. He did what was required of him, but with ill grace. Communication was still a problem, but he had learnt a few words of English and I had picked up a few in Norse. Coupled with hand gestures and demonstrations, we got by.

My companions didn't trust him, of course. As far as they were concerned he was the enemy. However, he had given me his oath and I was confident that he wouldn't break it. Honour was more important to Borg than his life.

I ate the vegetable pottage and dressed before sending for the ealdormen. So far those from

Edinburgh, Dunbar and Selkirk, the three shires into which Lothian was divided, had arrived. They were all veteran warriors in their thirties or forties and, although I had met them when I had accompanied my father on several of his regular tours of Lothian as a boy, I didn't know them well, and they didn't know me. Now I was called on to lead them as a boy of fourteen. I was large for my age with a slightly darker complexion that more Anglo-Saxons – a characteristic of all of my family – but my beard had yet to put in any sort of appearance and my voice was still at the stage when it suddenly changed from the treble of a young boy to a more manly pitch and back again. To say that I was apprehensive as they filed into the cramped space inside my tent would be an understatement.

'My lords, thank you for coming,' I began nervously.

I spotted the look of contempt that two of them exchanged and anger replaced my anxiety.

'You may not like being ordered what to do by me,' I told them, 'but I am the earl's eldest son and you owe me the same obedience and respect as you owe him.'

'Respect has to be earned, boy,' Osmond, the ealdorman of Edinburgh said with a sneer. 'What have you ever done that entitles you to lead men?'

'He has killed a Norse jarl in one to one combat, can you say the same Osmond?' a voice said from the tent entrance and Ulfric entered, shaking the excess water from his cloak.

He pointed at Borg, who came forward to take the cloak from him.

'His father was a bigger man that any of you three and, not only did Lord Uhtred kill him, but it was his plan which ensured that we wiped out a patrol that outnumbered us and all without loss. I doubt that any of you could have achieved that.'

The other three men looked affronted by Ulfric's lecture; after all they ranked only second to the earl in our hierarchy and Ulfric was no more than a household warrior, but he had a fearsome reputation and they held their tongues.

'You've come back with news of the enemy host, I assume, Ulfric.'

'Yes, lord.'

It was the first time he had called me that. I knew it was because of the three ealdormen but it felt good all the same.

'They have moved north, out of the Tyne Valley, to a place called Bellingham on the North Tyne. From there I believe that they are likely to move on to Otterburn and then over the Cheviots to Jedburgh. I have left the others to shadow them but I thought you should know where they are.'

'Thank you Ulfric. Ask Borg to fetch you some pottage and get some rest before you return. From Jedburgh I would expect them to either move north-east to the Tweed valley and the coast, or north-west towards Edinburgh. Whichever route they choose we are in the wrong place here.'

'But we must stay here. It's where the Bernicians have been told to muster and it's where the Scots will come,' Osmond objected.

'I'll send messengers to meet the contingents from Bernicia and I'll leave a few men here to tell the earl where we have moved to.'

'And is my town to be the new camp?' Osmond asked.

I thought for a moment.

'No, we don't want to be trapped against the Firth of Forth,' I said. 'We'll muster at Penicuik in the Pentland Hills. I'll send a messenger to find my father and let him know.'

~~~

Penicuik was a small village on the banks of the northern branch of the River Esk. The latter would provide water for the camp and it was close enough to the Pentland Hills for us to retreat into if the Norse army arrived before the Scots did – always assuming that my father could persuade King Kenneth to join us, of course.

Over the next few days the weather improved and the men managed to get everything dried out in the heat of the late July sun. The contingents from Bernicia slowly arrived over the same period and, by the time that the thanes and fyrd from Durham arrived I was commanding a host of two thousand three hundred men.

At the end of the week two of Ulfric's scouts arrived to report that the Vikings had sacked

Jedburgh and Melrose. They were now camped on the banks of the River Tweed. The question was, would they move westwards, or east towards Berwick and the coast?

They did neither. Three days later Ulfric arrived to say that they were advancing north along the valley of Eddleston Water towards Edinburgh. Penicuik lay right in their path and I began to worry where my father was. If he didn't arrive with the Scots in the next few days I would be faced with a stark choice: face the Norsemen with the army I had, or retreat into the Pentlands and hide.

The former meant almost certain defeat as I had only a third of the number of experienced warriors that the enemy had and I couldn't rely on the fyrd standing against the fierce heathens. On the other hand the latter option, although preserving the army for now, would be seen by everyone as a defeat without a blow being struck. Morale would plummet and, in any case, my pride wouldn't allow me to make that choice.

I spent a sleepless night, tossing and turning as I tried to imagine what my father would do. In the end I didn't have make any decisions. Just after noon one of the outlying pickets rode in with the news that a great host was advancing from the west. My father had come and he had brought Kenneth's cousin, Malcolm Forranach, and over two thousand wild Scotsmen with him.

~~~

Osmond was furious, as were most of our people. In exchange for Kenneth's help Waltheof had agreed to hand over the shire of Edinburgh with its stronghold to him. This would give the Scots a substantial foothold south of the Forth and, as far as I could see, it would be the first step to losing the whole of Lothian to them. The firth was a natural obstacle which provided us with a clearly defined border. The River Tweed was the next obstacle to the south and, once the Scots had their foot in the door, there was little to prevent them from expanding their territory until they reached it.

My father refused to listen to our objections, however. He had given his word and that was that. Of course, he realised the implications, but he seemed to think that, once the Vikings had been defeated, then we could retake Edinburgh at some stage in the future.

When I pointed out that no one had ever captured Edinburgh since the Angles of Bernicia had defeated the native Britons – the Goddodin – over three hundred years ago he roared at me to get out of his sight before he hit me.

Word of our argument spread, of course, and Osmond derided me openly now that I no longer had my father's favour. I had thought that the man would have supported me as I was trying to keep his shire from falling into Scottish hands. Then Feran told me that Osmond had been seen coming and going from the Scottish camp. It seemed that he and Malcolm had done a deal whereby Osmond would become the Mormaer of Edinburgh once he'd sworn allegiance to the King of Scots. For Osmond it meant that he would retain what he had now and for the Scots it gave them a bridgehead in Lothian

However, that was a problem for the future. The Vikings were now only one day's march away and I went to join the war council which would advise my father on possible tactics for the coming battle.

When I entered the small church in Falkirk I found the ealdormen, a few of the most important thanes and my father's senior warriors already there. Just after I'd entered I was pushed out of the way by a large man with a bushy ginger beard who was wearing little other than a saffron tunic and a leather belt from which was suspended a sword with an ornate hilt. He was followed by Malcolm and twenty Scottish nobles, both mormaers and thanes. Mormaers was their equivalent title for earl and I'd heard that the mormaers of Athol, Fife and Strathearn had come with Malcolm.

I was surprised that the Mormaer of Gowrie, in which St. John's Town of Perth lay, wasn't present with his men but I later learned that Kenneth had kept him by his side. The Mormaer of Moray, the region adjacent to Gowrie, was one of those who was in dispute with Kenneth over the throne.

My father and Malcolm embraced and the Scottish leader introduced the hulking red headed brute who had barged me out of the way as his cousin, Drest, and his right hand man.

'Uhtred,'

I heard my name called with surprise. I had expected my father to still be angry with me, but his face was wreathed in smiles.

'Come here lad.'

I saw him beckoning me and men moved out of my way as I went forward to join the party in front of the altar.

'This is my son, Uhtred, who had the distinction of drawing first blood against the heathen Vikings. He killed a jarl and his men, almost single handed from what I hear.'

At first I basked in my father's praise but it was a gross exaggeration. I frowned as I saw the incredulity on the faces of the two Scots. He'd made me look a boastful fool, but if I contradicted him in front of everyone he would never forgive me.

'Father, you give me too much credit. True the plan was mine and I did kill the jarl in single combat, but Ulfric and the half a dozen men with me also deserve your praise for killing the other Vikings.'

'Yes, of course,' my father said, continuing to smile, and I breathed a sigh of relief.

The Scots still looked unconvinced that a stripling like me, who scarcely came up to Drest's shoulder, could kill a Norse jarl in fair fight, but at least the tale was now more credible.

'What are your suggestions for tomorrow, Earl Waltheof?' Malcolm asked, bringing our attention back to the matter in hand.

I was thankful that I was no longer the centre of attention, but then my father thrust me back into the limelight once more.

'I would like to hear what my son thinks. After all he devised the plan that enabled him to wipe out the Norse patrol without losing a man, even though they outnumbered him.'

I think that it was then that it finally sunk in that my father wasn't doing this out of pride in me. Ulfric had been too fulsome in his praise and it had evidently irritated my father. Perhaps he thought that I was too pleased with myself and needed to be put in my place. Certainly it seemed that he wanted to belittle me in front of the Scots and, more importantly, the ealdormen and thanes on whose support I would have to rely when he was gone. I couldn't let that happen and so I had to come up with something quickly.

'Well, this is only an outline suggestion which needs refining,' I began, more to gain thinking time than anything. 'Olaf Tryggvason, the leader of the Norse army, believes that he is faced just by the Earl of Bernicia. Let's not disabuse him of that idea. Furthermore, the Norse are used to fighting in the shield wall. They are not used to facing a charge by horsemen. I suggest that we find a suitable killing ground where we can ambush these Norse invaders and teach them a lesson that they won't forget in a hurry.

'We don't need to merely defeat them, we need to annihilate them to teach them to keep well away from Northumbria, and Scotland too, of course,' I added hastily.

'That's all very laudable, but it isn't a plan,' Drest said with a sneer.

'I'm coming to that,' I replied looking him in the eye and trying to convince myself that he didn't intimidate me. 'We need to find a small valley in which to hide so that the Norse think that their advance is blocked by the army of Northumbria on its own. They need to believe that an easy victory awaits them when they see that the majority of our warriors are members of the fyrd.'

I went on to explain the rest of my plan and, much to my astonishment, my idea was adopted after various nobles on both sides had tried and failed to find flaws in it. After that my father and I rode out with Malcolm and Drest to find a suitable location for the coming battle.

Father seemed pleased with the plan once we had settled the final details and I forgot about my earlier suspicions. It was nearly dusk by the time that we rode back to camp to grab a bite to eat and brief the other leaders. I spent another sleepless night wondering what on earth had possessed men who should know better to put their trust in a strategy dreamt up by a lad of fourteen.

Chapter Three – The Battle of Penicuik

August 985

Borg seemed even more surly than ever when he helped me into my byrnie, but that was probably because he knew that we were about to fight his people. As I left my tent the sun was in my eyes as it emerged over the distant skyline that was the Lammermuir Hills. Borg had my horse ready and I rode out of camp at the head of my father's fifty mounted warriors.

He had been opposed to entrusting me with the most important part of the plan, no doubt fearing I would earn more glory for myself but, to my surprise, Prince Malcolm was insistent that the task should be entrusted to me.

Ulfric rode to one side of me and Leland, the captain of my father's household warriors, rode on the other. In the row behind us Borg carried the Wolf banner of Bebbanburg. He had been pleased and managed to shake off his surly mood when I gave him the honour of carrying it, but my real reason for taking him along was because I worried that, despite his oath, he might sneak away and warn Olaf. I doubt that he knew our plans, but I wasn't prepared to take that risk.

I had allowed him to wear his armour but I had replaced his Norse helmet with an Anglo-Saxon pattern one. I hadn't allowed him to carry a weapon so, of course, he was defenceless. However, it wasn't part of our plan to enter into a melee, so he should be safe enough. If not, well then, he was expendable.

We rode out of camp and headed due west, up onto the slope of Carnethy Hill. From there we watched as the rest of our combined forces marched north east. After an hour the head of the column changed direction and headed up the steep valley between the two hills which the locals called Castlelaw and Caerketton. At the head of the valley lay two more hills, Capelaw and Allermuir and it was on the col joining the two hills that my father would take up his position. The Scots would form up on the reverse slope of Caerketton Hill and wait until the right moment.

My horsemen had two tasks. They sounded simple but the whole plan depended on the success of the first one and the decisive victory we needed might well depend on the timing of our second task.

Just as the last of the Scots, who had less distance to cover and who were therefore at the rear of the column, disappeared up the valley the two scouts who I had sent to the summit of Caernethy Hill to the south west returned to say that the Norsemen were in sight.

'How are they deployed?' I asked.

'Right across the area between the river and the hills,' one of the scouts replied. 'They are in no particular formation; more like a vast herd of sheep on the move.'

'Have they put out any scouts?'

'There is a screen of about twenty mounted warriors travelling three hundred yards or so in front of the leading elements.'

'Then they are our first target, but not until they are further along the road.'

As the Viking horde advanced they must have seen us on the slopes above them but they ignored us. I prayed fervently that that wouldn't last.

Just before they reached the village of Penicuik we suddenly kicked our horses into a mad gallop down the grassy sides of the hill and headed for the enemy scouts. They were taken by surprise and milled about in confusion. Someone evidently kept their head because they suddenly dismounted and rushed to form a shield wall to fend off our attack.

It was what I had expected. Neither the Norse nor the Danes fought on horseback. We each carried two spears and, as we came within ten yards of the shield wall we hurled our first spear and then wheeled and rode away.

About half of our spears stuck in shields, but others hit exposed legs and a few even found the gap between the helmet brim and the top of their round shields. When they saw us riding away they roared their anger and chased after us, despite the yells of the more level headed to keep the shield wall intact.

After a hundred yards we wheeled back and charged again. This time the Vikings were exposed and we charged into them, spearing them and then drawing swords and axes to cut them down. After a few minutes I gave the signal and Ulfric blew his horn and we broke off the fight. As we cantered away we left all but five of the scouts either dead or badly wounded.

By now the mass of the main body were running towards us and it was time to withdraw. We rode away, skirting the village to the north, towards the entrance to the re-entrant. A few hot heads chased after us but they stopped, out of breath, when they realised that they weren't going to catch us.

I turned back and saw that a group of men had got themselves separated from the main body and were dejectedly retracing their steps. They were a good three hundred yards from the rest and so I ordered another charge. We had covered half the distance between where we had halted and the nearest stragglers before they realised their danger. To give them credit, they didn't panic but turned to face us, hefting swords, axes and spears to meet our charge.

Most horses would baulk at charging into a man but ours had been trained for war. We barrelled into the dozen men, knocking them down to be trampled by hooves or cutting them down as we burst through their hastily formed shield wall. Then we kept going, cutting down other individual warriors as they turned to meet our unexpected charge.

By then we were getting close to the main body again and our horses were getting blown, so Ulfric blew the signal to break off the engagement once more. We trotted back out of reach of the Norsemen, who were now furious with us.

When we reached the entrance to the re-entrant we halted and watched as the Norsemen came towards us. They were moving much faster than I had expected at a sort of jog and the front ranks were only a quarter of a mile away now. We collected the spears, which we had positioned there stuck into the ground, so that we now had three more each.

As the Norse ran towards us we moved into an extended line and rode at them, throwing our spears high over the leading ranks to strike the men behind them. It was unexpected so the men who were our targets still had their shields on their backs; many of them must have been hit. We cast our second spears and then rode away again.

A roar of anger from thousands of throats followed us. It was, of course, exactly what I was aiming for. We repeated the manoeuvre one more time and then we rode up into the re-entrant.

The Vikings yelled with excitement. It looked as if they had us trapped. The steep sided hills surrounding us were covered in rocks and they thought that they had us at their mercy. Certainly it was not possible to ride a horse up into the hills and any sort of charge was out of the question. We picked our way carefully along both banks of the burn which ran down the re-entrant. Because we were anxious not to lose horses with broken legs, the Norsemen slowly gained on us. Then, just as someone spotted the Bernician army standing on the skyline at the head of the re-entrant, we turned to follow an animal track off to the left.

The Vikings forgot all about us and formed up to advance towards my father's army. Our task was over, for now. We continued up the track until we reached the col between Capslaw and Castlelaw Hills and then we paused to look back across at the battle taking place between our army and the Norsemen. The front ranks of the Vikings had now engaged with our shield wall and I expected that any second the Scots would pour down the hill from their position the other side of the ridge and crash into the Vikings' right flank. We needed to make haste if we were going to be in position ready for the next phase of the plan.

~~~

The first part of the descent on the far side of the col was as difficult as the ascent had been and I fretted at our slow progress. However, the slow pace allowed our mounts to recover. The lower we went the less steep the slope became and there were fewer and fewer rocks. After a while we were able to mount. At first it was unsafe to ride at more than a walk but soon we were able to increase the pace to a trot, then a canter.

We could hear the faint noise of combat as we rode along the base of the hills towards the re-entrant where the battle was taking place. I had expected to see some of the Vikings already fleeing by the time we turned into it but I was amazed to see that our men were still fighting the Norse army on their own. They were doing their best to hold the ridge line but it was evident that they were close to defeat.

I didn't know what to do. It was obvious that the Scots had betrayed us; they should have joined in the fray as soon as battle was joined. Then, just as I had made up my mind that I couldn't sit idly by and was about to give the order for us to charge to our certain deaths, the sound of horns came from behind Castlelaw Hill and the Scots ran downhill in a disorganised mass of warriors towards the right flank of the Norsemen.

I breathed a sigh of relief as the surprised Vikings broke off the fight with our army and tried to form a shield wall to face the new threat. It was all in vain, however. The Scots cascaded down the hillside, leaping from rock to rock at great speed. Of course a few misjudged it and broke an ankle or a leg and I saw one fellow fall and bash his brains out, but there were few casualties in comparison to the numbers that crashed into the shield wall.

Some Scots leaped into the air and landed deep inside the ranks of Norsemen; others just seemed to flow over the row of shields like waves crashing against the shore. A third of the Vikings were unable to break off the fight with our men and many hundreds were caught in the open trying to move to reinforce the hastily formed defensive line against the Scot's onslaught.

Now was our moment and I gave the order to advance up the re-entrant at a canter. Some of the enemy saw us coming towards them and hesitated, not knowing whether to rush to the aid of the thousand or so Vikings facing Malcolm's army or form a shield wall to face my fifty horsemen. Their hesitation was their undoing. Small groups tried to lock shields to defend themselves, others ran hither and thither to avoid us and some crouched down behind their shields, but they did so individually or in twos and threes, not as a shield wall.

We swept around the groups like water around rocks and concentrated on spearing individuals or cutting them down with our swords. I used my shield to brush aside the spear of one man who tried to gut me and chopped down at his neck. I felt my arm jar as I half severed his head from his body and was nearly dragged from my saddle as I tried to extract my blade.

It came free and the corpse fell away just as an axeman aimed a blow at my horse's head. I yanked the reins viciously to the right and my horse turned out of the way just in time. He would have a bruised and bleeding mouth but he was still alive. I shoved my shield into the Viking's head and he fell away to be trampled to death by the horses behind me.

We carried on until we hit the rear of the Vikings still attacking my father's army. We had arrived just in time. Despite the fact that only a few hundred of the enemy were still attacking what remained of our shield wall, we had suffered grievously. I learned later that we lost six hundred killed and almost as many badly wounded that day. Bernicia had lost so many men that it would take a generation for us to recover. No doubt that was Malcolm's intention when he delayed his attack until the last possible moment. I could forget any notion of trying to recover Edinburgh and its shire from the Scots for a long time to come.

~~~

I was so angry at what I regarded Malcolm's betrayal that I would have gone to confront him in the aftermath of the battle, and no doubt have been killed for my temerity, but I had more important things to worry about. One of those grievously wounded was my father. A Norse axe had cut deeply into his thigh, right down to the bone, which had snapped.

By the time I reached him he had lost a lot of blood and he was deathly pale. I looked around desperately seeking a priest, most of whom were also healers, but couldn't see one. Then to my amazement, Borg appeared with a satchel and pushed me out of the way.

'I clean and sew up,' he said in halting English.

I had half expected him to join the few hundred fleeing Vikings who had survived the massacre. But I was later told that he had followed me closely in our mad charge and had saved my life. Ulfric had seen a Viking with a spear run at me from behind with the obvious intention of thrusting it through my chain mail and into my back. Even if he hadn't killed me I would have been unseated and, once on the ground and wounded, I would have then been a dead man in any case. Several of my horsemen had been dragged from their horses and none had survived.

Ulfric had tried to reach me but he was too far away. The only horseman near me was Borg but I had forbidden him to carry a weapon. However, he still had the Wolf banner of Bebbanburg and that had a sharpened tip at the bottom so that it could be thrust into the ground. He had reversed his hold on the standard and drove the sharp base into the spearman's neck.

Now he was about to save my father's life as well. He uncorked a flask of mead and washed the blood and muck from the wound before producing a clean strip of linen, some moss and a needle and length of catgut from his satchel. He stitched the gaping would together and then tied the moss over it with the bandage.

'Now he rest. Not move. Erect tent over him.' He instructed me.

'Thank you, Borg. You were never a slave but now you are not only free but one of my companions.'

I'm not sure if he understood but he nodded and smiled.

To make my meaning clear I looked around and saw my father's sword lying nearby. I picked it up and presented it to him. He looked at me blankly so I took his hand and folded it around the hilt.

'You now warrior. My friend.' I said in my poor Norse.

He beamed and turned away. I was puzzled until I realised that he was hiding his tears from me.

I gripped his shoulder and squeezed it briefly, then looked at Ulfric, expecting him to be appalled at the fact that I had made a Norse boy one of my companions. He wasn't.

'That was well done, Uhtred,' he said before sending men to the baggage train to find the earl's tent.

We were busy for the rest of that day and the next tending to the wounded, piling up our dead ready for burial in a mass grave and looting those Vikings we had killed for weapons, armour, coins and valuables. The Scots seemed happy to steer well clear of us and only looted the dead that they had killed. I had thought of going to see Malcolm now that I had calmed down somewhat, but by the time I'd made up my mind to do so, they were already leaving for home.

I rode across to the head of their column nevertheless but found out that Malcolm had left the previous day, leaving the three mormaers to deal with the aftermath. They smirked at each other when I asked why they had delayed their attack and I felt my temper rising again.

'One day you will all pay for your perfidy,' I said, but they just laughed.

'Go home and lick your wounds, boy. Kenneth gave his oath not to attack you but he's getting old. Malcolm will succeed him soon and then we'll come back and take the rest of Lothian from you,' the Mormaer of Fife boasted.

'Aye, and Bernicia too if he's a mind to do so,' another added.

I rode away fuming impotently, determined that we would be ready for that day and this time it would be the treacherous Scots who would pay dearly.

Chapter Four – Saint Cuthbert's Bones

Summer 995 to Spring 996

I stormed out of the hall at Bebbanburg, furious with my father and with my brother Eadwulf. Waltheof had survived thanks to the ministrations of Borg after the battle but the broken femur had mended badly and he walked with a limp once he'd recovered.

For some reason he blamed me for this, and for making Borg one of my companions, despite the fact that the former Norse boy had saved his life. We had never got on well but now we couldn't speak together without arguing. Of necessity I had taken on many of his duties as earl as he couldn't ride or walk any distance. However, every decision I made was criticised and, as often as not, reversed once I returned to Bebbanburg and reported to him.

Eadwulf, who was now nineteen, had become my father's favourite and he indulged him. My brother was by nature, indolent and dissolute. He rarely bothered to train with weapons or help me to administer the earldom. Instead, he got drunk, bedded the female slaves and indulged in acts of petty spite.

Perhaps my mother might have been able to curb some of Eadwulf's excesses, but she had died five years ago when he was fourteen and only just beginning to indulge his passions.

This most recent disagreement was over a request from Aldhun, still called the Bishop of Lindisfarne even though the seat of the diocese had been moved to Chester le Street a long time ago. Now Aldhun wanted to move from there to Durham where he felt he and his monastery would be safer. This had been agreed by the Archbishop of York and by my father in whose earldom both Chester le Street and Durham lay.

Moreover Bishop Aldhun had requested my father's support to encourage the local people to help build the new church in which Saint Cuthbert's body would be laid to rest. He had been a venerated man during his lifetime and had attracted hundreds of pilgrims after his death.

It was expected that everyone would help to build the church, which would be the resting place of his remains for all eternity an act of piety, but it would help enormously if the earl, or a member of his family, was present to lead by example.

The Ealdorman at Alnwick had recently died without a male heir and, pro tem, I was carrying out his duties as well as most of my father's as earl. When I was told that I was to lead the escort to Durham and then remain there until the new church was built I practically exploded.

'Father, you know how busy I am, looking after the shire of Alnwick as well as helping you. I can't possibly be spared at the moment,' I had protested.

'Eadwulf can help me administer my lands and I have decided to appoint him as the new ealdorman for Alnwick as well. So you see you can't use that as an excuse for shirking your duty.'

'Eadwulf! He doesn't know how to run a pig sty led alone a shire! What are you thinking of? You know how hard I'm working to build up our army again after Penicuik. Eadwulf has no more idea of how to lead men that I have about sewing.'

'That's enough! One more word and I will cut you off without a penny and make your brother my heir.'

'Then God help Bernicia; you might as well make a present of it to the Scots or the Danes.'

I thought my father was going to have a heart attack, so purple in the face had he become. I quickly left the hall before he had a chance to carry out his threat. Shortly afterwards I rode out of Bebbanburg with Ulfric, Borg and half a dozen of my companions. They included Kenric but Feran had long since deserted my side. He was now my dear brother's closest companion and shared his love of decadence and idleness.

I bitterly resented wasting time, as I saw it, on this fool's errand but my attitude changed as soon as I met the bishop or, more correctly, as soon as I saw his daughter. Ecgfrida was nineteen, five years younger than me, when we first met but she looked younger. However, her intellect was not what you might expect of a young girl. I sat between her and her father on the high table that evening and I found that she could hold her own on any subject in which I was interested. Moreover she made me look like a dullard when the conversation turned to topics I knew little about.

I wondered why she was still unmarried. Most girls were married long before they reached her age. I didn't think it was because she was the child of a priest. Daughters of members of the clergy were not as common as they used to be - Rome frowned on married priests - but the practice had yet to be forbidden. Only monks were expected to remain celibate. I tried to probe gently for the reason behind her spinsterhood but she immediately changed the subject.

I retired to bed that night intrigued by Ecgfrida and, I readily confessed to myself, smitten by her. She was unlike any other girl I had ever met. Most had seemed to me to be superficial and more interested in my status and potential wealth than in me as a person. My father often made withering remarks about my lack of a wife but I was determined not to wed just to beget an heir. I decided to wait until I found someone who would be my soul mate. Now I thought I might have done just that.

The six mile journey from Chester le Street to Durham was uneventful, if tedious. The monks carrying Saint Cuthbert's lead lined coffin moved slowly and had to rest and change over pall bearers frequently. I had hoped that Ecgfrida would ride so that we could talk as it wasn't far, but Aldhun decided that his daughter should ride in one of the wagons with the other ladies rather than on horseback. I was disappointed but, of course, I was at pains not to show this.

I had visited the Ealdorman of Durham before but he preferred to live at Monkwearmouth on the coast where there was a monastery and a thriving port. Durham itself was a fortified town, called a burh, sitting on the top of a steep sided hill surrounded on three sides by a bend in the River Wear. I could immediately see why Aldhun would prefer to live there instead of staying at Chester le Street. After the Viking raids that the monks from Lindisfarne had suffered, both on the island and since they had left it, Durham offered security.

However, it wasn't there that we were headed. For some reason there was no church within the fortifications, so we headed along the west bank of the river, around the southern end of the bend and back up the east bank. The little whitewashed wattle and daub church, known as the White Church for obvious reasons, stood on its own surrounded by a small cemetery.

The first task was for everyone to cut timber from a nearby wood and build temporary shelters in which we could live pro tem. That night it rained and we all took shelter in the only available building - the church.

The next morning dawned bright and sunny. We ate a rudimentary breakfast of stale bread, cheese and berries before starting work again. As the wet undergrowth and pile of cut timber steamed under the growing heat of the sun, Aldhun, Ecgfrida, the prior and I rode north to where a ferry crossed to the north bank of the Wear. It was only small and it took two trips to take us and our four horses across. The operators of the ferry were a man well into middle age and his son. When they heard the bishop saying that we would need to build a bridge over the river the man got agitated and the brawny son became belligerent.

At first I was tempted to draw my sword to cow the two, but I could tell that Ecgfrida sympathised with them. I overheard her whispering to her father that we must not take away their livelihood.

'Perhaps the father could act as your toll collector and I'm sure we can employ the lad as a labourer. After all, there will be plenty of work once we start to construct the new church and the monastery,' I suggested.

Once they realised that they would still be employed the two ferrymen were much happier. However, the bishop wasn't altogether pleased with the proposal.

'I had hoped that the people of Durham would give their labour for nothing. I can't afford to pay them as well as the skilled masons and other artisans we'll need.'

'They might give you one day a fortnight as an act of piety but I was thinking that we could employ the lad permanently. If that's a problem I'll pay him. We need the local population's support and putting some of them out of work won't help us.'

'Thank you, my son. You're already giving up your time, but I won't say no to some financial help as well.'

I gathered from that that I was expected to stay and help with the work. I could understand that seeing the son of the earl getting involved would encourage the others, but I wondered how open ended this commitment would prove to be. It could take some time to build a timber church and buildings for the monks and even longer to replace the buildings in stone. However, I was more than content to remain in the company of Ecgfrida and I was in no hurry to return to the unpleasant atmosphere at Bebbanburg.

~~~

I stayed throughout the winter and in the following April I rose early to put on my best tunic, trousers and cloak. Cædmon, the man who had replaced Borg as my body servant, told me to stop fidgeting as he wrapped red ribbons around my blue trousers below the knee. I did as he asked with difficulty. It wasn't every day that a man got married.

Once I was fully dressed I walked across to the newly completed timber church to hear mass before coming back to the monk's refectory to break my fast with bread, cheese and water. It was a wattle and daub building, like the rest of the new monastery. Gradually they would be replaced in timber or, in a few cases, in stone. The foundations of the new monastic church, which Aldhun insisted on calling a cathedral after the practice on the Continent, had already been dug, but it would be years before it replaced the present small timber structure.

The monastery almost filled the plateau at the summit. The houses cascaded down the north side of the hill and, as that side within the timber palisade was now full, new dwellings were being built to the south and east. The slope to the west was too steep to build on. The only other building on the plateau was the thane's hall. Originally a simple oblong building consisting of one room where the local thane, his family, household warriors and servants all lived together, now it had been extended to provide separate chambers for the thane's family, for me, for Aldhun and for Ecgfrida.

Although it was mid-April a chill wind swept across the plateau, making me glad that I had worn my thickest woollen cloak rather than the thinner richly embroidered one that would have been more appropriate for the occasion.

I arrived early at the church as was the tradition. It wouldn't have done for the bride to be kept waiting by the groom. Ulfric was my groomsman and the thane's eldest girl attended Ecgfrida.

It seemed an age but eventually my wife-to-be emerged from the hall dressed in a yellow cotton under-tunic and a surcoat of green wool. As was the practice for unmarried girls her glorious long auburn hair was worn unbound with a silver circlet to keep it from blowing across her face. She looked beautiful and I couldn't help thinking that it was be a pity that, after today, she would have to appear in public with a wimple covering her hair.

I had naturally sent my father and brother an invitation to attend but they had declined. I was stung by the insult but at least all the ealdormen from Bernicia and even the one from Berwick in Lothian had come with their wives.

It would be inappropriate for Aldhun to officiate at his own daughter's wedding and so the archbishop had travelled up from York to marry us.

I remember little of the ceremony save how pretty my wife looked. Even the feast afterwards passed in a blur, despite my remaining sober. It wasn't until we had been bedded amongst much hilarity and bawdy jests that I later recalled all too vividly what had then happened.

Perhaps it was my fault; I was too eager, or Ecgfrida was not eager enough, but our first attempt at coupling was a disaster. Try as I may I didn't seem able to get my new wife in the mood. I later discovered that the wretched wife of the thane had told her of her own experiences with her brute of a husband and consequently Ecgfrida came to my bed dreading what was about to happen.

Our unsatisfactory love-making almost made me regret marrying her, but there were compensations. Not least of these were the three estates the bishop had bestowed on me as Ecgfrida's dowry. Officially they were church lands, but they had been bequeathed by thanes without heirs and were Aldhun's to do with as he wished.

Two of the vills lay to the south of the River Tweed; one at Carham and one at Norham; and one to the north in the province of Lothian at Duns. I was told that both Carham and Norham had a simple hall but there was a larger fortified hall on the top of Duns Law, the site of an earlier hill fort. That's where I decided we would live. In May, we witnessed the ceremonial removal of Saint Cuthbert's casket from the White Church up to Aldhun's partially built cathedral. Then Ecgfrida and I left Durham accompanied by her maid and my original escort of warriors.

Out of duty we travelled to Bebbanburg first but I wished we hadn't. Our welcome was scarcely warm. My father had grown even more irritable since I'd left, if that were possible, and his only welcome to my wife was a scowl. Eadwulf kept looking at me like a cat who has been given a bowl of cream and I wondered why my brother seemed so pleased with himself. That louse Feran stood near him grinning like an idiot. I soon found out.

'I hear that Bishop Aldhun has given you land,' my father barked at me as soon as I'd introduced Ecgfrida to him.

'Yes, father. The vills of...'

I got no further before he interrupted me.

'Good. It makes what I've got to say a lot easier. I've decided to make Eadwulf my heir now that you have some income of your own to support you and your wife.'

I was thunderstruck. At first I stared at him in disbelief but the smug look on my brother's face told me that our father wasn't having a jest at my expense.

'You can't,' I exploded. 'I'm the eldest and this worthless piece of dung could no more defend Bernicia from the Scots or the Vikings than he could keep his penis in his trousers.'

'That's enough!'

My father got to his feet and for a moment I thought that he would strike me but he staggered and nearly fell until Eadwulf gave him his shoulder to lean on.

'Get out of here before I have you put in chains for your impudence.'

'And which of your men would like to try and do that,' I challenged him, putting my hand on the hilt of my sword.

It was Ecgfrida who calmed the situation.

'Uhtred, it's not worth it. Let's leave this miserable place and go to our new home.'

I nodded and turned to leave.

'Wait, boy!' Waltheof commanded me. 'As one of my thanes you will kneel and swear allegiance to me and to Eadwulf as my heir.'

I slowly turned around and walked back to confront him. He shrank back in his chair and Eadwulf, coward that he was, scuttled behind him. Feran looked as if he was about to mess his trousers.

'Never!' I spat at him before turning back to look at those of my father's warriors who had crowded into the hall to watch the drama play out.

'What, are you going to bar my exit? Come, which of you wishes to face me in fair fight?'

Leland, the captain of the household warriors, shook his head.

'None of us want any trouble, Uhtred. We are sworn to serve the earl but what he has done in disowning you is not only despicable; it is stupid. We all know that Eadwulf is no warrior. I hope that, when the Scots or the Vikings next invade you will return to lead us.'

My father was apoplectic at this and screamed at Leland that he released him from his oath.

'Get out of my sight! You are no longer my captain.'

'Would you serve me, Leland?' I asked with a smile.

'Yes, in a heartbeat.'

'Release me from my oath too, Earl Waltheof,' Ulfric asked, as did two score of men in the hall.

My father paled but he'd backed himself into a corner.

'Very well, but there is no way that Uhtred can pay all of you on the income he'll get from three paltry vills. I hope you all rot in hell.'

So it was that I rode into Bebbanburg with six men and rode out again with thirty. Some of those who had initially supported me had been frightened at the prospect of serving a man who might not be able to pay them and had decided to stay, especially those with families.

I stopped on top of the ridge before dropping down into the valley on the far side and took a last look at the stronghold sitting proudly on top of its rock above the grey waters of the North Sea and angrily blinked away a tear from my eye. It had been my home, the place where I grew up. Now it belonged to my enemy. I used the word advisedly because I had no illusions about the seriousness of the rift between me and my father and brother. Eadwulf, in particular, wouldn't rest easy until I was dead.

Chapter Five – Thane of Duns

Winter 996 to Autumn 997

When Ecgfrida told me I was elated. Although sex between us was joyless, we continued to make love from time to time as I wanted an heir. Now it seemed that my prayers had been answered.

'How far gone are you?'

'The wise woman says the baby will be born in the summer.'

That night I got uproariously drunk with my household warriors in my new hall at Duns Law.

When we left Bebbanburg we had ridden to Norham first. The village lay on the south side of a ford over the River Tweed some six miles inland from Berwick, the seat of the Ealdorman of Berwickshire at the mouth of the river. The vill consisted of the village of Norham itself and two large farmsteads to the south. They grew some crops and vegetables but the main occupation was looking after livestock: cattle and sheep.

There was a small timber church at Norham with an elderly priest and a hall where the rather portly bailiff lived. He was alarmed when so many armed men rode into the village but was reassured by the presence of my wife and her maid and a few other women in the carts, some of whom were servants and more than a few were attached to my men as wives or whores.

One of Ecgfrida's accomplishments was the ability not only to write, but to keep accounts. We stayed for three days at Norham and in that time she discovered that the prosperous looking bailiff had been defrauding the bishop ever since Aldhun had acquired the vill. I could have sent the wretched man to Durham for trial, but instead I contented myself with expelling him and his wife from the vill with no more than the clothes on their backs.

I appointed Ulfric as my representative at Norham and left six men with him to defend the vill and ensure that the taxes due were paid. I also held court there before I left and gave judgement in a number of petty cases.

Far from resenting the stricter rule which had been imposed on them, the freemen seemed pleased. No doubt this was because the bailiff had been open to bribes whereas I had been scrupulously fair.

Carham was a rather different matter. The bailiff was a young cleric who also acted as the village priest. It was smaller than Norham but had been yielding greater revenues, which reflected well on the honesty of the bailiff. I rewarded Kenric's service to me by leaving him in charge with another five of my warriors. Of course, both he and Ulfric would have to pay their men from their share of the income from the two vills, thus relieving me of the need to do so.

Duns was very different to the other two. Not only did it have a stronghold on top of the hill to the north of the town, but the town was quite large.

There were some three hundred residents and there were a dozen hamlets and farmsteads dotted around it. In all the population came to well over five hundred. Of course, most of these were slaves, bondsmen, women or children, but there were some seventy freemen who held land from me and more than a score of artisans.

I soon discovered that the training of the fryd had been neglected and my remaining nineteen companions and household warriors were kept busy training everyone between the ages of twelve and thirty five to fight.

I also decided that, as the vill bred horses for sale, the ablest of the boys between twelve and fourteen would be given training to fight on horseback. There were twenty one of them initially and, when they were ready, it would give me a mounted force of fifty men; a formidable number.

All of this kept me busy and I realised that I was happier than I had been since my mother had died, despite the problems that Ecgfrida and I had in bed. Her pregnancy gave me the excuse to leave her alone for the next six months and I took to sleeping with my men on the floor of the hall. If anyone thought this strange they were too sensible to say so.

Our son, Aldred, was born in the summer of 997 and I felt that my life was complete. I was happier than I had ever been. I should have known that it couldn't last, and it didn't.

~~~

One of my passions was hunting. Not only did I enjoy the sport it offered, but it provided our larder with game birds, boar meat and venison. Much of this was smoked or preserved in salt for the winter, which were harsh in this part of the country. About three months after Aldred was born I set out with Leland, Borg, three more of my warriors, and three huntsmen to look for boar in the woods in the wooded hills to the north west of Duns.

We were still looking for boar trails when Borg rode up to me and said that he thought that there were men following us.

'I can't be certain, lord, but I'm sure I caught a glimpse of the sun shining off a helmet or weapons once or twice.'

I trusted Borg. He wasn't of a fanciful disposition and I couldn't think of anything else that would cause the flash of light amongst the trees that he'd seen. It wasn't a particularly sunny day; clouds hid it for much of the time but the sun had appeared for brief periods. I chewed my lower lip, trying to think what to do.

Before I'd reached a decision armed men flooded onto the track in front of us. They wore byrnies and helmets and carried shields and spears. We were dressed in tunics and, although we wore swords and daggers at our sides, we were armed for hunting with boar spears and hunting bows. Besides, there were a dozen of them and evidently there were more coming up behind us to cut off our retreat.

I had to think quickly or we were dead men. I didn't think for one moment that these warriors had

73

come to capture me. I suspected that they had been sent by Eadwulf. Even though my father had chosen him as his successor, my dear brother was frightened of me and no doubt feared that somehow I would cheat him of his promised inheritance.

It was Leland who spotted the animal track off to our right. It was only wide enough for men on horseback in single file and we would have to beware of overhanging branches, but it was better than trying to fight our way through the shield wall that our adversaries had now formed.

We suddenly turned off along the narrow trail following Leland. The ambushers rushed forward with a roar of rage when they saw what we were up to. I felt guilty about leaving my men to bring up the rear but Borg insisted that I was the next to take the escape route after Leland. Borg, the three household warriors and then the huntsmen followed on. Unlike us, the latter were on foot; necessarily so as they had the dogs on leashes. The four powerful boar hounds had sensed the tension in the air and were barking and straining at the leash to attack our pursuers. The handlers let the dogs go and then darted down the narrow path after us. Unsurprisingly the four hounds were no match for so many armed warriors, but they bought us enough time for everyone to disappear into the trees. In the distance behind us we could hear the enemy pounding down the trail on foot. No doubt they had horses somewhere but they had no time to reach them and remount.

The huntsmen knew what they had to do without being told. They all carried bows and a quiver full of arrows. As we were hunting boar they had narrow points, rather than being broad headed, and although hunting bows were smaller than war bows, and thus less powerful, they were deadly at close range.

The huntsmen climbed the lower branches of trees alongside the trail and waited for the first of our pursuers to appear. Like us they were in single file and, when the first three came into sight, the leader dropped with an arrow in his chest, quickly followed by the second and the third man.

The rest paused out of sight before they started to cut their way through the undergrowth on either side of the track, no doubt hoping to get behind the archers and cut off their retreat; but by then my men had dropped down to the ground and disappeared.

It delayed the enemy enough for us to reach open ground. From there we could ride at speed back towards my fortress but I wanted to capture one of the enemy. Hopefully I could extract enough information from him to confirm my suspicion that Eadwulf was guilty of attempted murder.

'Leland, I'm staying here with Borg and the huntsmen. Take the other men and our horses and ride back to Duns Law as fast as you can. Bring my warband back here.'

'Lord, you can't stay. What's the point? You'll be killed, and the others with you.'

'We'll be fine. I have a plan. Now do as I say; and quickly, before they get here.'

Reluctantly he nodded and they cantered off across the grassland, scattering a flock of sheep as they went.

'Now, back into the trees. I want you three up into the trees again. Your task is not so much to kill our pursuers but to delay them. Borg and I will work our way behind them. I want to capture one alive so he can tell me who's paying them.'

From the way that they were dressed I knew that they were Danes. Even my brother wasn't stupid enough to use his own men.

We made our way slowly through the thick undergrowth, getting our clothing snagged on thorn bushes and the like, until I was confident that we would be behind the Danes. We then turned and eventually reached the trail we had followed to escape the ambush. I was about to set off, with Borg close behind, to come up behind the rear of the enemy when I heard the muffled sound of horses. We withdraw back into the undergrowth.

As we watched from cover a boy passed us leading four horses on long reins. Because of the narrowness of the trail they were in single file with the reins of one tied to the stirrup of the one in front. I let four boys pass us but, when the last one reached us, I stepped out and knocked the lad out with the pommel of my dagger. The lead horse of the string was startled and was about to neigh when Borg grabbed its reins and rubbed its nose to keep it quiet.

I glanced along the track to see if any of the other boys had heard anything, but the nearest one was separated from us by four horses and he was evidently unaware that anything was amiss.

We slung the boy over one of the horses and tied his hands to his feet under the horse's belly. Then we mounted and set off back down the trail to meet the main track through the wood. After a while we emerged out of the trees and I could see my men cantering across the pasture towards the exit from the woods where I hoped that my huntsmen were managing to keep the Danes at bay.

'Well done Leland,' I said, clasping his wrist in greeting. 'Take half the men back through the woods and come up behind the Danes to cut off their escape. Borg, take our prisoner back to Duns Law and see what you can get out of him. The rest of you come with me.'

We arrived back at the point where I'd left the huntsmen to find one of them lying dead under a tree at the edge of the wood. The other two still seemed to be keeping the Danes busy. We dismounted and I led my men into the woods to find the Danes clustered around tending several of their wounded. A few more lay dead with arrows protruding from their chests. I learned later that they had tried to rush the archers and had succeeded in spearing one before they were driven back. However, we were only just in time. The huntsmen were almost out of arrows.

The ensuing fight was a blur. I recall being attacked by two men and, as I was unarmoured, I sustained a cut to my biceps before my attackers were killed by the warriors on either side of me. Luckily the cut was to my left arm and, although it was deep, it eventually healed, leaving no ill effects.

Another wounded Dane lying on the ground swept his sword around in an attempt to cut my legs off at the ankle but I jumped into the air just in time and put the point of my sword through his neck as I landed. Shortly after that it was all over. The few remaining Danes fled back to where the boys were holding their horses and they rode straight into my men waiting at the other end of the trail. None survived.

One of my men cleaned my wound, stitched it up with cat gut and bound it with strips of a cotton tunic taken from a dead Dane. We took their armour, weapons, coins, ornaments and horses and left their bodies for the crows and the wolves to feast on.

Of course Ecgfrida and her women fussed around me when I got back to the hall. The wound was washed in mead, my wife clucking like an old hen about the filthy bandage and the likelihood of infection. Once it was bound up again with clean linen I was allowed to go and find Borg to see what he'd learned from our Danish lad.

'Not much,' he told me. 'But I don't think he knows much. He's the son of a warrior serving one of the jarls who owns land near York. All his father told him was that they had been promised a pouch full of gold each for killing you but he doesn't know who had paid them. They had received half of the payment now and were to receive the balance on production of your head.'

'Are you certain that's all he knows?'

'Yes, the boy's terrified, especially after I told him what had happened to his fellow Danes. What do you want done with him?'

'He can stay on here as a slave. Ask the cook if he needs any more spit boys.'

Standing close to the fire slowly turning a spit to ensure that the carcass of a cow, pig or sheep was roasting evenly was a task done by slave boys. It was extremely hot and sweaty work and, if the boys weren't to become as well cooked as the meat, they had to be changed frequently. I was sure that another one to share the load would be welcome.

I examined the coins that we'd recovered from the Danes. There were some coppers and even a silver one or two in the pouches we looked at, but amongst them there were a few gold half angels bearing the likeness of my father. It was proof enough that they had been paid half their fee in coins minted in Berwick. The question was, what should I do about it?

~~~

Leland and Borg rode up to the closed gates of the fortress of Bebbanburg leading two pack horses. They stopped just out of arrow range and unloaded four wooden chests from the pack horses and piled them up in the middle of the track. Then they mounted their horses and rode away.

'Did you see them opened?' I asked after the pair had returned to Duns.

'Yes, we stopped at the bottom of the slope and waited to see what would happen. The earl limped out leaning on a stick accompanied by your brother. Eadwulf walked forward with a few men and opened the top box. Needless to say, he recoiled in horror when he saw the contents,' Leland said with a grin.

Leland had gone back to the scene of the fight first thing the next day with some of my younger warriors and they had taken the Dane's heads. It must have been a gruesome task as animals and birds had already started to feast on the bodies; in particular, none of the heads still had their eyes.

We had chosen the younger men, some no older than sixteen, deliberately to prepare them for the realities of warfare. Chopping the head off a dead man should harden them to doing the same without hesitation to an armed opponent.

We had washed the heads and doused them in vinegar to preserve them, and to reduce the stench somewhat, before putting them into the chests. I wanted Eadwulf to know that the attempt at assassination had failed and, furthermore, that I knew who was behind it. My hope was that he wouldn't attempt anything similar in the future.

Chapter Six – Return to Durham

Early Summer 998

The new cathedral was ready for consecration and Ecgfrida and I had been invited to attend the ceremony by Bishop Aldhun. Durham was the first cathedral to be built in Northumbria; the main church at York - and the seat of the archbishop - being called a minster to reflect its status as a missionary teaching church.

I knew from Aldhun's letter that both the archbishop and King Æthelred would be present but he'd said nothing about my father. The presence of the earl was almost mandatory, especially as the king would be there. However, as far as I knew he hadn't gone more than a few miles from Bebbanburg since he'd been wounded.

As we rode up to the hill towards the burh surrounded by its palisade the sun appeared from behind a cloud and bathed the place in sunlight. I had brought an escort of twenty mounted warriors, not because I thought I would be in any danger in Durham, but because I thought that we might be attacked on the return journey. As it turned out I was wrong on both counts.

A surly looking man in a rusty helmet and a padded gambeson stood with his hand on the hilt of his sword outside the gates of the burh. Beside him a youth of sixteen or seventeen holding a spear edged behind the older man, as if he was frightened of the approaching cavalcade. The older sentry held up his hand for us to halt.

'Don't you recognise the banner of Lord Uhtred?' Ulfric asked.

Both he and Kenric had accompanied me whilst Borg rode behind me bearing my banner. I had kept the snarling black wolf's head, the badge of my family and of Bebbanburg, but I had replaced the golden yellow field on which it sat with a blood red one.

The man looked confused so Ulfric pointed to the carriage behind Borg in which sat Ecgfrida, her maid and the nurse holding little Aldred.

'That's the bishop's daughter. I don't suppose that he'll be that pleased with you for denying her entry.'

'I'm sorry, lord,' he muttered with downcast eyes, 'but the burh is full. I've been told to tell all latecomers that they must camp by the river.'

'Very well. But that doesn't apply to me or my wife as Aldhun has invited us to stay with him,' I told him firmly, giving Ulfric a warning look.

He looked as if he was about to kick the unfortunate member of the local watch out of his way. He controlled himself with an effort and, muttering profanities, he went to order my escort to turn around.

The man driving the carriage urged the horses forward and I went to accompany it through the gates with my servant bringing up the rear. However, the two sentries continued to bar the way.

'I'm sorry, thane, but the king is lodging with the bishop. You'll have to go with your men.'

'I have a letter from Bishop Aldhun inviting my family and I to stay with him. He must have known that the king would also be lodging with him when he sent it. Now either you get your fat belly out of my way or I'll dismount and see how good a swordsman you really are.'

'I'm just doing what I was told to do,' he said defensively.

Reluctantly he and the other sentry stood to one side and allowed us through.

We made our way up the streets of Durham towards the monastery and the thane's hall at the top. The place was crowded, the taverns were evidently full and men were knocking on doors of even the meanest dwelling seeking accommodation for ealdorman this and abbot that. I began to wonder if there would be room for us in the bishop's hall after all if the king was staying there. He would hardly be travelling alone.

The new cathedral looked magnificent. The last time I'd seen it had been when the foundations were barely out of the ground. It was twice the size of any other church I'd seen and, instead of being the usual rectangular shape, it had been built in the shape of a cross with a tower emerging from where the four parts of the roof met. I doubted if the cathedral at Canterbury was any more splendid.

The bishop's hall – the only other place constructed in stone – lay at right angles to the cathedral alongside most of the other monastic buildings. Opposite them across an area churned to mud were the dormitory for the monks, the guesthouse for visitors and the stables. Stable boys came to take our horses and the carriage away and we walked, slipping and sliding, across the mud patch towards the bishop's residence. Once we got there we were again halted by guards. This time the men wore polished byrnies and helmets and held shields displaying the dragon of Wessex.

'You can't come any further, go back to the burh and seek accommodation there,' one of them said officiously.

'I'm getting very tired of this. My wife is Bishop Aldhun's daughter and she and I are invited to lodge in his hall. Now get out of my way.'

The man shook his head and his companions lowered their spears slightly, as if threatening us.

I was about to explode with anger when the prior appeared.

'Ah, Lord Uhtred, how are you? I'm glad to see you and the Lady Ecgfrida. The bishop was wondering when you'd arrive.'

'I'd have been here sooner if certain numskulls didn't keep barring my way,' I said heatedly.

Ecgfrida put her hand on my arm to calm me down.

'I'm sorry, lord,' the man in charge of the guards said insincerely. 'No one told us to expect you.'

I ignored him and escorted my wife and servants past them to follow the prior across to the bishop's hall. It was a long building two storeys high; the hall itself, which also served as the administrative centre from where the business of the diocese was conducted, was located on the first floor. It was approached via a narrow external staircase to make it difficult for an attacker to assault. The bishop's private solar lay at one end of the main hall and this had been vacated pro tem for King Æthelred to occupy.

The ground floor consisted of four chambers, each with its own entrance, normally storerooms, but which were now being used to house the bishop's guests. We had been allocated one of these. There was a truckle bed for Ecgfrida and me to share and straw palliasses for the servants. A small cradle in the corner was just big enough for Aldred, who was now fourteen months old.

Whilst the servants went to fetch our paniers and unpack them into the solitary chest in the room, my wife and I went to greet her father. A guard stationed at the bottom of the steps up to the first floor told us to wait there. I was getting used to this by now so did my best to maintain my composure. It was struggle and I was beginning to get impatient when he returned and allowed us past.

We found Aldhun deep in conversation with three other men. The one with the gold circlet around his fair hair was obviously King Æthelred and I assumed the other cleric was Ealdwulf, Archbishop of York, from the richness of his habit and the gem-studded pectoral cross hanging from a gold chain about his plump neck. He had a florid complexion and I came to the conclusion that he ignored his vows about fasting and living a simple life. The other man was the only one I'd met before; Leofwine was the Ealdorman of Durham and, as such, was one of my father's senior nobles.

'Ah, Cyning, may I present my daughter, Ecgfrida and her husband Thane Uhtred,' Aldhun said, getting up to greet us.

The king frowned, no doubt irritated at the interruption, but nodded in our direction, whilst the other two men ignored us.

'Lord Uhtred is the eldest son of Earl Waltheof,' my father-in-law went on to explain, seemingly undaunted by our cool reception.

'The disinherited one,' Leofwine told the king with a sneer.

'Disinherited?' Æthelred asked.

'Yes, his father took against him and has appointed the younger brother, the sinful Eadwulf, as his heir,' Aldhun explained with a sniff, indicating what he thought of my father's decision.

'Sinful?' the king asked, clearly puzzled by what he was being told.

'He has a reputation for being lazy, a fornicator and a drunkard,' Aldhun said with a meaningful look at Leofwine, who looked as if he was about to come to my brother's defence.

'Is this true?' the king asked me.

'That I've been disinherited, yes, Cyning. As to my brother's character I would hesitate to cast any stones. You should ask others.'

'The young man is due here for the ceremony, Cyning,' Leofwine pointed out. 'Perhaps you can make up your own mind when you have met him?'

'Very well. But it is not up to Waltheof to decide who should be earl after him. He has done little to protect my border from the Scots, whereas I have heard good reports of Lord Uhtred in that regard. If Eadwulf is as indolent as his father he will never be Earl of Bernicia.'

I was pleased to hear that, but I was far from reassured. The rulers of Wessex had called themselves kings of the English for several decades now, but their grip on Northumbria was tenuous. I was fairly certain that Æthelred wouldn't be able to do much about it if Eadwulf, secure in Bebbanburg, decided to ignore the king's edicts. In reality Bernicia was part of England in name only. Even the southern part of Northumbria, Deira, whose earl, Ælfhelm, was a Saxon, might have been appointed by Æthelred, but the Danish jarls living in his earldom paid him scant regard.

'At least the Scots under King Kenneth have been relatively quiet in recent years,' I pointed out.

'That won't last much longer,' Archbishop Ealdwulf said. 'From what I hear, the King of Scots is now an old man and his heir, Malcolm, wants to expand the enclave the barbarians already have south of the Firth of Forth. He won't rest until he's moved the border south to the Tweed.'

'All the more reason to have an earl in Northumbria who is capable of thwarting Malcolm's ambition,' the king said with finality.

We were dismissed but Aldhun invited us to join him later on for the feast he'd organised in the king's honour.

~~~

I had probably drunk more than I should have. The women had long since retired but tradition dictated that the men should stay until the king had left the hall. Not all those present had a bladder equal to the task and the foul stench of urine began to emanate from the corners of the hall as several men made use of the cover provided by the shadows where the candlelight didn't reach.

I noticed with distaste that my brother was one of those who did so, not once but twice. He and I had studiously avoided each other at the feast and I was glad that, despite being the official representative of our father, the earl, he had to find lodgings in the burh. The ealdormen and senior churchmen present having been given all the available beds in the guest lodgings in the monastery itself. If I could steer clear of him at the ceremony the following day we should be able to avoid an unpleasant confrontation.

I had more dignity than Eadwulf, despite the fact that I was dying to relieve myself. At last the king rose unsteadily from his chair and made his way out of the hall, no doubt to use the monastery latrines sited at the eastern edge of the plateau. Two of his gesith followed him as he went nowhere without a bodyguard.

I might not wish to piss inside the hall but I wasn't too proud to make use of a convenient bush in the darkness away from the hall. I breathed a sigh of contentment as I emptied my bladder but then some sixth sense warned me and I lurched sideways into a roll just as a sword cut at where my neck had been a split second earlier.

I came up into a crouch, my right hand scrabbling for my eating knife in a sheath on my belt. No one was allowed to carry weapons in the presence of the king but the knife I used to cut up my meat was four inches long and sharp. My would-be assassin had overbalanced when his sword met no resistance and staggered away from me before recovering quickly. The night was illuminated by a new moon so there was some light but my eyes had not grown accustomed to the gloom after being in the candle-lit hall, whereas my assailant had presumably been lying in wait in the darkness for some time before I'd emerged.

I was still in the couching position trying to ascertain where my attacker had gone when I heard a faint noise alerted me. His sword cut down at my unprotected head but I managed to stab blindly at my attacker's legs before the blow landed. I was lucky and the blade sank up to the hilt in the man's thigh. He yelped in pain and tried to move backwards. Consequently his sword missed me again.

Before he could recover I sprang to my feet and my fist connected with his jaw. He fell to the ground, dropping his sword. I scooped it up and went to strike him with it; not enough to kill him, but to wound him badly enough to incapacitate him.

Then my world went black.

When I awoke my head felt as if someone had stuck red hot irons into it and I moaned in agony. I tried to move but I couldn't get my limbs to obey me.

'Lie still, lord. You have a nasty cut in your scalp right down to the bone. You are lucky to be alive.'

I tried to see the speaker and, although I could see that the room was well lit, everything was a blur. Whoever was tending to me washed my face with a wet cloth and I felt marginally better. I drifted back into unconsciousness and when I woke again the room was dark.

I went to call out but all that emerged was a dry croak. My head still felt as if it was on fire and, when someone lifted it so that I could drink some water I screamed in pain. I continued to drift in and out of consciousness with occasional sips of water for what I later learned was three days. Then one morning I woke up and the unbearable pain had been replace by a dull ache. Furthermore, I could see clearly.

A tonsured head appeared and opened each eye in turn so that he could peer into them. He lifted my head and I saw that he was wearing the black habit of the Benedictine order and I correctly surmised that he was the monastery's infirmarian, or one of them.

He seemed satisfied and gave me more water to drink before disappearing. I called out but my voice couldn't manage more than a croak. I swallowed and tried again.

'Where am I? What happened?' I managed to utter this time, albeit hoarsely, but there was no one there to hear me.

An elderly monk came in and examined me and then stood aside to reveal the bishop and a tearful Ecgfrida looking down at me, concern written all over their faces.

'We thought we'd lost you, my son,' Aldhun said with a smile. 'However, God has seen fit to spare you.'

'What happened?' I asked again, my voice a little stronger this time.

'Someone tried to cleave your head in two with a sword. Thankfully the blade must have been blunt or rusty and your skull is thicker than most men's,' he explained. 'The sword broke and that saved your life. The sentries outside the hall heard a scream and the sounds of a scuffle and came running to investigate. They saw you lying on the ground with blood seeping out of your head and raised the alarm.

'You must have wounded your assailant and they followed a trail of blood using torches but found the man with his throat cut. He also had a knife in his thigh. He couldn't have got that far on his own so presumably there were two of them. I can only surmise that, when the chase got too close, one killed the other, no doubt to stop him talking.'

I tried to nod but that caused a blast of pain to shoot through my head.

'Yes, I wounded my attacker and took his sword off him. The other man must have attacked me before I could use it,' I managed to get out slowly and in short bursts of speech.

'Do you know who did this to you?' Aldhun asked.

'No, but I have a fair idea. However, I have no proof.'

'Eadwulf,' my wife hissed.

'Why?' her father asked.

'No doubt because he heard that the king would prefer Lord Uhtred to be the next Earl of Bernicia,' another voice said.

I couldn't see the speaker but I recognised the voice.

'Borg, is that you?'

'Yes, lord,' he said stepping into my field of vision with a smile.

I returned the smile and then lay back exhausted. Within seconds I had fallen asleep again.

~~~

It was over two months before the infirmarian pronounced me fit enough to travel. During the time that I was bedridden my muscles had wasted and I had lost quite a lot of weight. Gradually I exercised and ate, ate and exercised until my clothes no longer hung on me as if I had stolen them from a giant.

It was late September before we left to return to Duns. Leland and Ulfric were determined that my brother wouldn't have any further chance to try and kill me and so we set off escorted by thirty mounted warriors, fully armed, with scouts riding ahead and on the flanks. Kenric wasn't there because he'd taken half a dozen men to watch Bebbanburg from afar. If a large party of warriors left we'd have plenty of warning.

My head still throbbed at times and I wasn't as quick as I used to be when exercising with sword and shield, but otherwise I had recovered well. Ecgfrida was determined that I'd rest until the spring to give me the chance to fully recuperate, but it wasn't to be.

Chapter Seven – Raiders

Winter 998/999

That winter was a harsh one. The snow came early and by the end of November there was a foot of the stuff everywhere; more where blizzards had blown it into deep drifts. Travel was nigh on impossible; even hunting was difficult, and usually fruitless. I was grateful that that summer had yielded a bumper harvest and that we had managed to smoke or salt enough meat to provide some variety in my hall to the gruel and broth made with root vegetables.

As the winter wore on with no let-up in the cold weather, hungry wolves got ever bolder and more than one family in isolated farmsteads were wiped out. Humans were also starving and reports of raids by those more improvident than those living in my three villages began to emerge.

Despite the difficulties of journeying through the snow, Ulfric's messenger managed to reach us to say that Norham had been attacked by raiders from the north. The River Tweed had frozen and the raiders had been able to cross it, avoiding Ulfric's hall sited above the ford, usually the only crossing point for miles.

I had just returned from a wolf hunt feeling pleased with myself as we had found a den this time and killed the majority of a large pack, with only two of the beasts escaping. We had lost one man in the fight but that seemed to me a price worth paying to get rid of the immediate menace to Duns.

'Where are these raiders now?' I asked the messenger once he had given me Ulfric's message.

'They were beaten off with heavy losses, lord, and retreated back across the Tweed.'

My suspicion was that these raiders had come from the other side of the Lammemuir Hills; in other words from the Scots enclave around Edinburgh. Since my father had been fool enough to allow King Kenneth to take control of the region south of the Firth of Forth the ealdorman, Osmond, had done little to discourage his people from raiding into Selkirkshire and Berwickshire. In fact, I suspected he secretly encouraged it despite the treaty between my father and the King of Scots.

However, my immediate problem was the marauders who had attacked Norham. According to Ulfric's messenger, they had driven off the livestock which were being overwintered in various barns outside the village to provide everyone, including those on the isolated farmsteads, with breeding stock for the coming year. Without them there would be no calves and no lambs to sell or eat.

The messenger said that he'd seen no sign of the raiders or their plunder on his way to Duns. That road had been difficult enough for him to traverse and I couldn't see them heading further west up over the hills. To even try would be suicidal in these conditions. No, they had probably come down the narrow coastal plain between the hills and the sea, avoiding Berwick as being too strong for them to assault, and then followed the Tweed valley west to Norham. If so, they would probably return the same way.

It had taken the messenger a day to reach me but the Scots would be moving slowly, partly because the need to dig their way through snow drifts, but also because they had to drive livestock along a narrow trail through the snow. I calculated that they would be lucky to make much more than five or six miles in the few hours between dawn and dusk at this time of year.

I gathered my warriors and loaded packhorses with food for us and fodder for the animals, ready to leave as soon as it was light the next day. By my calculations it would take the raiders the best part of three days to reach the road that ran along the coast between the villages of Ayton and Eyemouth. North of that lay an open area called Coldingham Moor and beyond that they would cross the border between the shires of Berwick and Edinburgh; effectively where England ended and Scotland began.

We needed to catch them before they reached the moor and that meant making our way along the snow blocked track between Duns and Ayton – some dozen miles of hard going.

There were places where the snow lay a mere six inches deep, which we could ride through at a slow walk; but then we would hit deep drifts and have to dismount and use our wooden shovels to clear a path. It was hard work and I detailed five at a time to clear a path until they were worn out, then another five would take over. I did my fair share and worked until the muscles in my arms and shoulders screamed in protest.

By nightfall we had reached a narrow river called Whiteadder Water, which was frozen solid just as the Tweed at Norham was. We crossed over and camped on the far bank. Even with camp fires that spat and hissed as the ice in them melted to water and then evaporated into the air, we spent a cold and uncomfortable night. It didn't help when fresh snow started just before dawn. I had thought that it was too cold to snow but realised that it wasn't quite as cold now. When I looked up the moon, which had been fringed with an icy halo the last time I looked, was now hidden by dark clouds.

The temperature continued to rise as the morning wore on and the snow turned to sleet. If anything that hampered our progress even more as snow turning to slush was heavier to move than powdery crystals of the stuff. I consoled myself with the thought that the thaw would be a little faster on the coast and, hopefully, would slow the raiders down even more.

We reached Ayton just as the sun sunk below the Lammermuir Hills to the west. The thane, a man named Sicga, sounded the alarm as twenty frozen and bedraggled mounted warriors emerged through what was now a mixture of sleet and rain. When he realised who it was he stood down his five household warriors and the twenty members of the fyrd who had answered his summons.

Leaving my men to warm themselves and dry their clothing by the fires in Sicga's hall and the houses of his freemen, I continued, accompanied by Borg, to the coast road that ran from Berwick all the way to Edinburgh. It was difficult to find at night and in the prevailing conditions but, as I'd hoped, my memory served me well and the area between the low hills inland and the cliffs that dropped steeply to the rocky shoreline below was no more than two hundred yards wide.

We were leading our tired horses so when Borg, who was in front of me, fell through a melting bank of snow into a small burn no real damage was done. Had we been riding his horse would undoubtedly have broken its leg. As he got up cursing and swearing because all of his clothes were now sopping wet, I told him to be quiet. We could now hear the faint sound of lowing cattle and of men talking.

Borg was in danger of freezing to death so I sent him back to Ayton whilst I investigated. Tethering my horse, I scrambled down the side of the burn until I could see campfires below me. The burn entered the sea at a natural harbour surrounded by half a dozen fishermen's hovels. The Scottish raiders had evidently killed the local inhabitants and were using their dwellings for shelter. Not all could fit inside and so a few were using upturned boats with one side propped up by oars against the prevailing north-easterly wind to shelter under. They had lit fires in front of these improvised shelters to cook their evening meal.

The stolen livestock had been allowed to roam free in the steep valley – no more than a wide gully really - to scrape away the slush to find what grazing they could, which wasn't much. Suddenly I heard a noise to my left and a boy of between ten and twelve appeared slipping and sliding his way across the hillside. No doubt he, and a few others, had orders to make sure the animals didn't escape from the gully.

I waited to see if he would see me. I didn't want to kill a young lad but I'd have to if I was discovered. Luckily he was too intent on stamping his feet and rubbing his hands together to keep warm to pay much attention to his surroundings and a few minutes later he turned back the way he'd come.

I scrambled back up the gully, retrieved my horse, and made my way back to Ayton.

~~~

We waited in the cold and dark at the far side of the ford through Eye Water, the river that ran into the sea at Eyemouth. I prayed that my anticipation of what the Scots would do was correct.

I reasoned that, not having looted either the fishing village of Eyemouth or the rather more prosperous area around Ayton on the way out, they intended to do so on the return journey. It made sense as otherwise they would have been encumbered with livestock all the way to Norham and back again.

If I was the leader of the raiders I would send my warriors to launch a dawn attack on Ayton and the surrounding farmsteads whilst the boys, with just a few men as escort, drove the Norham livestock across the Eye Water and north-east towards Coldingham Moor.

With Sicga and his men I estimated that I probably had the same numbers as the raiders. However, only six of Sicga's men were trained warriors; the other ten were members of the fyrd. Normally I would have regarded inexperienced freemen as a liability on an operation like this, but Sigca had chosen them at my request because they were skilled archers, albeit with hunting bows, not war bows.

Whilst I waited in ambush on the track between the ford over the Eye Water and Ayton, Sicga and his men had hidden themselves a few hundred yards from the ford, along the track to Coldingham. His task was to kill the drovers and their escort and recover our stolen animals. Mine was to eliminate their main body.

Thankfully the sleet had stopped and the temperature continued to rise, albeit slowly. However, it wasn't very warm lying on wet grass under a bush which dripped cold water down my neck no matter where I lay.

As the sun's first rays turned the oily black surface of the sea into various shades of orange and yellow I heard the faint sound of ponies splashing through the ford before I caught sight of shadowy figures heading towards where we were hidden. I waited anxiously for the sound of animals being driven through the ford. If we sprung the ambush before the stolen livestock entered the trap set up by Sicga they might get away.

Just when I thought my plan was doomed to failure I heard boy's voices faintly on the wind urging the animals into the river. A few minutes later I felt confident that all were across the river and should by now have entered Sicga's trap.

I tapped Borg on the arm and he blew his hunting horn. By now the leading riders had passed my position and a score and half of raiders on foot were abreast of our position. We arose like wraiths out of the ground and charged forward into the enemy, attacking from all sides.

Ulfric and four of his men had swiftly mounted and now attacked the Scots leaders. Unarmoured men on ponies were no match for my armoured warriors riding much larger horses and they cut them down before they knew what was happening. The Scots on foot weren't so easily overcome.

We were outnumbered by two to one and, despite their lack of armour and the advantage we had of surprise, they quickly recovered and resolutely defended themselves.

As I raced into the melee I was attacked by two men at once. The one to my right hacked at my head with a small axe whilst the other thrust a spear at my chest. I reacted without conscious thought, lifting my shield to deflect the spear and my sword to slice into the forearm of the axeman. He dropped the axe with a cry of pain and I forgot about him; the other tried to jab at me again but I was now too close to him to be worried about the spear.

I smashed the boss of my shield into his face and, whilst he was blinded by the pain of a broken nose, I slashed my sword down onto his shoulder. He fell to the ground and a quick thrust of the point of my sword into his throat put him out of his misery.

Suddenly I felt a sharp stab of pain in my calf and I realised that my other opponent, far from being put out of action by the deep wound to his forearm, had dragged his dagger from its sheath and stuck it into me from his prone position on the blood soaked ground.

Another quick jab with my sword at his neck made sure that he was really out of the fight and I hastily checked my calf. Thankfully my thick leather boots had prevented the dagger from doing more that give me a shallow cut and I sought out my next adversary.

It was only then that I saw Borg lying on the ground with a bloody wound to his head. A huge Scotsman wielding a two-handed battle axe was standing over him and was just about to administer the coup de grace when I chopped sideways into his bull-like neck with all the strength I could muster. I had expected to see his head topple from his body but, to my amazement, the blade stuck less than halfway through.

With a roar he turned to face me, wrenching my sword out of my hand. He raised his axe and instinctively I lifted my shield to block the blow without any real expectation that it would do more than slow it before it fell apart. I braced myself, but the blow never came. Suddenly the light went out of his eyes and he toppled sideways, crashing into the ground.

I rushed to Borg's side to try and stem the flow of blood from his head wound but it had stopped of its own accord when his heart had stopped beating. I felt inordinately sad that the captured Norse boy, who had turned out to be one of my closest companions, was dead. Normally I could steel my heart against feeling emotion for the death of one I knew well, at least until I had the time to grieve, but for some reason Borg's death deeply affected me.

I got to my feet slowly, telling myself to get a grip; I still had a fight to win. However, when I looked around, it was all over. A few of the raiders had got away but most were dead or wounded. The latter soon joined the others in death. Our losses were comparatively light; in addition to Borg three other warriors had been killed and four more were wounded. Their wounds weren't serious and hopefully they would make a full recovery.

Sicga had suffered no casualties, but then his had been the easy part. His archers had taken care of the four warriors with the livestock and then the ten boys herding them had either surrendered without a fight or had fled into the snow covered hills. I didn't give much for their chances of survival. Although a thaw had started, it would take a long time before all the snow melted. They would die of hunger or the cold; that is if the wolves didn't get them first.

Six boys had been taken prisoner and I let Sicga keep all but one. He wasn't a Scot; he was an Angle – the son of Ealdorman Osmond. It proved that the raid had Osmond's blessing. No doubt his people had suffered this winter but it was the first indication that he was prepared to break the unofficial truce between Scottish Lothian and the part still ruled by my father. My hope was that his son, Hacca, would prove to be a valuable hostage against Osmond's future good behaviour.

We borrowed a cart from Sigca to take our dead to the monastery at Coldingham for Christian burial. The dead Scotsmen – plus a few Lothian Angles who appeared to have sided with the Scots - were thrown into the sea from the top of the nearby cliffs.

Chapter Eight – Lothian Under Threat

Summer 1000

My hope of persuading Ealdorman Osmond to respect the border proved to be a vain one. During the latter part of that wretched winter he had fallen ill and died. I offered to free the fifteen year old Hacca so that he could succeed him, intending to extract the boy's oath not to raid our territory before I did so, but instead of allowing Hacca to inherit, Malcolm persuaded King Kenneth to appoint Malcom's bastard son, Angus, as ealdorman instead.

As soon as Angus had taken possession of the fortress on the rock high above the town of Edinburgh, he set about replacing the existing Anglian thanes with Scots, some of whom were of Pictish descent but the majority were Britons from Strathclyde.

This was a worrying trend because the western part of Angus' shire joined Strathclyde at Stirling and it meant that what remained of Bernician Lothian was now under a co-ordinated threat from both the north and the west.

The border between Selkirkshire in the east and Strathclyde in the west had always been ill-defined

105

but, as the area was largely unpopulated uplands which stretched for some thirty miles between the two, it didn't used to matter very much. Now we learned that Owain ap Dyfnwal, King of Strathclyde and nominally Kenneth's vassal, had been surreptitiously settling these uplands for several years so that he could lay claim to the area as far as Ettrick Forest. That brought the eastern edge of his kingdom to within a few miles from the burh of Hawick in Selkirkshire and not that far from Selkirk itself.

The two ealdorman of Anglian Lothian had approached my father for help to counter the growing threat. They had in mind a pre-emptive attack on the Britons who had settled in the west but Waltheof did nothing, other than reply urging caution.

In early June Gosric, the Ealdorman of Selkirkshire, called a meeting to discuss the threat to us. Iuwine of Berwickshire and most of the thirty odd thanes from the two shires attended. Although they were officially my deputies, I took Ulfric of Norham and Kenric of Carham with me, along with a small escort. I also took Hacca.

The meeting was held in the monastery of Melrose, partly because its refectory was large enough as a venue and partly because it was more or less central. After the abbot had celebrated mass and blessed our deliberations Gosric outlined the threat, something which most of us were only too well aware of. Iuwine followed on by saying that our task was to discuss what action we should take to deal with the growing threat to our continued existence.

After he'd finished speaking he invited anyone who wished to do so to take the floor. To my surprise Hacca was first on his feet, although he had no right to speak as he was neither ealdorman nor thane. However, both Gosric and Iuwine seemed eager to hear what he had to say.

'I am not the only Angle to have been dispossessed by the encroaching Scots,' he began. 'There are fifteen thanes and perhaps sixty of their loyal household warriors who have been forced off their land and who now live as outlaws in the Pentland, Moorfoot and Lammemuir Hills. It is not to be borne.'

His young voice had grown more excited as he spoke and I managed to catch his eye in an effort to tell him to take a more measured tone. Whether he understood my look or not, he continued more calmly.

'We need to make contact with these men and invite them to join our army. Seventy five trained warriors who have a serious grievance against Angus mac Malcolm in particular and the Scots in general would be a valuable addition to our army.'

'You speak as if we have already decided to go to war with Angus, boy,' an elderly thane I didn't recognise called out from the back of the chamber.

'No, but does anyone here not see the encroachment from the west and the growing power of the Scots south of the Firth of Forth as menacing? All I'm saying is that we need to prepare to resist any further inroads into the two shires and my father's former thanes will join us, provided we can make contact with them.'

'What the lad says makes sense to me,' Sicga of Ayton said, getting to his feet as Hacca sat down. 'However, we have other matters that need to be resolved. The Scots warriors are ill disciplined but they are all trained as fighters from young boys. Our fyrd are farmers who carry a spear if they possess one but have little idea how to use it. How many men can we muster in total? Perhaps seven hundred in total if everyone between the ages of fourteen and forty five attends the muster. Of these no more than two hundred are proper warriors. Yes, the seventy five that Hacca mentions would be very helpful, but our main problem is the woeful state of training of the fyrd.'

'What is your solution, Sicga?' Gosric asked.

'With no disrespect to you, lord, or to Ealdorman Iuwine, we need someone who can organise the training of the fyrd and has the military skills to lead us effectively. Only then do we have any chance of defeating an invasion.'

'I take no offence. I am nearly fifty and too old to do as you suggest,' Gosric said with a smile. 'My sons came to me late in life and are too young and inexperienced.'

He stopped and looked at Iuwine, raising a questioning eyebrow. His fellow ealdorman was young, but he was a few years older than me. However, he didn't have a reputation as a warrior or a commander. Had he not been an ealdorman I suspected he would have chosen to become a monk or a priest.

'You have someone in mind?' Iuwine asked, ignoring the unspoken question in Gosric's expression.

'Yes, lord. I saw first-hand how Thane Uhtred of Duns defeated a large band of raiders despite the fact that we were outnumbered. They were practically annihilated and, although we did lose men in the fight, their losses were four or five times ours.'

'I can support what Sicga says,' Hacca put in. 'I was there, albeit on the losing side.'

That raised a chuckle from quite a few of those present. The upshot of the meeting was that I was elected as Bretwalda of Lothian. I was pleased, of course, but I had no illusions as to the difficulties of my task. In contrast, most there seemed to think that their troubles were over, having shouldered me with them. They weren't, of course, they were only just beginning.

~~~

My problems were threefold. I needed to make contact with the disposed thanes of the shire of Edinburgh and persuade them to join us without reward, except food and shelter; I needed to provide armour and weapons for the fyrd; and I needed to train them. Because they were farmers in the main, although some freemen were fishermen or artisans, they resented anything which took them away from providing for them and their families. Most of them took the attitude that life was hard enough without devoting time to learning the art of fighting.

I decided to tackle the first task without delay. There had to be a certain urgency to it. If the dispossessed thanes and their oath-sworn warriors were raiding local farmsteads in order to survive it wouldn't be long before Angus decided he needed to hunt them down.

Three days later I said goodbye to Ecgfrida and Aldred and set off with Hacca, Leland, my body servant, Cædmon, and four of my household warriors for the Lammermuir Hills.

My northernmost farmstead was at Longformacus in the foothills. Beyond that lay uplands that covered an area of some twenty miles by ten miles before you reached the first of the villages in the shire of Edinburgh. The boundary between it and Berwickshire was ill defined but I suspected that our quarry lay in the north-western part of the hills. From there they had a variety of places they could attack. The south-eastern hills were far less populated.

We stayed at Longformacus on the first night and then climbed up into the trackless waste above the hamlet. We saw nothing all day except some sheep and a boy with two large dogs who guarded them. The weather had started out fine but clouds soon scudded in from the east. By early in the afternoon the sky had turned dark grey and the wind had picked up. It was obvious that we were in for a wild night and I began to think about where best to seek shelter.

I thought that there was little hope of finding a building but I reasoned that the shepherd boy must live somewhere. Although he was the only person we'd seen, there were bound to be others somewhere as we'd seen several flocks on distant hillsides. Then as the big, fat raindrops began to fall, Hacca spotted a hovel below us beside a small river that he said was called the Whiteadder. It was the same river as the one we'd camped by the previous year, just before we'd captured Hacca, but now we were much further upstream.

As we neared the hovel the wind lashed rain in our faces and it became difficult to see much. Nevertheless, somehow I knew that the place was deserted. I half expected to find the dead bodies of the family who'd lived here, but there was nothing. The cauldron hanging above the dead fire still had a vegetable stew in it but it had started to go mouldy. It was obvious that the outlaws we sought had been here; the fate of the occupants was less evident.

We stabled the horses in a lean-to attached to the hovel and fed them from the bags of fodder we had brought with us. Normally we'd have allowed them to graze, but not in this weather. Cædmon emptied the cauldron outside and scrubbed it clean before lighting a fire and preparing a stew made with some dried venison from his pannier and root vegetables growing in a patch outside. I cursed the weather. Leland was a good tracker but any trail that the outlaws had left would be destroyed by the rain.

The next morning dawned bright and clear. The only sign of last night's storm was the puddles of water lying here and there.

'Any idea where outlaws are likely to hide?' I asked Hacca as we saddled our mounts.

'I doubt if they'll use anywhere out in the open as a base,' he replied. 'It might be worth going to Monynut Forest. That would give them cover from view as well as providing timber for huts.'

'Where is this forest?'

'I've never been there but I seem to recall being told that it lies between two small rivers that flow under a ridge that runs between Bransley Hill and Heart Law.'

'Do you know where they are?'

'To the north of here, I think.'

I glanced at the sun as it climbed into the sky in the east and judged where due north must lie. There was a ridge that ran north-west to south-east in that direction so we set off to climb it. When we reached the top we could see that the wide valley below us was covered in trees. It had to be Monynut Forest. However, it stretched for miles in all directions and to search it would take forever.

Suddenly Leland pointed to the far hillside. Looking to where he was indicating I saw that it was dotted with sheep. We'd seen others before, of course, but not in this density. There were cows as well. It was further confirmation that we had come to the right place to find the outlawed thanes. I surmised that they had gathered in the local population, with their livestock, as well as raiding further afield. It would explain the deserted hovel below us.

I was about to descend towards the forest when Hacca drew my attention to the north-western end of the forest. It was a good four or five miles from where we sat but I could just make out movement.

'Your eyes are better than mine, Hacca, what can you make out?'

At twenty nine I was hardly an old man but Hacca was half my age and I knew he had the eyes of a hawk.

'It looks like three men on horseback in the lead, then perhaps a dozen mounted on ponies. One is carrying a banner, but I can't make out any detail. Then they're followed by a score of men wearing byrnies; at least I think they are. The sun is glinting off their torsos. Then there is a mass of men behind them, capering excitedly.'

'How many?'

'In total? Perhaps a hundred.'

More than enough to deal with a score of outlaws, even if they are all trained warriors, I thought gloomily. We had arrived too late.

'We should have brought more men,' Hacca said, almost weeping. 'Can't we do something?'

'What? Throw our lives away in a futile gesture of support? What good would that do?'

Just then I saw small figures emerge from the wood and start to drive the livestock up the slope and over the ridge towards the coast. Angus' Scots, for it had to be them, ignored the boys and continued on into the trees.

As we watched impotently people emerged from the forest. Some wore byrnies and helmets but they included men in normal tunics, women and even children. They headed south-east over the moorland towards where one of the small rivers joined the Whiteadder. Beyond that I knew that there was a small hamlet and I smiled to myself. The hamlet lay in Berwickshire and therefore out of Angus' jurisdiction.

'Come on,' I yelled, digging my heels into my horse's flanks and cantering off along the ridge.

My men were taken by surprise but quickly set off after me. The ridge slowly descended and a short while later my horse splashed through the shallow waters of the narrow river and on down the east bank of the Whiteadder until I reached the hamlet. There I halted, my horse blowing hard with exertion, and waited until the first of the fugitives came into sight.

'Come on,' I yelled. 'Get behind us.'

The leading men halted uncertainly and glanced behind them.

'Lord Hacca is with us. You are in Berwickshire now; you're safe.'

That seemed to do the trick and the group started to move again. The last of the women and children had just reached the hamlet behind us when a group of mounted warriors came across the stream and headed towards us. Most carried spears and they levelled them, seemingly about to charge us.

Two of my warriors were archers and they had dismounted and drew back their bows as the Scots charged us.

'Kill the leaders' horses,' I said quietly.

The first two arrows brought two of the three horses down and the next two took care of the third horse and the pony bearing a man carrying a banner. The latter was blue with a golden dragon embroidered on it – the emblem of the Kings of Scotland. I knew then that Angus, the bastard son of Malcolm of the House of Alpin, must be present. All four riders sprawled in the dust and the one horse that wasn't dead cried pitifully in agony. I held my hand up and yelled for the rest to halt.

'You are in Berwickshire and, unless you want to provoke a war, you must go back whence you came.'

One of the three riders got to his feet and held his side for a moment, evidently badly winded. He snatched up a gleaming steel helmet with a gold band around the rim and jammed it back onto his head.

'I'm Angus, Ealdorman of Edinburgh, and I say you lie.'

'I am Uhtred, Thane of Duns and son of Earl Waltheof of Bernicia. I do not lie; not ever. I say again that you are trespassing on my father's lands. Unless you wish to explain to King Kenneth that you were the man responsible for breaking a truce that has lasted for fifteen years, I suggest you withdraw.'

Angus scowled at me, chewing his lip and cursing for a few moments.

'Very well. I'll do so if you hand over the outlaws sheltering behind your paltry warband and pay me five gold angels for the horses you've killed.'

I shook my head.

'The horses were killed to stop your aggression. Much as I regret it, their death was your fault; you must pay.'

Angus swore again in frustration.

'I won't press the point, but only if you hand over Swefred and his outlaws.'

'Swefred was the Thane of Dunbar,' Hacca whispered to me.

'And you can hand over the boy beside you as well,' Angus added, his eyes lighting up as he recognised Hacca.

'No, sorry. They are all now under the protection of Earl Waltheof.'

'And you are going to stop me from taking them, are you?' he sneered.

I looked Angus in the eye. He was young, perhaps eighteen, and likely to be impetuous. His father had been itching to invade the rest of Lothian, and no doubt Bernicia as well, but Kenneth had managed to keep his younger cousin in check so far.

'Yes, and if you try you are a dead man.'

Angus licked his lips nervously. He was very conscious of my two archers and, although they had relaxed their aim on him, they had their arrows strung and could raise their bows, draw back and release in the time it would take him to give the order to charge.

116

By now Swefred and his warriors had formed up behind us with the unarmed men, women and children behind them. I didn't turn around to see how many there were but I later found out that there were twenty seven of them. Angus might have three times our number but many of his men were youths from Edinburgh whose idea of a fight was a brawl in a tavern on a Saturday night.

The ealdorman raised his hand.

'You may have won this time but the next time we meet I'll kill you,' he snarled.

'You are very welcome to try. No one has yet come close, not in a fair fight at any rate.'

'Goodbye, Uhtred, Bretwalda of Lothian. Soon you will be leader of nothing and no one.'

So Angus had heard that I'd been elected as war leader of Berwickshire and Stirlingshire, had he? It wasn't surprising, I suppose. Secrets were hard to keep these days, even from one's enemies.

~~~

Finding the other bands of outlaws now took on a new urgency and I sent Hacca to Glentress Forest in the Moorfoot Hills and Swefred to the Pentland Hills to find the other dispossessed thanes. This time I sent as many warriors as I could spare to escort them and it proved to be a sensible precaution. The Pentland Hills were further away and Swefred reached the outlaws before Angus had found them but Hacca ran into trouble.

I had given Hacca twenty mounted warriors, six of whom were archers. They had spent the night in an ancient hill fort to the south of the confluence of the River Tweed and Eddleston Water. Here the Tweed formed the boundary between Selkirkshire and the shire of Edinburgh. As soon as they crossed the river and entered Glentress Forest they would be in Angus' territory.

'We forded the river near where Letther Water joins the Tweed and then followed the Letther north to enter the forest in the valley between Black Law and Whitehope Law. They are two of the hills which dominate the forest,' Hacca explained.

I nodded and he continued. I was prepared for a tale of failure as he had returned to Duns without any of the outlaws he'd been sent to find. What puzzled me was the fact that Hacca seemed very pleased with himself.

'We saw no sign of anyone, not even when we scaled the highest hill, Dunslair Heights,' the boy said. 'However, we heard the sound of distant fighting coming through the trees and we followed a narrow animal trail downhill until we emerged at the edge of the forest. Across the valley we could see another of the old hill forts built by the Goddodin.'

I knew that the Goddodin had been the tribe of Britons who had inhabited Lothian when our ancestors – the Angles – had conquered the area several centuries ago. Hacca went on with his tale.

'It was quite a small fort and consisted on the usual concentric rings of earth ramparts but on the top someone had recently constructed a palisade. I

118

assumed, correctly as it turned out, that the dispossessed thanes from this area had erected it to use the place as their base.

'Over a hundred Scots were trying to scale the palisade,' Hacca continued, 'but the defenders had managed to keep them at bay up to now. I could see at least a dozen dead Scots lying at the base of the palisade and several more wounded men were being helped away to an area where there were several carts. Presumably the attackers' baggage train was being used as an infirmary. I could see three or four monks tending to men lying in carts.

'Apart from the men assaulting the ramparts, there were a dozen more mounted on horses or ponies watching from a distance of a hundred yards or so back from the fighting. I saw the same blue banner with a dragon couchant embroidered on it in gold that we had seen at our last encounter with Angus on the River Whiteadder.

'On this occasion I sent my six archers forward to dismount eighty yards short of the group of riders. They didn't notice them at first as they were watching the assault on the fort intently. When the first flight of arrows landed, three of the horses were hit as was the man holding the banner. He was wearing a pot helmet with a nasal which offered no protection to his neck. It was a lucky shot and it hit him just below the rim of the helmet, killing him instantly.

'The second volley hit two more horses and wounded another man in the thigh. Chaos ensued initially but the remaining riders quickly sorted themselves out and charged the archers. The latter could have got off another volley but instead they got back on their horses and led the Scots towards where we were hiding in the cover of the trees. I had never fought a man in earnest,' Hacca confessed to me, 'and I was scared.'

'I've fought many times,' I told him with a smile, 'and I always feel my guts clenching in terror until the first blow. Then instinct takes over and I don't have time to feel fear.'

The boy nodded.

'Yes, I found the same. One of the men on horseback came straight for me. He was much larger than me and I saw that he had an axe which he swung at my head as his horse came level with mine. I fully expected the axe to bite into my side but I thrust my sword towards his exposed armpit anyway. It was like trying to push it into a tree but I was in a blind panic and I put all my weight behind it. After a moments initial resistance it slid into his body.

'He was gravely wounded and all power went out of his blow. When his axe hit my back as I leaned forward, it glanced off my chain mail doing little damage, except to bruise me and crack a rib or two.

'I suppose I must have been in pain but I didn't feel it until later. I slid from my saddle just as he fell to the ground and I thrust the point of my sword into his neck. Blood spurted out but quickly stopped as he died. It was only then that I noticed the gold circlet around his helmet.'

'Angus?' I asked, not quite believing that Hacca had killed him.

The boy nodded, looking proud.

'What happened then?'

'The other warriors killed the rest of the mounted Scots. Of course we outnumbered them two to one so it was an easy victory; our only casualties being two men with minor wounds. One of my men chopped off Angus' head with the man's own axe and he stuck it onto the spear to which Angus' banner was attached. We rode out of the trees towards the main body of the Scots who broke off their assault to watch us as we approached. A great wail went up when they saw their leader's head impaled on top of their banner.

'Just at that moment the gates opened and the men inside sallied out to take the Scots in the rear. At the same time I signalled for my warriors to move into extended line and we started to canter towards the Scots. They may have lost their lord but they still outnumbered us by over two to one. However, the heart had gone out of them and they were leaderless. Apart from Angus himself, the senior thanes and chieftains had been amongst the men we'd killed in the trees. A few of the Scots started to flee and the rest soon followed suit. We rode after them and must have cut half of them down before they crossed the South Esk River and I called off the pursuit.'

'Well done, Hacca. You've done far more than I could have expected of you, but where are the dispossessed thanes and the men who you rescued?'

'I came on ahead to report back to you myself, but they have gone to raise the Lothian fyrd and then besiege what's left of Angus' men in the fortress of Edinburgh.'

Hacca doubtless saw his chance of recovering what he'd lost, but I could see the danger inherent in the lad's success. Killing Angus removed one threat but it would inevitably enrage Malcolm. Whatever Kenneth said, he would want revenge. It was true that we now had the opportunity to regain that part of Lothian which we'd lost but, if we did so, then even Kenneth might be forced to retaliate. I needed to think.

~~~

Discussing my options with Leland, Ulfric and Kenric proved unhelpful. All three thought that I should mobilise our forces and go to the aid of Redwald, the thane in charge of the siege of Edinburgh. When I met with the two ealdormen, Iuwine and Gosric, they were equally bereft of ideas. I tried to discuss my quandary with Ecgfrida but my wife's sole concern seemed to be the safety of our son, Aldred. She urged me to try and make peace with Kenneth before it was too late.

I had a feeling that the King of Scots, who was facing trouble with the Norse settlers in the West and North of Scotland, would prefer peace on his southern border, but he couldn't afford to lose face by allowing Edinburgh to fall. The solution I eventually came to was a compromise. I doubted very much if Hacca would be pleased with it, but I hoped that it would be accepted by everyone else.

Chapter Nine – The Treaty of Falkirk

Autumn 1000

'King Kenneth has agreed to meet with you, Lord Uhtred,' the Abbot of Melrose told me, once he had washed and changed into a clean habit after returning from his mission to the Scottish monarch. 'You are to be at Falkirk on the first day of October and are to bring no more than thirty men with you.'

'That's unreasonable. How do I know that I can trust him? I intend to take every man who can bear arms just in case he, or more likely his grandson, Malcolm, plays me false.'

'He has offered his son, Giric, as a hostage.'

'Giric? If he is Kenneth's son, why is Malcom his heir?'

'Because Giric is only nine and, in any case, Kenneth accepted his cousin as his heir some time ago to avoid a challenge for the throne.'

'Can I trust him, even with his son as hostage? More to the point, can he keep Malcolm from doing something stupid? After all, Malcolm has nothing to lose if Giric is killed.'

'Malcolm has been told to stay away, or so Kenneth assures me.'

'Hmmm, very well. Will you accompany me, Father Abbot, as the facilitator of this meeting?'

'You think that the support of Holy Church will help? Very well, but why don't you ask your father-in-law to accompany us as well?'

'Thank you, I'll do that.'

~~~

Having one hard winter I had hoped that the next one would be better. It was a vain hope. Late September had been unusually cold with frosts in the morning but at least it had been dry. The weather turned milder just before I set out and rain swept in from the west. It seemed as if it would never stop and the once rock hard earth of the roadways turned to a muddy quagmire.

I had hoped to reach Oxton in Lauderdale by nightfall but we had to keep stopping to rest our exhausted mounts as they battled against the slimy mire underfoot. As dusk descended we had only reached the tiny hamlet of Thirlstane. We were soaked to the skin and Bishop Aldhun had developed a cough that none of us liked the sound of.

We spent the night on the floors of the hovels or in barns and outhouses, but at least we were dry. We had three days to reach Falkirk before the day appointed for the meeting but we still had over forty miles to go. As we had only travelled nine miles on the first day it looked as if I had seriously underestimated the time needed to get there; and that was without the delay imposed by the bishop's poor health.

The next day was dull and overcast but at least the rain had stopped for now. Our clothes were still damp from the previous day but by midday the sun appeared and our cloaks began to gently steam as they slowly dried out. Aldhun was no better and so I persuaded him to remain at the hall of the Thane of Oxton when we reached there. Now the going got a little easier but it was two hours or so after dark before we reached Oxenfoord, where Redwald, the thane who had been in charge at the old hill fort in the Moorfoot Hills, had his hall.

I awoke the next day with a thick head. Redwald himself was still besieging Edinburgh, but his brother and family had insisted on laying on a feast for us. Hacca had been greeted as something of a hero and it showed the regard in which he was held as normally food was hoarded this late in the year; the only feast being held at Christmastide.

I would have liked to see how the siege was progressing but there was no time. We pressed on as fast as we could all that day as the roads continued to dry out. As twilight fell we reached the village of Ratho, which meant hill fort in Brittonic, the language spoken by the Goddodin. Now we were only a dozen miles from Falkirk and I was confident of reaching there on the next day, the thirtieth of September and the day before my appointed meeting with Kenneth.

I should have paid more attention to the nearby hill fort. The Thane of Ratho could have warned me but he was a Briton, not an Angle, and his loyalties lay

125

with his fellow Britons in Strathclyde and their allies, the Scots. As we rode past the hill on which it sat a horde of armed men erupted from the top rampart and ran down the slope towards us, taking such great strides that any stumble on the uneven ground underfoot would surely result in a broken leg.

They cascaded down the hill like a swarm of wasps disturbed from their nest. They were all on foot and few wore any form of armour but they outnumbered us by at least three to one. If they caught us we were doomed.

'Do we fight, lord?' Leland asked, drawing his sword and swinging his shield around from his back where it rested for travelling.

'No, we bloody well don't. Ride as if the devil was after you.'

I kicked my heels into my horse's flanks and he shot forward into a gallop. The rest of my men streamed after me, but then I remembered the Abbot of Melrose. He could ride, but not well, and there was not a cat in hell's chance of him keeping up with us.

~~~

The leading runners had reached the flat area at the bottom of the hill by the time that I'd managed to turn my horse around and head back to where the abbot was trailing along a hundred yards behind my rearmost warriors. He was clinging onto his horse for dear life as it galloped along, seemingly without any control by the abbot; merely driven by some instinct to stay with its stablemates.

'Grip with your knees,' I told him as I turned once more and came alongside him.

His face was panic stricken but he nodded and did as I said. I interposed myself between him and the advancing Scots as they raced to cut us off. Then I was aware of more and more of my men turning and coming to form a screen between us and the enemy.

The speed at which the Scots were running slowed now that most of them were on the level ground at the base of the hill. However, the nearest men were only fifty yards or so from us and still ahead of us. Given our respective positions and directions of travel, they would intercept us in a minute or two. I would have veered further south to avoid them but we were hemmed in by a small river with steep sided banks. Then, mercifully, the river curved south-west and we followed it, leaving most of the horde of warriors behind.

They screamed their frustration but a few managed to reach my screen of warriors. Their exertions had exhausted them, but our horses were beginning to flag as well. A dozen or so darted in to try and spear my rearmost warriors but they were ready for them. As they levelled their spears to thrust them into the horses' flanks, their riders pulled the galloping steeds' heads around. As I glanced behind me I saw half a dozen horsemen charge into the Scots and cut them down. Then they turned once more and cantered after us.

We had all slowed our mounts to a canter now, fearful of them dying under us. About a score of our attackers ran after us for a hundred yards or so, then stopped. They stood hands on knees, trying to get their breath back. The rest, now some distance behind them, also stopped and started to trudge back the way they'd come.

'Archers, with me,' I called and, to everyone's surprise I started to canter slowly back towards the leading Scots.

My order might have taken my men by surprise but those with bows quickly followed me. There were only a dozen or so of the enemy close to us and they started to run away as we approached. They were too tired to manage more than a stumbling pace and we narrowed the gap quickly. However, some of the others had seen their plight and turned back towards us. It would be a close run thing.

Once we were about fifty paces behind the isolated group my archers jumped out of the saddle, strung their bows and nocked an arrow in place. By then their targets were some eighty yards away but still well within range. Two quick volleys brought all but two down. Most were killed but three were wounded: one in the thigh, one in the calf and one in the shoulder.

The man with the calf wound carried on limping away but the other two had fallen.

'Quickly, knock the two wounded out and hoist them over your horses. I want to question them.'

Two men lifted each unconscious body onto the horse held by a third and then turned and sent two more arrows each into the crowd of yelling Scots running towards us. Seconds later we were all mounted and heading back to join the others of our band.

The Scots gave up the chase and we trotted away until we were safely out of range. Then we dismounted and the abbot led us in prayers of thanks for our salvation. We let the horses graze and drink from the river whilst the wounds of our captives were roughly attended to. I wanted them alive but I couldn't care less how much pain they would be in when they recovered consciousness.

We tied them across two of the packhorses and set off again for Falkirk. Their interrogation could wait until we got there, but I wanted to be certain who had sent them. I was fairly sure it was Malcolm, but I needed evidence before I met King Kenneth.

~~~

The King of Scots did not look in the best of health. His face was haggard and it had an unhealthy grey pallor. However, he held himself well and his voice was strong when he spoke. I hoped for all our sakes that he still had a few years life left in him. However, it was obvious to me that the day was coming when Malcolm would ascend the throne. I prayed that I had long enough to prepare for his inevitable invasion of Lothian.

But that wasn't my immediate problem. I had to convince Kenneth to keep the peace for now.

'I'm told that you call yourself Bretwalda of Lothian,' the king barked at me as soon as we came face to face on the wooden bridge over the River Avon at Falkirk.

Drest mac Cináeda, who I had first met at Falkirk a dozen years before when Malcolm and my father had united against the Norse horde of Olaf Tryggvason, stood behind the king. I had thought that he was Malcolm's man so I wondered what he was doing here. I later learned that, although he was Malcolm's cousin, he was Kenneth's champion first and foremost. He had a few grey hairs now and his face was more lined, but he was still a giant of a man and one who, from the expression on his face, still held me in contempt.

'Not quite, lord king. The ealdormen and thanes of Anglian Lothian elected me as such. It was not an honour, or a burden, that I sought.'

'Would you like to tell me why you slew Drest's nephew,' Kenneth asked.

I was puzzled. Drest was Malcolm's cousin but that didn't make him Angus' uncle. What I didn't know until later was that the giant was married to Malcolm's sister. However, my immediate concern was for our security. I wasn't about to enter into negotiations from a position of weakness.

'Before I say anything further, where is Giric?' I asked. 'I understood that he was to be surrendered to me as a hostage for my safety.'

Kenneth pursed his lips then nodded.

'Fetch my son.'

Drest lumbered away across the bridge, making it creak in places, and came back with a boy of about nine who scarcely came up to the warrior's waist. I had no idea if the lad was indeed Kenneth's son but he was dressed like a prince. As he passed Kenneth he gave him a nervous look and the king gave him an encouraging smile so I thought that he probably was his son.

The boy glared at me as he approached me and spat at my feet.

'What a charming son you have, lord king,' I said with a smile. 'Now I have something for you.'

I turned and beckoned towards Leland and he pushed our two captives forward. Their hands were tied and their ankles hobbled. Regrettably they looked the worse for wear. Quite apart from the bandaged wounds to their shoulder and calf respectively, their faces and torsos had taken a battering. Their interrogation had not been gentle.

After a while Leland had discovered that, fortuitously, they were brothers. He had persuaded the older man to talk by the simple expedient of brandishing a flensing knife and threatening to peel the skin off the younger man strip by strip. The threat had quickly induced the older man to confirm that it was indeed Malcolm that had sent his followers to ambush us. Thankfully they had proved inept at the task, mainly because they had underestimated the speed at which our horses could gallop; something they had based on the smaller ponies that they were used to.

'These are two of the hundred or so of your warriors who ambushed us yesterday.'

'What? No, that cannot be. I would never be party to such a thing!' Kenneth spluttered, furious at me for suggesting it.

'I don't think you had anything to do with it. This man confessed that it was Malcolm.'

Kenneth turned to glare at Drest.

'Did you know about this?'

Drest shook his head but I didn't believe him, and I don't think his king did either.

By producing the two captives I had wrong footed Kenneth and I now held the moral high ground. He had promised me safe conduct and he should have ensured that his promise was fulfilled.

'Very well. I apologise for the unauthorised actions of my cousin. You may rest assured that I will hold him to account for this,' he said stiffly.

'Thank you lord king.'

I doubted he would do anything other than make his displeasure known, but I didn't expect him to do more. He had enough problems without upsetting his heir unduly.

'Let us return to the slaying of my cousin Angus. I expect blood money and the head of the man responsible.'

'You know that Angus mismanaged the shire you gave him. What did he expect when he dispossessed so many thanes and drove them and their warriors out of their homes? That they would go quietly? No, they had a legitimate grievance and he brought their revolt on himself. He died in battle with them as a consequence. There is no blood debt due, nor was the man who killed him in fair fight a murderer.'

'They were outlaws; he was entitled to eradicate them as they were condemned men.'

'If they were outlaws, although no court had decreed that was the case, then he had made them so by acting unjustly. He was the cause of his own death.'

Kenneth made an impatient gesture and I knew that he had conceded the point and wanted to move on.

'I cannot accept the return of Edinburgh to the rule of your father, you must see that.'

'Of course, lord king, and I don't suggest it. He gave that to you in return for your help against the Norse. I have no intention of challenging that decision.'

'Then what do you propose?' he asked curiously.

'That the rightful heir to the shire, Hacca, becomes ealdorman but that he swears allegiance to you. As to the vills, all of the thanes Angus appointed have fled and those who they had replaced have been restored to their lands; I suggest that we leave things as they are.'

Kenneth paced up and down whilst he considered what I'd proposed. Finally he nodded.

'Very well. Provided that Edinburgh remains subservient to me, I agree to Hacca succeeding his father.'

'And his thanes are restored to their lands?'

'You're pushing your luck, Uhtred. You need to learn to be more cautious. Boldness is all very well but it can land you in an early grave.'

He chewed his lip and seemed lost in thought as he stared down at the water flowing under the bridge. Finally he turned back to me.

'On one condition; they must all swear fealty to me individually as well as to Hacca and pay me a tenth of the worth of their land.'

It was a harsh condition but no doubt the thanes would be allowed time to pay, perhaps years. A lot could happen in that time.

'It is for Hacca and his thanes to agree, but I will support such terms for the treaty between us.'

'They are to come to my camp and take their oaths to me before sunset tomorrow. That should give you enough time to round them up. I will not bargain further. You have wrung more out of me than I intended to give and I blame Malcolm's foolishness for that. Count yourself fortunate, Uhtred the Bold.'

It was a sobriquet that was to stick to me.

Chapter Ten – Saint Brice's Day Massacre

November 1002 to August 1003

I stayed at Falkirk for three days until the treaty, drawn up by the Abbot of Melrose and the Bishop of Saint Andrews, was signed. Then I left to return to Duns. Kenneth's men escorted us to the border of Selkirkshire and then returned, taking Giric back with them.

Giric had ignored me for the first part of our journey together but our mutual loathing for his father's heir thawed the boy's attitude to me. Unsurprisingly he felt that it was his right to succeed his father; furthermore, even at his age, he knew that his cousin would naturally regard Giric as a rival and would no doubt seek his death.

'When the time comes, you are welcome to seek sanctuary with me, Giric,' I told him quietly just before we parted.

He didn't reply but nodded, smiled briefly, and rode away. If only he had lived how different things might have been.

When I returned the council of ealdormen and thanes were generous with their praise and, modesty not being my greatest quality, I basked in their acclaim. But I wasn't lulled into a false sense of security by the respite I had secured. We needed to maintain our preparations for the day when Lothian was invaded by Malcolm.

However, it wasn't the Scots who posed the next danger.

Later that year I heard that Olaf Tryggvason had been killed; something that I paid scant attention to at the time. I hadn't thought much about the Norse leader after we'd defeated him at Penicuik all those years ago and his death in battle seemed irrelevant.

After he'd fled from England his luck had changed and in 995 he'd been crowned as King of Norway after defeating and killing his predecessor, Haakon Sigurdarson. However his reign lasted less than five years.

He was sailing home after raiding Pomerania when his ships were ambushed in the Baltic by the combined fleet of Sweyn Forkbeard, King of Denmark, Olaf Eiríksson, King of Sweden, and Eric Håkonsson, Jarl of Lade. Olaf was drowned and Sweyn Forkbeard appointed Eric Håkonsson to rule Norway as his vassal.

Two years later, in the summer of 1002, King Sweyn decided to raid the south coast of England. In the decades after the collapse of the Danelaw and the creation of a united England several Danes had risen to position of power and influence outside the old Danelaw. Amongst these was Pallig Tokesen, the Ealdorman of Devonshire.

Pallig was married to Gunhilde, Sweyn's sister, and he was suspected of assisting his brother-in-law's pillaging of the south by providing him with information. The raids provoked a backlash against the Danes, and whilst those living in Deira and Mercia were too numerous to be attacked, outbreaks of violence against Danes elsewhere became more and more common. On Saint Brice's Day in November scores were killed in London, Bristol, Gloucester and Oxford, which was the scene of the greatest atrocity. Amongst those killed was Pallig Tokesen and his wife, Gunhilde.

Whether King Æthelred was behind the Saint Brice's Day massacre, as was widely believed, wasn't clear. If he was it was a remarkably short-sighted policy. At first I thought that it wouldn't affect us in the far north of England, but I suppose I should have realised that the Danes of Deira would have had relatives who'd been killed and, in any case, they were incensed by the slaughter of hundreds of their compatriots.

Of course, in the decades after the Danes initially settled in Deira, East Anglia and part of Mercia there had been a great deal of inter-marriage between them and the local Anglo-Saxons. This had mostly been between men of Danish descent and Anglian women, but not exclusively so. However, although they were now all Christians, men with Danish blood were proud of their Viking heritage and their culture remained different to ours.

The real trouble in the north started with a quarrel between a Danish jarl and an Anglian thane over the ownership of land. The Dane had taken the land when the thane's father had died and his son, being too young to do much about it at the time, had fled to Mercia. When he was seventeen he'd returned with a small warband and killed the jarl and his hearth warriors.

The jarl's brother had then tried to drive the thane off his land and the conflict had spread with other landowners taking sides. The Earl of Deira, Ælfhelm, had proved incapable of halting the escalating violence and King Æthelred had grown alarmed at the prospect of his kingdom descending into civil war between Danes and Anglo-Saxons.

Because of sporadic Danish raids in Wessex and East Anglia he decided he couldn't come north himself so he sent a messenger to me with a letter.

'What does it say,' Ecgfrida asked when she saw me frown deeply at the contents.

She had been sitting playing a game with Aldred, who was now five and a half. Much to my son's evident annoyance, she left him and came across to me. I handed her the letter to read for herself.

'The king appoints you as Bretwalda of all Northumbria and charges you with the task of putting down the unrest in Deira,' she exclaimed after scanning it. 'How does he expect you to do that? You don't have anything like the number of warriors the Danes have and the fyrd won't want to get involved in a matter that doesn't threaten them and their families. Furthermore, all you've done to secure peace with the Scots has come at a cost to us. I don't see the king promising to recompense you for any expenditure involved.'

'That's true, and money is becoming a concern. Perhaps I need to raise the matter with him? He says I can call upon my father's warriors as well but he cautions me against making the situation worse by using excessive force.'

'What does he expect you to do? The situation is one of his making in the first place. He may be the king, but he has little or no common sense as far as I can see.'

'This isn't a problem that can be solved through fighting; it requires negotiation.'

'You plan to talk to the Danes? They'll kill you and leave me a widow and our son without a father to protect him.'

I had the distinct feeling that my wife was more worried about her situation, and that of her son, rather than having any concern for me. I scowled at her, feeling resentful.

'Not just the Danes,' I muttered savagely. 'I need to knock everyone's head together and seek a reconciliation.'

'What you need is a common enemy to bring them together. It's a pity that the Scots aren't a threat to them at present.'

'Not the Scots, no,' I said thoughtfully.

I forgot her apparent lack of concern for me; a germ of an idea had begun to develop in my mind, prompted by what she had said.

At first my father was unwilling to cooperate but, when I threatened to call a council of ealdormen and ask them to rule on the matter, he relented. Waltheof didn't derive all his income from taxes and rents. For a long time our family had traded across the North Sea and we maintained a small fleet of birlinns – a type of warship not that dissimilar to the Scandinavian longships – to escort our trading vessels to and fro across the pirate infested North Sea.

~~~

A week or so later I was heading north along the coast of Scotland feeling wretched and being constantly sick as the birlinn he had reluctantly lent me charged down one wave and rose up the next. The wind howled in the rigging and the rowers strained to keep her on course. I had been warned that to set out in February was foolhardy as it was still the season of storms, but I couldn't afford to wait. Once winter was over fighting between Dane and Anglo-Saxon would recommence in Deira.

My destination was Caithness in the north of Scotland. The Norse had settled in the Orkneys and Shetland Isles centuries before and eighty years ago they had invaded the north of Scotland, wresting control of Sutherland and Caithness from its Scottish mormaer. Now Sigurd the Stout, Jarl of Orkney, ruled the far north of the Scottish mainland from his base at Thurso - my destination.

Eventually the gale abated and we were able to raise the sail. Four days after we set out from Budle Bay near Bebbanburg we rounded Duncansby Head and headed west along the north coast towards Thurso Bay.

The settlement itself lay at the mouth of the river of the same name, but soon after we had rounded

Dunnet Head half a dozen longships put out from Thurso and surrounded our Birlinn.

'Who are you and what is your business here?' a voice called out in Norse.

'I am Uhtred, Bretwalda of Northumbria, come to seek an audience with Jarl Sigurd. Is he here?'

I was thankful that Borg had been able to teach me Norse before he had been killed.

'Bretwalda? It's not a title I know,' the voice called back.

'It means war leader.'

'You come here for war?'

The man sounded incredulous.

'No, to discuss something to our mutual benefit with Jarl Sigurd.'

'Very well. But only you and a servant will be allowed ashore, and you must come up to the hall unarmed.'

My body servant, Cædmon, didn't look happy at the prospect of accompanying me into the lion's den, but he didn't have much of a choice. I did and, as we were marched up to the jarl's hall by a score or more of fierce looking Norsemen, I wondered if my decision to come and see the Viking lord who ruled the north and the islands with an iron fist had been a wise one.

Jarl was a Scandinavian term for which the nearest English term was earl. However, many who called themselves jarls equated to no more than thanes, but this one was more like a minor king. Sigurd sat in a carved throne on a raised platform at the far end of his dimly-lit hall. At first I couldn't make out his features but as I came closer I could see a heavily bearded face marred by a scar which ran from his right eye across where his nose should have been and ended on the left hand side of his jawbone. No hair grew on the puckered scar tissue and the absence of a nose gave him a look that would give children nightmares.

His biceps were hidden by silver and gold arm rings but his forearms bore several scars. This man was a warrior of some experience – and luck to have survived such wounds. I half expected to see Thor's hammer, the charm worn by many Vikings, hanging around his neck, but instead a large silver crucifix lay on his chest suspended from a gold chain. Then I remembered hearing somewhere that Olaf Tryggvason had converted to Christianity at some stage and he had imposed the religion on his subjects, including the inhabitants of the Orkneys and Shetlands.

'Greetings, Jarl Sigurd, I come in peace seeking to discuss something to our mutual advantage.'

'Have you brought me a gift, you Saxon turd?'

It was not the most auspicious of beginnings. I refrained from pointing out that I was an Angle, not a Saxon.

'I have, lord. It is on my ship. May I send for my men to bring it here?'

'No, my men will fetch it. It had better be enough to make it worth my while to listen to your bleating.'

He nodded and half a dozen men left the hall. Meanwhile I was biting my tongue, trying hard not to respond to the man's insults. We withdrew to the side of the hall to wait for the return of his men whilst Sigurd heard petitions and issued judgements. It rapidly became apparent that Sigurd ruled through fear and the punishments he meted out were harsh. It shouldn't have surprised me. He had started as Jarl of Orkney but he now held sway over the Shetland Islands, the northern Hebrides off the west coast as well as Caithness and Sutherland on the mainland. He paid homage to Sweyn Forkbeard but, in reality, he was left alone to rule his petty realm as he saw fit.

Sigurd held up his hand to halt a man who was claiming that another had stolen his wife when his men returned with the gift I'd brought him. He got up from his throne with difficulty and waddled down the steps to where the chest had been put down. One of his men opened it to reveal a quantity of hack silver and silver coins. His eyes lit up at the sight of it, as well they might. It represented the best part of my income for a year. I prayed that it would be worth it.

'Very good,' he said, giving me a grotesque smile. 'I accept your gift. Now all you have to do is to defeat my champion and I will listen to your proposal.

~~~

Sigurd's champion proved to be a warrior who made the Scottish giant, Drest, look like a midget. He stood head and shoulders above me and his arms were as thick as my legs. He held a two handed battle axe in his right hand and a sword a foot longer than mine in his left. Neither of us wore a byrnie or a helmet. I had been offered an axe but it wasn't a weapon I was familiar with and, to Sigurd's amazement, I opted for a dagger as my second weapon.

My adversary had a wolfish grin on his face and seemed to be relishing the prospect of cutting me into little pieces. I regarded that as a good sign; it meant that he was overconfident.

'Is this to the death?' I asked Sigurd as I my opponent and I circled each other warily; at least it was warily on my part.

'Not necessarily,' Sigurd replied, giving me a chilling smiles. 'You can make him submit or you can kill him. Then I will hear you. On the other hand, if you lose I have no further interest in you and it is up to him whether he lets you live or not.'

The Norse giant whose name I hadn't caught lumbered forward and swung his axe at my head, I turned and moved sideways, straight into the path of his sword as he aimed a blow at my side. I parried it with my own sword but his blow had such force behind it that I nearly lost my grip on the hilt.

As we squared up to one another again I moved as soon as I saw him tense for another attack. This time I rolled on my right shoulder and both his axe and sword swung at a body that was no longer there. As I came up into the kneeling position I slashed my dagger at his hamstring and dug the point of my sword into his thigh.

He roared in pain and his right leg collapsed under him. He must have been in agony but he still tried to swing his axe at my legs. I jumped up with both feet and, as I landed, I swung my sword, cutting

144

into his right forearm. His hand opened and the axe fell from his grasp.

I backed away and invited him to yield but the man wouldn't give up. Instead he tried to spit me on his sword. I was taken by surprise as I had relaxed, expecting him to surrender. I took a step back but the tip of his sword still struck my shin. Blood ran down my leg and I suspected that he had chipped the bone.

I was furious, more at myself for letting my guard down than at him. I had intended to spare him but I realised that a defeated champion was a nithing - a man with no honour or worth - and I suspected that he would rather be dead. I decided to oblige him.

I dropped my sword and dagger and picked up his discarded axe with two hands. It was even heavier that I had expected and I wondered how anyone, even a giant like him, could wield it one handed. He tried to stab me with his sword again but I moved out of the way with ease and then darted in, swinging the axe as I moved. The sharp edge struck his bull-like neck cleanly and, such was the weight of the head, that it cut straight through, muscle, sinew, blood vessels and bone. The head flew from the body and bounced once, coming to rest at the feet of Sigurd the Stout.

The jarl looked astounded for a second then clapped his hands together.

'Very well, Saxon, I will listen to what you have to say.'

'I'm not a Saxon any more than you are a Dane,' I replied calmly. 'My ancestors came from Angeln in the south of the Jutland peninsula, not Saxony.'

Sigurd looked at me, and for a moment I thought that I had gone too far in standing up for myself, but then he roared with laughter.

'I can see why they call you Uhtred the Bold. Very well, Angle, let's drink a horn of two of ale together and you can tell you what you are doing here.'

~~~

I was in York when news began to filter through about a series of raids by Danes throughout eastern Deira. I had taken Ecgfrida and Aldred to visit Bishop Aldhun at Durham on the way and then continued south on the pretext of visiting Earl Ælfhelm as Bretwalda of Northumbria to discuss mutual defence arrangements.

I wasn't surprised when Ælfhelm refused to see me, saying that he did not recognise my appointment as Bretwalda; as far as he was concerned he was the war leader of Deira.

My next visit was to see the archbishop. Ealdwulf, who had officiated at my marriage to Ecgfrida, had died in the spring and the new appointee was Wulfstan Lupus. Originally a Benedictine monk, he was also Bishop of Worcester and a favourite of the king. He was no soldier, but he was a noted scholar and a drafter of laws. Thankfully he shared my low opinion of Ælfhelm.

He had a horror of Vikings, and of anything else which disturbed the tranquillity of his life of prayer, his work to reform the Church and to make England a more law-abiding kingdom. The current strife between the Danes and the Anglo-Saxons of Deira was therefore abhorrent to him. He promised me his support, and that of the clergy, in restoring order to the earldom.

The next day tidings reached the city of several raids on the lands of the Danish jarls. At first these were thought be the work of Vikings from Denmark. However, instead of pillaging the coastal settlements, as was usual, they rowed up various rivers to strike at villages and towns several miles inland. Unlike the coastal villages, who were used to such raids and had long practiced procedures for fleeing inland with their valuables and livestock, the targets of these raids were taken unawares.

Ælfhelm's reaction was to barricade himself in York until the danger had passed. This reduced his standing amongst his nobles even further, if that were possible. In contrast, my men and the archbishop's messengers rode to every ealdorman, jarl and thane in Deira with a letter signed by both Wulfstan and me calling a muster at Selby.

This place was no more than a large village but it was a good site for a muster with lush grazing for the horses and flat land for the camp. Moreover it lay on the River Ouse, which was central to the plans I had made with Sigurd the Stout.

Less than three weeks after the summons had gone out the majority of Deira's warriors and the fyrd had arrived outside Selby. I had the Danes camp separately from the rest to avoid any outbreaks of trouble and, thankfully, there weren't more than a few incidents.

Five shires now made up Deira: based on Catterick in the north-west, Whitby on the coast, York itself, Beverley in the south, and one centred on Leeds which had been the Kingdom of Elmet centuries ago. The ealdormen of York, Beverley and Leeds were of Danish descent and the other two were Angles, like me.

That said, it was true that most of my ancestors had been Angles, but there was the odd Saxon amongst them, and the founder of our family, Catinus, had been a Briton who had come from Mercia as a slave. However, he had married an Angle and most of my ancestors since then had been Angles. In fact much of England had been settled by the Angles – Northumbria, East Anglia and most of Mercia, for example.

The Jutes had conquered Kent and parts of the south coast whilst the Saxons had taken the south west, Essex and the land immediately to the north of London. It was only the eventual dominance of Wessex that led to foreigners lumping us all together as Saxons. It was a small comfort that the name of the kingdom – England - and our common tongue – English – was derived from the name of my race.

Once all five Ealdormen and most of the jarls and thanes had arrived with their warriors and the fyrd the archbishop called a war council. In all there were nearly sixty of us and somehow we all crammed into the small timber church at Selby. It would have been better to have met in the open, but it had started raining.

I pushed my way to the front, clearing a path for Wulfstan as I went. Some objected to being shoved out of the way, but they bit back their protests when they saw the archbishop. The place stank of wet wool and unwashed bodies. Since I was a small boy I had bathed in the sea at Bebbanburg and I liked to wash as often as I could. However, few Anglo-Saxons were so fastidious, bathing only occasionally. In contrast the Scandinavian races were much more particular about cleanliness and their appearance.

When we reached the altar we turned to face the others. I had prevailed upon Wulfstan to accompany me because I needed his authority to bolster my own. After Saint Brice's Day Æthelred wasn't popular in the north and I didn't want to rely on his appointment of me as Bretwalda alone. However, Wulfstan seemed tongue tied and the silence grew until it became embarrassing.

'Pretend you are delivering a homily,' I whispered to him and he nodded.

'Brothers in Christ,' he began. 'We have come here to defeat the pagan Norsemen and throw them back into the sea before they can wreak any more havoc.'

I didn't like to point out that they were Norsemen, but ones who had had been converted to Christianity, and were therefore not pagans. After all, I wasn't meant to know anything about them.

My part of the deal was to provide Sigurd with information about where plunder could be found in places where the inhabitants wouldn't have a chance to bury or carry off their valuables. It remained to be seen if he would adhere to his part of the plan.

Naturally, I was a little apprehensive that my involvement might be uncovered. I had no illusions that the men of Deira would kill me, and probably quite painfully, if they ever found out. However, only Cædmon knew the details of what had been agreed.

Of course my warband had crewed the birlinn to the Orkneys and might put two and two together. However, I trusted the latter implicitly; after all they had sworn an oath of loyalty to me that was binding unto death. My body servant was a different matter and when Leland reported that he had seen him deep in conversation with a servant of one of the Danish jarls my suspicions were aroused.

'Take him somewhere quiet and find out what they were talking about,' I said, not without a great deal of regret.

I had liked Cædmon and he was a good servant; however, I couldn't afford to take any risks. I didn't need to tell Leland that he would have to kill my servant and dispose of the body once he'd questioned him. Even if innocent of trying to betray me, I could hardly expect Cædmon to remain loyal once he'd suffered interrogation.

When Leland came back that evening to say that Cædmon had been bribing the jarl's servant to let him have some apples for me to eat I felt a great deal of remorse, but at least I wouldn't have to worry about the man's loyalty any more.

That left me without a servant and I decided that I would clean my own armour and weapons and groom my horses myself as penance for having had an innocent man killed. That didn't last long, however;

the following day Ulfric returned from patrol and came to see me. He found me using sand to burnish my helmet and asked where Cædmon was.

'I don't know. He seems to have vanished.'

Ulfric had been out of camp when Leland had questioned my servant and, although I trusted Ulfric above almost anyone else, there was no point in more people than necessary knowing about Cædmon.

'How strange,' Ulfric mused. 'I would never have expected him to run.'

'Perhaps he fell in the river and drowned. He never did learn to swim,'

'Maybe, anyway I came to tell you that the Viking host is about three hours away, coming upstream in some twenty longships.'

Longships varied in size, the largest carrying seventy warriors or more and the smallest about thirty. Assuming an average fighting crew of fifty men, that meant that Sigurd the Stout had brought around a thousand warriors with him. Our force numbered two and a half thousand, but only about eight hundred were trained warriors; the rest were members of the fyrd. Those accompanying the Danish jarls were better trained and equipped than the Anglo-Saxon freemen, but they wouldn't be a match for the Norsemen. Not that I intended to fight.

'From previous reports it would appear that that's the whole Norse fleet.'

'Yes, it seems so. However, the ships are crammed full. It seems that they had taken a lot of our people as slaves.'

I was immediately alarmed. I had made an agreement with Sigurd but I didn't altogether trust him. When our armies faced each other he was to negotiate and then withdraw, taking his loot with him. That was to be his payment in return for the information I'd given him on where to raid and what the defences were. He'd promised not to enslave Deirans, or to kill any more than he had to. If he had decided to ignore that part of our pact, would he abide by anything else he'd agreed to?

We formed up for battle south of Selby between the river and a large wood. It was a good defensive position as we lined up on the north bank of a tributary of the Ouse, called the River Aire. It was relatively narrow but the muddy banks would make it into something of an obstacle for attackers.

The plan was for Sigurd to disembark his men on the left bank of the Ouse and then march forward to face us; I would then negotiate with him.

At least I could see that Sigurd had stuck to the first part of our agreement. His men advanced until they were a few hundred yards from the banks of the Aire. The land hereabouts was flat and the nearest trees were the best part of a mile away. I was therefore confident that I was looking at the sum total of his warriors and there was none hidden away to surprise us if things didn't go as planned.

I had sent scouts out on our side of the river at dawn and so I was as certain as I could be that none had crossed the Aire further upstream and were now waiting to take us in the left flank.

I rode forward with the archbishop, the ealdormen of Deira, together with Leland and Ulfric, halting a few yards back from the river. Sigurd did the same, bringing half a dozen of his chieftains with him and a boy of about eleven. Unlike us they were all on foot.

'I'm Uhtred, son of Waltheof, Earl of Bernicia. I represent the people of Deira, many of whom you have pillaged and made captive. Who are you?'

'Sigurd, Jarl of the Orkneys, the Shetlands, Caithness, Sutherland and the Scottish Isles. I go where I like and take plunder from those weaker than me. How are you going to stop me? With that rabble? Most scratch in the dirt for a living and have no more idea of how to fight than my son here has about how to read Latin.'

I looked at the boy dubiously. Those of Sigurd's sons I had seen at Thurso were grown men. This lad was wearing a fine blue woollen tunic with silver embroidery at the hems and the neck but it was too large for him, his face was filthy and his hair was lank and matted. Norsemen and Danes were much more diligent about personal hygiene than this boy. Their hair, in particular, was kept clean and well groomed. I guessed that this boy was a thrall – a slave – who had been dressed up to look the part.

I stared at him and the lad refused to meet my eye, looking down as if ashamed at the deception he had been forced to take part in. Any Norse boy, especially the son of a man as powerful as Sigurd the Stout, would have stared back at me with defiance, and like as not hatred.

I decided to let the matter be. I had agreed with Sigurd that he would hand over his youngest son as a hostage to ensure he kept his word about leaving Northumbria alone in future. At least giving me this thrall had the appearance of leaving a hostage.

Ulfric edged his horse close to mine and said loudly in English, a language that luckily Sigurd didn't understand.

'That boy is no more Sigurd's child than I am a sheep's dropping.'

'I know; but if I challenge him that he'll have no option but to fight. I want to end this without bloodshed, if I can.'

I had said this for the benefit of the ealdormen. Ulfric didn't know the details but he knew enough to guess that this was all a charade. I dismounted and walked forward to the edge of the river where we wouldn't have to shout at each other. Sigurd did the same, waving his men back but bringing the boy with him.

'If you let us depart in peace with our plunder then I swear not to harm your lands further. I'll leave my son with you as hostage. Reject my terms and you'll all die.'

'You'll swear by your gods to keep faith?'

'I'm a Christian, not a pagan,' Sigurd replied, affronted. 'I'll swear on the Holy Bible.'

I knew that, of course, but I had to pretend that I knew nothing about the man.

'Very well. One of my men will ride across and collect your son, then the Archbishop of York will come over to administer the oath. But first you have to release all the captives you've taken.'

'They are all Scots,' Sigurd said blandly.

I doubted that very much. Some might be as no doubt the Vikings had done a little raiding on their way south along the coast, but most would be from Deira. However, I couldn't call him a liar openly.

'Nevertheless you will release them. I have a treaty with the King of Scots.'

That gave Sigurd pause for thought. He might decide to defy me, but Kenneth was trying to recover Caithness and Sutherland. If I brought the armies of Northumbria north to help him it was probable that we could defeat him. However, taking the Northumbrians all the way up to northern tip of Britain was as likely as snow on a hot day in August. For a start my father would never agree to my leading the men of Bernicia anywhere, and I doubted that the rest would want to leave their homes to fight so far away. However, Sigurd couldn't be certain of that.

'Very well, we will release them and send them across to you. Let's get on with this.'

And it was as simple as that. Whilst the banks were slippery and men on foot who tried to cross would keep sliding back down into the water, horses found it easier to climb the soft mud. Ulfric rode across with Wulfstan and he administered the oath, then they returned with Sigurd's pretend son on the back of Ulfric's horse. I rode across with fifty mounted warriors and followed the Vikings back to where the fleet was beached.

The captives were released and Sigurd and his men departed without another word being spoken. I heard later that he had raided the coast north of the Forth and no doubt replenished their supply of thralls to make up for those I had persuaded him to leave behind. I never met him again.

Naturally both the Danes and Angles of Deira were ecstatic about their bloodless victory over the Norsemen, as they saw it, and, as I had hoped, it served to bond them together again, at least for now.

As I suspected, the boy was indeed a thrall. He was a Pict from Caithness called Uuen, the rest of whose family had been killed when Sigurd attacked their village. He protested and fought like a tiger when my men stripped him and washed his filthy body in the River Ouse but I allowed him to keep his thick woollen tunic and leggings, rich though they were and far too good for a servant. He was grateful for that and, when I gave him a choice: become a swineherd, his occupation whilst a thrall of the Norsemen, or serve me as my new body servant, he had the sense to choose the latter.

Chapter Eleven - The Battle of Monzievaird

1004 -05

I was out riding with my son when the summons came. Aldred was now seven and was a more than competent rider of the pony I'd bought him for his last birthday. We'd raced back home and, although I had given him a head start, he managed to gallop in through the gates in the palisade, whooping with delight, just ahead of me.

As I handed my sweaty horse over to a stable boy to unsaddle and rub down, Ecgfrida came out of the door to the hall.

'The king has sent a letter,' she told me without preamble, wringing her hands in dismay.

I knew immediately that it wasn't good news. King Æthelred's foolish collusion in the massacre of the Danes in 1002 continued to haunt him. Sweyn Forkbeard, King of Denmark and Norway, had ravaged the Wessex coastline in 1003 and then returned to invade eastern England the following year. The Earl of East Anglia, Leofsige, had raised the fyrd to oppose the invasion by Sweyn and his Danes but Leofsige had been killed and his army routed near Bury St. Edmund's, leaving the east of England undefended.

The letter said that Æthelred was gathering a mighty host to drive Sweyn out of England for once and all. The king ordered me to gather as many men from Northumbria as I could and bring them to Nottingham. I was to meet the muster from Mercia there and he would join us as soon as he could with the men of Wessex.

I showed the king's letter to Leland.

'The man's mad,' he scoffed. 'The Danes of Deira haven't forgiven him for the Saint Brice's Day massacre and, in any case, they are hardly likely to be reliable allies against other Danes. I can't see your father letting you take the Bernician fyrd anywhere either, and the men of Lothian are needed here.'

He was right. The last reports I had of Kenneth indicated that he and Malcolm, his putative heir, had fallen out. The story I heard was that Kenneth had changed his mind and had now made his fourteen year old son, Giric, his heir. The rumour wasn't exactly correct. A few weeks later I learned that Giric had been installed as co-ruler with his father. Presumably Kenneth thought that this would ensure a smooth transition of the throne from father to son when the time came. Predictably Malcolm had been incandescent with rage. He denounced Kenneth as foresworn and a traitor, and set about trying to instigate a rebellion amongst the mormaers. I would much rather have Giric as King of Scots than Malcolm, but he was too young to command that much support north of the border.

'What will you do?' Ecgfrida asked me when we were alone.

It had been a long time since we had shared a bed but we were still close and had no secrets from each other now, at least not on my side. Not only were we good friends but increasingly I relied on her advice on important matters. She had never let me forget the risk I'd run in going to Orkney and making a pact with Sigurd the Stout. Ever since then I'd confided in her before making important decisions.

'I'll have to make it clear to the king that his northern border is too volatile to strip it of fighting men at the moment.'

'He may never forgive you if you desert him in his time of need,' she pointed out.

'It's a risk I'll have to take. My duty is to Northumbria. Æthelred's writ barely runs up here anyway.'

The reply was duly sent and I heard nothing further that year. As it turned out there was no pitched battle between the armies of Sweyn and Æthelred. When the latter advanced into eastern England he found the place a wasteland with nothing left of the towns and villages except charred timbers, but no Danes opposed him.

It transpired that, whilst that summer was warm and relatively dry in England, it had never stopped raining in Denmark and the harvest had been ruined. The population was in danger of starving during the coming winter and there was general unrest at Sweyn's absence. He had little option but to return home in haste.

That winter was another harsh one and everyone, Malcolm included, was too busy ensuring that most of his people survived to cause much mischief. Our grain stores were full, the livestock well protected against hungry packs of wolves, the rafters of my hall were hung with smoked meat, and the piles of cut wood would see us through the cold days and nights ahead. We settled down for a comfortable, if dull, winter.

It wasn't until the middle of January that the snows came. It had been bitterly cold from early December onwards but the daytime skies were blue and those at night twinkled with stars. Of course the absence of cloud cover meant that the frosts were severe and the ice often didn't melt from one day to the next. The ground was frozen solid and that meant that travel, though unpleasant was feasible with care.

Apart from riding around the outlying hamlets and down to Carham and Norham to see that everyone was alright, I didn't stray very far. However, travellers came to us from time to time. We heard the worst of tidings from a mendicant friar who was returning to his mother house in York and begged a night's rest with us. It was our duty to help and give him food as well as a bed for the night. In return he was a fund of gossip.

'I saw no signs of preparation for war, but that was hardly surprising in this weather,' he confided in a hoarse whisper that could heard a hundred yards away. 'But there was talk of it in the air everywhere I went north of the Forth.

'Malcom is supported by the Mormaers of Fife, Angus and Perth whereas the others, including Hacca of Edinburgh, support Kenneth and Giric, or so it is rumoured.'

'That would give Kenneth numerical superiority, wouldn't it?' I asked him.

'I'm not a military man, far from it, but it is also said that Owain ap Dyfnwal of Strathclyde will change his allegiance to Malcolm once battle is joined.'

'You mean he will turn his coat on the battlefield and stab Kenneth in the back?' I asked, aghast.

'That's what I just said, isn't it?' he asked peevishly.

'We must stop him,' I said decisively, though I had no idea how I could do that.

~~~

Hacca was pleased, but somewhat surprised, to see me when I arrived at his stronghold of Edinburgh. Over a tankard of mead I told him what the friar had told me.

'Yes, it's only too true, I fear,' he confirmed with a sigh. 'Kenneth is gathering his forces in the south before marching north to confront Malcolm. I am ordered to join the king's muster at Dunblane. That's where Owain and the men of Strathclyde will join us.'

I hadn't mentioned what the friar had said about Owain being ready to betray Kenneth up to now and I debated whether I should confide in him. I decided to try an oblique approach.

'Have you heard any rumours about Owain?'

Hacca shifted uncomfortably in his seat.

'I don't listen to gossip,' he said a trifle stiffly.

161

'Then you should. At the very least they provide a line of enquiry to follow up. You'll learn that the key to survival is often knowing more than the next man.'

He looked unconvinced but admitted that he'd heard stories that Owain had been in secret negotiations with Malcolm.

'I don't give them much credence. If Owain became an oath breaker then he would be despised by all honest men.'

'Perhaps what Malcolm has promised him will make the disapproval of his inferiors unimportant in comparison?'

Hacca sat lost in thought for a moment.

'What are you suggesting?' he asked at long last.

'That we harry and delay Owain's army so that he arrives too late to take part in the battle. By that I mean raids on his baggage train; attacks by my horsemen to force his men to deploy, followed by a quick withdrawal; night attacks on his camp; that sort of thing.'

'But supposing these rumours are false and that Owain intends to aid Kenneth and Geric?'

I shrugged. 'The Britons are a threat to Lothian anyway, so I won't lose any sleep over killing a few of them.'

'You say that that you need my help but I am duty bound to answer the summons to Dunblane.'

'Do we know where Malcolm is at the moment?'

'The last I heard he was still gathering his forces in Angus.'

'If Owain is mustering his men at Dumbarton, and I've sent scouts out to verify that, then I'd expect him

162

to take the road from there to Stirling, cross the River Forth, and then head north to Dunblane. If you lend me your household warriors, preferably mounted, you can still head for Dunblane with your fyrd.'

Hacca still looked dubious and so I added: 'Your warriors can join you there, or follow you if Kenneth has already left to confront Malcolm. I need men who can fight well and move swiftly for my plan to work and, being mounted, they will easily catch a slow moving army up.'

'Very well. I'll let you have twenty horsemen. How many will that give you in total?'

'About a hundred. It's nothing like the numbers Owain will have in his army, but it should be enough for what I intend.'

In fact, when the scouts returned to confirm that the Strathclyde Britons were mustering at Dumbarton, they estimated the numbers already there at fifteen hundred.

~~~

Owain's Britons had halted for the night beside Endrick Water, a river which ran from its confluence with the River Carron to Loch Lommond. They evidently felt safe within their own lands and didn't bother to put out any piquets. The only sentries we could see were at the horse lines and outside King Owain's tent. Most of the Britons slept in the open, only the chieftains and nobles having tents. That made our task simpler.

163

The night was chilly, as you might expect for the middle of March in the Scottish glens, and there was a light frost on the ground, illuminated by the full moon above. It meant that each group kept their campfire banked up to provide a little warmth, although only those closest to the fire would really get much benefit. The good news was that it gave us light to see what we were about.

The signal to move was the hoot of an owl repeated four times in quick succession. It was unlikely to occur in nature but it would arouse less interest than a blast on a horn. We moved forward in a long line which stretched from one side of the camp to another.

At first we walked our horses and started to methodically spear the sleeping men as they lay on the ground. It wasn't long before someone saw us and started to shout a warning, but by that time we must have killed the best part of a hundred men. We continued at a walk, thrusting our spears into men as they rose groggily to their feet until someone had the sense to try and organise some form of defence.

Groups of Britons coalesced into ad hoc groups armed with weapons and shields but we didn't try to tackle them. I gave the signal and a horn blared out the charge. By this time we were near Owain's tent and he emerged just as I reached it. I thrust my spear towards his bare chest; had I succeeded in killing him history might have been very different. However, one of the sentries managed to interpose his shield in front of his king and jabbed at me with his own spear.

Thankfully he was unused to fighting horsemen and he aimed at me instead of my much more vulnerable horse. Had I ended up on foot I would have been either dead or a prisoner. I ducked and the spear went over my left shoulder, scraping a couple of links from my chain mail as it went. I kicked out with my boot and the man went tumbling back into the side of the tent.

One of my companions had disposed of the other sentry but now several armed warriors were heading our way. Owain had a sword in his hand and he attempted to slash my thigh open. I steered my horse away from the blow with my knees and the sword cut deep into the wooden part of the saddle instead of my flesh. There it stuck fast, much to Owain's fury as he tried to pull it free.

I stabbed down wildly with my spear and felt it sink into flesh. I had no ideas how much damage I had done to the king but we were now coming under attack and it was time to go before we lost too many men. I waved frantically at my signaller and he blew the signal to disengage on his horn. Everywhere my men broke off fighting and kicked their heels into their steeds. We galloped through the rest of the camp, scattering men or riding over them if they were too slow to get out of the way.

We heard the sound of pursuit behind us but we didn't stop until the ground started to slope upwards towards the hills known as the Campsie Fells. There I discovered that we had lost six men killed or so badly wounded that they had fallen from their horses.

Eight others had minor flesh wounds which were washed, sewn up with catgut and bandaged.

By the time we had done this, and our blown horses had recovered, we could hear the sound of the Britons searching for us. We had scattered their herd of ponies and a few horses as we left the camp so I suspected that our pursuers were on foot. We listened intently and silently Kenric pointed towards a spot three hundred yards away where we could dimly make out a few men as they breasted a ridgeline below us. I quickly counted those I could see and came up with an estimate of about thirty.

Handing the reins of my horse to Uuen I took a firm grip on my sword and shield and headed downhill on foot, angling to the right of the oncoming Britons. I took seventy men with me, leaving the rest with Uuen and our horses.

We kept to the shadows as much as possible and moved slowly so as not to alert the Britons to our presence. The skittering of a dislodged stone would sound very loud in the stillness of the night. However, our quarry was making enough noise to hide any inadvertent sounds we might make. Once we were close to the enemy, but still a little above them, I gave a hand signal and we moved into a wedge formation.

They didn't know what had hit them. We drove through them like a spear through a straw target, killing and wounding as we went. By the time we'd emerged on the other side of the group we must have caused over a dozen casualties with no losses to ourselves. Moreover, they were disorganised and demoralised. We turned and attacked the remainder and a melee ensued. The outcome was never in doubt as we outnumbered them quite significantly.

I was faced by a yelling Briton waving his spear around as if trying to scare me. I batted the point aside with my shield and thrust my sword into his guts. He dropped his spear and clutched his stomach as he dropped to the ground.

I stepped over him to confront a large man with a double handed axe. Had it struck me neither helmet nor byrnie would have saved me. He raised his axe on high and aimed at my head but I stooped low and to the side. The axe missed my left leg by inches as I drove the point of my sword through his neck. He gurgled and died, spurting blood everywhere.

It was all over. We had killed thirty two of the Britons and the rest had fled. There were no wounded to worry about because my men slit their throats before stripping the corpses of anything of value, not that there was much, and making our way back up to our horses.

We camped for the rest of the night further into the hills and slept to recover from out exertions until the sun was high in the sky. As soon as we had had a bite to eat the scouts left to find Owain's army whilst the rest of us made our way into the Gargunnock Hills north east of the Campsies.

In the middle of the afternoon the scouts came back to say that the Strathclyde army had only managed to advance five miles after recovering from our night attack. They were now on the flat ground to the south of Flanders Moss. It took us an hour and a half to reach a small village that lay just to the south of the road that Owain was following.

We waited, hidden from sight but only a few hundred yards from the passing army, until the baggage train came into sight. There were thirty lumbering carts drawn by oxen and filled with everything from food and tents to spare spears and arrows. They were guarded by a hundred men on foot walking beside the carts and a further hundred bringing up the rear.

Half of my horsemen were armed as normal but the rest carried small pitchers of oil in one hand and a flaming torch in the other. I raised my arm and as soon as I lowered it we galloped out of the village and spread out, heading for the long line of carts. They weren't aware of us until we were almost upon them and by then it was too late. Whilst some cut down the nearest guards the rest smashed their pots in the wagons and threw the torches after them.

Every cart went up with a whoosh that must have been heard at the front of the column. Our task was done and we galloped back to the village where the twenty men who had bows dismounted and grabbed their quivers before standing in a line just in front of the outermost hovels.

They managed to get two more flights of arrows into the air before the first one had landed. The sixty arrows wrought havoc in the leading ranks of the rear guard as they charged towards us. They halted, uncertain what to do as the fourth volley tore into them.

'That's enough,' I called. 'Mount up and let's get out of here.'

The Britons camped in the open by a small lake that night and set so many sentries that I doubted if anyone got much sleep. They had no tents and precious little food. Moreover their bundles of spare spears and arrows had been lost, seriously hampering their ability to wage war.

Early the next morning I sent some scouts out again. Half a dozen went to keep an eye on Owain's men, but the rest went to find out if Kenneth had left Dunblane yet. I led the remainder to a timber bridge over the River Forth. There were fords but the bridge lay on the direct route from Owain's current position to Dunblane. The only other bridge was near Stirling and to use that would add nearly a day onto his journey.

We arrived to find that Owain had taken the precaution of sending a party of men on ponies to take possession of the bridge. Thankfully there were only thirty of them and they fled back toward their army as soon as we appeared.

It took us two hours to chop through the supports so that the bridge collapsed into the river. Now Owain would have to backtrack to one of the fords upstream or head for Stirling. The fords were passable but the water was high and could only be done slowly and with care. It would certainly take a lot longer to use any of them compared to using the bridge. Either way we had delayed him by another day or so.

My own scouts had crossed unopposed at Stirling and came back to report that, although Kenneth was still at Dunblane, it looked as if the camp was preparing to move out. That probably meant that Malcolm had left Perth and was on the move. Kenneth would have been in something of a quandary; should he move to counter Malcolm or wait for Owain? It seemed that he had opted for the former. I was tempted to head for home, my duty done, but I decided that I'd better remain for a little longer and made sure that Owain didn't catch up with Kenneth.

~~~

Although the bridge had been destroyed it would be quite possible to rebuild it using timber from a nearby wood. My plan was therefore to hold the far side of the crossing point and use my archers to hamper any re-building work. At this point the river was too deep for men on foot to cross as, even if they could swim, the current was strong enough to sweep them downstream and drown them. On the other hand, our horses could cross back further down river by swimming with us hanging onto the saddle horns when it came time to withdraw.

We camped for the night on the far bank of the River Forth and at dawn we prepared our position, using timbers from the destroyed bridge to make an improvised palisade to protect out twenty archers. The enemy vanguard appeared at noon and halted uncertainly on the far bank. They started to call insults across and caper about but whoever was in command didn't seem to know what to do.

When Owain arrived he did something I hadn't expected. He sent his men to cut timber and make rafts. As soon as the first twenty were ready he loaded a score of men on each and launched them further upstream from us. They used poles to try and direct them but, in truth, they were out of control as they rushed past us in the middle of the river. Our archers managed to hit quite a few of the rafts' occupants and then they were out of range and still heading downstream.

'Ulfric, take half a dozen men and go and see where they come ashore,' I told him and he rushed off.

It was a good hour before they returned and Ulfric had a grin on his face.

'They all grounded back on the far bank except for a couple who capsized,' he told me.

I had seen Owain send riders to find out what had happened to his rafts and they returned shortly after Ulfric had and obviously reported the same thing. Ten minutes or so later the Strathclyde army set off along the south bank, presumably heading for one of the fords or the bridge near Stirling.

'Do we take the other bridge and destroy it?' Ulfric asked.

'No, we need it to cross back into Lothian,' I replied, shaking my head. 'Leland,' I called out. 'Get everyone mounted. 'We're going home.'

There was no plunder to pay my men with so I had to pay them out of my own dwindling resources.

Money was becoming a bit of a worry but at least Kenneth and his son were now free to deal with Malcolm without Owain stabbing him in the back.

As it turned out all our efforts had been in vain.

~~~

I later heard what had happened from one of Geric's gesith – the companions who formed his bodyguard – who had managed to survive.

'We had camped at Loch Monzievaird about fifteen miles west of Perth,' he told me as he sat at dinner the evening after he'd arrived. We thought that Malcolm was still at Perth, but evidently he had stolen a march on us and the next morning the scouts came racing back to say that his army was less than two miles away, this side of Crieff.

'Geric and his father had mustered three thousand men; it should have been many more but Owain of Strathclyde had failed to answer the summons. By the time that Kenneth had summoned his mormaers and chieftains it was too late. We rushed into formation but Malcolm launched his attack before we were ready. Some warriors were still struggling into their byrnies when the first wave tore into us.

'We were probably equally matched in terms of numbers but Geric was determined to break the attack to give his father a chance to form the army up. He raced into the fray with five hundred men and for a moment we managed to hold them off. We were killing two of theirs to every one of ours, but then Geric was killed. Most of his gesith died trying to avenge him but I was knocked unconscious and didn't wake up until after Malcolm had won and his men were looting the dead.

'I later found out that Kenneth had been so grief stricken by his son's death that he had tried to fight his way through Malcolm's gesith to kill the man himself. He was killed within feet of him and then the heart must have gone out of our men and they fled.'

'So Malcolm is now the undisputed King of Scotland?'

'Yes. I heard that he was crowned at Scone two weeks ago. It took me a long time to get here on foot, hiding from Malcolm's men who scoured the land looking for survivors. Evidently he's keen to ensure that he rules unchallenged.'

I wondered what had happened to the bodies of Kenneth and his son but much later I heard that Malcolm had at least been magnanimous in victory. He had sent the bodies of Kenneth the Third and Geric the Second for burial on Iona with previous kings of the Scots.

Now I had an implacable enemy on my northern border and Æthelred was too busy coping with Danish invasions and revolts further south to help Northumbria.

Chapter Twelve –

Malcolm's Invasion

Early Summer 1006

Thankfully the new King of Scots spent the next year or so consolidating his hold on his kingdom and trying, in vain, to drive the Norsemen out of Sutherland and Caithness. I wasn't idle, of course. Far from it. I was busy supervising the training of the men of Lothian and travelled everywhere to see the ealdormen and thanes of Bernicia. My father and brother seemed content to sit in Bebbanburg, knowing they were safe from any Scottish incursion, but at least they didn't try to interfere with my activities.

As the year 1005 wore on I decided that I needed to try and persuade the jarls and thanes of Deira that we needed to make common cause against the Scots. However, when I tried to call them together for a meeting, Ælfhelm sent men to warn me to keep out of his earldom.

I was still debating what to do when news reached me of Malcolm's campaign in the north of Scotland. Eric Håkonsson - the jarl who had been one of the triumvirate who had killed Olaf Tryggvason in the

Baltic and subsequently became ruler of Norway as Sweyn Forkbeard's vassal - had invaded Moray.

Moray was an area of north-eastern Scotland south of the Moray Firth. Its mormaer, Findláech, had ruled the area as a virtually independent king but, faced with Eric's invasion with three thousand Norsemen, he had hastily submitted to Malcolm and begged for his help.

The tale reached me in bits and pieces but it seemed that Malcolm had made a pact with Sigurd the Stout, the virtual king of most of northern Scotland and the Isles. In return for the hand of Malcolm's youngest daughter, Olith, in marriage Sigurd had united with Malcolm to oppose Eric. I felt pity for Olith, who I was told had barely reached thirteen years, for having to sleep with the elderly and fat Sigurd. It was one more reason for me to detest Malcolm.

The combined forces of Malcolm, Findláech and Sigurd had defeated Eric's Norsemen near Aberdeen at the mouth of the River Don and Eric had fled back to Norway with scarcely enough men to row half the ships he'd brought with him. Reportedly Malcolm had made a pact with God that he would build a church at Aberdeen and install a bishop to convert the local Picts to Christianity in return for his help.

Such piety didn't sound like the Malcolm I knew but, as I heard the story from several sources, including my own father-in-law, I assumed it was probably true. It was disturbing news for Northumbria, of course, because it now left Malcolm free to attempt to seize the rest of Lothian.

That was bad enough, but soon wild rumours began to circulate that Malcolm was raising a great army with the intention of taking, not just the land north of the Tweed, but that north of the Tyne as well. Gradually the rumours grew even wilder and people began to mutter that he wanted to settle his southern border on the Humber, thus incorporating all of Northumbria within his kingdom.

I didn't believe it for one minute, but such tales served my purpose and I now ignored Earl Ælfhelm and contacted the ealdormen of Deira directly. They were worried by Malcolm's plans, but not enough to flout the orders of their earl. Something had to be done about Ælfhelm.

~~~

'Malcolm has moved south of the Forth,' Hacca told me as he dismounted outside my hall at Duns one day in the middle of April.

He had brought with him all those of his thanes and warriors who did not want to join the the Scots invaders. In total Hacca had brought nearly a hundred nobles and their trained warriors. They were welcome reinforcements, but there was no way that they and the men I already had trained could resist the Scots horde. Hacca told me that Malcolm had brought well over four thousand men with him, including the wretched Owain of Strathclyde and his Britons. Against that I would be lucky to field eight hundred from Lothian alone.

'What will you do,' Hacca asked me that evening after I had sent out the summons for the ealdormen and thanes of Selkirk and Berwick to muster at the latter town.

'We will need every man who can fight from Bernicia and Deira if we are to have a chance of defeating Malcolm. What I need to work out is how to weaken him whilst inducing everyone north of the Humber to fight against him.'

'Without the support of your father and of Earl Ælfhelm I can't see how you are going to achieve that,' Hacca said gloomily.

'No, so the first task is to neutralise them. I have an idea but first I need to send a messenger to King Æthelred.'

~~~

I sent Hacca to hold the small fortress at Dunbar against Malcolm. It was situated on a rocky islet within spitting distance of the mainland and it was little more than a small hall surrounded by a low palisade, but it was impossible to assault from the land and could be resupplied by sea, so it could withstand an indefinite siege. As I'd hoped, Malcolm wasn't interested in merely raiding Lothian, he wanted to conquer it. That meant he couldn't afford to leave a stronghold like Dunbar behind him.

My intention was to delay him as long as possible and it worked up to a point. Malcolm spent a week fruitlessly trying to take the place before he realised that he was wasting his time. Leaving a small force of his warriors to invest it, he moved on. The men he left were men he could rely on not to desert when they got bored and so they were amongst his best men; at least that was something.

When he advanced down the coast he found that, in accordance with my instructions, the people had fled up into the hills taking their livestock and any cereals left over from last winter with them. As it was still early springtime there were no crops to harvest and no root vegetables to dig up.

That meant he was reliant on shipping supplies down from Scotland by sea or sending them overland via Stirling. If only I had my father's fleet we could have cut off supplies by sea because the Scots had very few warships to counter our birlinns. But I didn't, not yet at any rate.

I could do something now about the overland route however, and I sent Ulfric with fifty horsemen to intercept the resupply conveys and hide the carts they captured up in the hills. I would have sent Leland but he was ill and, I feared, not long for this life.

Starving men quickly become unhappy and we became aware that small groups of Scots were deserting Malcolm and heading back to their homes. However, it was only a trickle as yet.

I decided not to try and hold Berwick and so, much against the wishes of Uuwine and the local thanes, we withdrew over the Tweed at Norham and headed for Bebbanburg. We were camping at Norham on the south bank of the Tweed for the night when the alarm was sounded just before dusk.

A group of riders forty or fifty strong appeared whilst there was still just enough light left to see the banner at the front. It was the dragon banner of Wessex, King Æthelred's personal standard, but the rider leading the cavalcade wasn't the king. It looked more like a boy.

It wasn't until he dismounted that I realised who it must be and I went down on one knee.

'Edmund Ætheling, you are a welcome sight.'

The boy was one of Æthelred's many sons. He was not yet fifteen but he'd presumably been sent by the king because his elder brother was busy trying to defeat the continuing Danish incursions in the south of Wessex.

'My father sends you his greetings, Earl Uhtred.'

'Earl? I am no earl. It's my father who is Earl of Bernicia.'

'Not anymore; nor are you now just Earl of Bernicia, you have been made Earl of Northumbria by the Witan.'

'I don't understand, lord. What of my father and Earl Ælfhelm? They will surely oppose any such move to make me their overlord?'

'You don't need to worry about Earl Ælfhelm. He's met with, um, shall we say an unfortunate accident? He was ineffectual and worse than useless as far as opposing the Scots was concerned.'

I took him to mean that someone in his entourage had killed Ælfhelm to get him out of the way. It didn't sound like Æthelred to me. He preferred to get what he wanted by more devious means. I began to look at Edmund with new eyes.

'And my father? Has he been disposed of as well?'

'Hardly, not sitting in the impregnable stronghold that your family seems to have hung onto for centuries. No, I've merely sent him a message informing him of his demotion to Ealdorman of Alnwick, a post I believe your father had given to your brother, but without seeking royal approval, so it was invalid.'

'I see. Thank you, lord.'

'Call me Edmund, lord sounds so formal,' the boy said with a grin.

'Thank you, Edmund,' I said returning his grin.

He laughed and we went into Ulfric's hall in search of mead and ale with which to celebrate my new status.

~~~

Now that I could officially call on every ealdorman, jarl and thane in Northumbria to muster their men, I wasted no time in doing so and announced that the muster point would be York. I set off for there with Edmund and our men the next morning. Even the drizzle that soaked us before we'd gone two miles failed to dampen my spirits.

I decided to travel via Bebbanburg and install my own garrison there, taking those who were loyal to my father and brother with me to York. It would also mean that I could leave my wife and son there where they would be safe during the coming conflict. It was a sensible move in the circumstances, but I have to confess I couldn't wait to see the expressions on the faces of Waltheof and Eadwulf.

It was mid-morning before the bulk of the fortress standing high on its rock loomed out of the rain. The two banners – the dragon of Wessex and my own wolf's head on its blood red background – hung sodden and limp from their poles so Edmund sent one of his companions forward to announce us.

At first there was no reaction and we sat there for a few minutes until both of us lost our patience.

I rode forward and yelled at the men watching from the tower beside the main gates.

'You know me, I am Uhtred, Earl of Northumbria, and this is Edmund Ætheling, son of King Æthelred. He speaks with his authority. You have five minutes to open these gates or everyone within the stronghold will be declared traitor and outlaw. This also applies to your families who live in the village of Bebbanburg. Your wives and children will be taken prisoner and sold into slavery.'

We could just make out the sounds of heated argument coming from behind the gates and then they opened and we rode through them.

'Would you have carried out your threat?' Edmund said softly as we halted before my father's hall and dismounted.

'If I made the threat I would have had to follow through or no one would trust my word again, lord.'

'Remind me never to cross you, Uhtred,' Edmund said with a grin.

Of course I would have had to carry out my threat or be seen as a windbag who didn't mean what he said, but I would have hated doing so. No one was more grateful than I was that I didn't have to make good on it.

The detestable Eadwulf was waiting on the steps of the hall to greet us, if that's the right word. The expression on his face left us in no doubt that we were about as welcome as the plague.

'Where is father?' I asked without preamble, wondering if he had simply refused to come out to meet us.

'In the ground,' Eadwulf said without a trace of grief. 'He died a week ago, just after getting a letter from that puppy there,' he said, pointing at Edmund. 'It broke his heart. I am now Earl of Bernicia, in accordance with his wishes.'

'Did you not read my letter, Eadwulf? There is no Earl of Bernicia anymore. In view of your attitude I doubt that my father will even agree to you becoming Ealdorman of Alnwick. He and Earl Uhtred need nobles they can trust.'

'Who is now the captain of Bebbanburg?' I asked whilst my brother was still spluttering in protest.

'I am, lord.'

The speaker was a large man dressed in byrnie and a helmet with a nasal guard and metal ear protectors. At first I didn't recognise him. He'd been a young beardless warrior the last time I'd seen him. He removed his helmet and bowed.

'Horsa? Man, you've changed. I nearly didn't recognise you.'

'Yes, lord. It's good to see you again too. I'm pleased to say that your brother hasn't yet asked for

182

my oath of allegiance so I'm free to serve you, if you'll have me.'

'Of course, you are most welcome.'

After he had knelt and given me his oath he stood and we embraced. Eadwulf gave a snort of disgust and turned to go back into the hall.

'Wait, brother. This is no longer your hall and Edmund and I are eager to get out of this accursed rain. Horsa, you first duty is to escort Eadwulf inside to pack up his belongings, only his mind, and then he is to depart immediately.'

'Where do you expect me to go?' he asked pathetically.

'I don't know and I don't care, just so long as I don't ever see you again.'

Shortly afterwards I went up to the ramparts to watch him take the road south. He had taken three horses, one each for him and his body servant, and a pack horse. Two women, who Horsa said were his favourite slaves and bedfellows, followed him on foot. Our paths were destined to cross again, but not for several years.

~~~

We left the next day. I put Horsa in command of Bebbanburg with twenty of my youngest and rawest warriors as his garrison. It was Horsa who had been responsible for getting the gates opened the previous afternoon, contrary to Eadwulf's orders, and he had to kill two of the men who'd opposed him. The rest of the previous garrison of Bebbanburg joined my army as we headed for York.

I had been told that it had originally been a Roman fort housing a legion enclosed in stone walls. It had become the municipal centre for the north of Britannia: the Roman name for the province which would later become England. The Roman oppidum which had grown up around the fort had been unprotected. However, the population in those far off days must have been much larger. Now the civilian population and the garrison fitted within what remained of the walls.

These had fallen down in many places over the centuries and people had taken the stone for the foundations of their houses. It had been used to build the monastery with its imposing cathedral church; though not one as imposing as Durham. The walls had been patched with sections of palisade but, even so, I saw with dismay that these days there were several gaps in the defences.

A camp had sprung up outside the burh, along both banks of the River Ouse, for the army that was beginning to gather. Judging by the number of tents, there were at least a thousand men here already. Ulfric took the men who had accompanied me off to find a suitable site upstream from the rest whilst Edmund's men headed for the banks of the smaller River Foss which joined the Ouse south of York. Once I had taken the oath of allegiance to him as the representative of his father he would be leaving without delay.

The ceremony would take place in the cathedral in the presence of Archbishop Wulfstan and the assembled nobles. It was intended to reinforce my status as Earl of all Northumbria. Afterwards all ealdormen, jarls and thanes would come forward in turn to swear to obey me as their superior. Needless to say, a careful note would be taken of all those who failed to appear to take the oath. I would have liked to have acted against them promptly, but their punishment would have to wait until the threat posed by the Scots had been dealt with.

To my surprise and pleasure none of the ealdormen and only a handful of the jarls and thanes failed to attend the service in the cathedral. The service, the homily and the administration of the oaths seemed to take for ever but at last it was over and we could start the real purpose of the meeting.

'I'm delighted to see all but a handful of the nobles of Northumbria gathered before me.'

I let my gaze sweep over the rows and rows of men standing in front of me from my vantage point on the raised dais on which the altar sat. Wulfstan stood on the other side of the altar with Edmund beside him.

'I don't need to tell you that Malcolm and his Scots are advancing down the east coast. From the last reports I received from my scouts, he has diverted inland to cross the Tweed via the ford at Norham and has now entered Glendale, skirting the wilderness that is the Cheviot Hills.'

'Of what concern is that to us, Uhtred?' a voice called out from the midst of the Danish jarls. 'It is a long way north of Deira. We don't understand why you have allowed the Scots that far south without any attempt to stop them. Do you intend to hand all of Lothian and Bernicia to Malcolm?'

There was a murmur of agreement and then another of the Danes called out.

'Is it your plan to allow him into our lands without opposition just so we are forced to fight for you?'

I held up my hands and gradually the angry voices died away.

'There is no point in fighting a battle I am certain to lose. That would just open up the road south into Deira for Malcolm and his barbarians,'

I didn't for one minute think of the Scots like that. Many were wild and ill-disciplined for sure, but they were Christians and as civilised as any Dane or Anglo-Saxon, except for the Highlanders perhaps. But it didn't do any harm to let them think of the Scots as quite different to them.

'That's all very well but why should we follow you? You're an Angle and the last one that was foisted on us as earl was useless, just like all of you.'

I was about to point out that they had just sworn allegiance to me but I realised that I was losing the argument as far as following me as their war leader was concerned, and so I looked towards the archbishop.

'You have expressed your concerns and the earl and I have heard what you say. Allow us time to consider them. I suggest we meet here again in two days' time.'

~~~

I was staggered by what Wulfstan had suggested to me within an hour of the end of the war council.

'But to do that would make an enemy of the Bishop of Durham,' I pointed out.

'You told me yourself that you haven't slept with Ecgfrida in years. Not only would you gain the support of the Danish jarls by doing as I suggest, but you would also gain the opportunity to sire more children.'

I sat back in my chair and thought about what the archbishop was proposing. Styr Ulfson was the Ealdorman of York and the most influential of the Danish leaders. Furthermore, he was extremely wealthy, having made his money as a merchant trading in gold jewellery. He had a daughter, Sige, who was fifteen. I didn't suppose for one moment that she would welcome marriage to a man twenty years her senior, but this wasn't about personal wishes; this was about the survival of Northumbria as part of England.

It was also about my own survival, I reminded myself. I wasn't so foolish as to think that Malcolm would let me live if he got his hands on me. After all, he had tried to have me killed before. If he succeeded in conquering even part of Northumbria and incorporating it into his kingdom, he knew that I would stir up trouble for him by whatever means I could with the aim of driving him back out.

'How do I marry Sige, even if I agreed, when I am already married?'

'You leave me to deal with that,' Wulfstan said with a grim smile. 'There are certain advantages in being an archbishop.'

'Let me sleep on it,'

'Very well, but don't forget the war council meets again the day after tomorrow. Don't take too long to make up your mind.'

Despite not sleeping together as man and wife for nearly a decade, I was still fond of Ecgfrida and if I divorced her I felt that I would be betraying her father as well, a man I liked and who had been my spiritual mentor for almost as long as I could remember. It wasn't an easy choice.

The next day news arrived which made my mind up for me. The Scots had reached Durham and had laid siege to it.

'Why would they do that?' Ulfric asked me as we broke our fast together after hearing mass. 'They have ignored Bebbanburg and the other major fortresses and now they are trying to take one of the most impregnable burhs. Is the man an idiot?'

'Far from it,' I replied, trying to chew a tough piece of mutton and sounding as if I had a cleft pallet.

I gave up on the meat and spat it out, only for one of the dogs that lived in the hall to snap it up. I kept my hunting dogs in kennels but my predecessor as earl had liked them to live with him and I hadn't got around to getting a new home built for them as yet.

'Malcolm is clever. By laying siege to the burh where my father in law is bishop he hopes that I will come riding to his rescue. That way he thinks he can defeat me in open battle.'

'What will you do?'

'Nothing in a hurry. Durham can hold out for weeks, months even and Malcolm won't be able to assault the place, not without siege engines which he doesn't have.'

'Siege engines?'

It wasn't a term that Ulfric was familiar with but I had studied old scrolls in Latin and had a modicum of knowledge about catapults, assault towers and the like. The trouble was they were not a great deal of use when the place you were attacking sat across a wide river and on top of a steep-sided hill.

'Never mind. I'll explain what they are later. My immediate task is to unite the fighting men of all Northumbria under my banner.'

'And how are you going to do that? The Anglo-Saxons might all follow you but you need the Danes and, judging from the council meeting yesterday, few seem inclined to trust you.'

So I explained. Ulfric was against the proposal that I should divorce Ecgfrida at first; they were good friends and he was upset by the whole idea, but eventually he saw the sense of it from a strategic viewpoint. Not only would it identify me more with the Danes, but it would serve me in good stead once I took up residence in York as the ruler of Northumbria.

So, my mind made up, I went to see Wulfstan first so that he could dissolve my marriage to Ecgfrida and then went to call on Ealdorman Styr. Of course, Sige wasn't with him; she was with her mother and other siblings in Leeds. However, I was pleased to find that

I liked her father. Although rich and one of the most powerful nobles in Deira, he was unpretentious and down to earth. He dressed simply and adorned himself with just two gold arm rings and a gold crucifix around his neck. Most Danes were ostentatious about their appearance, wearing as much gold and silver as they could to advertise their wealth.

His one weakness was his desire to enhance his status and his wealth further. Allying himself with the new Earl of Northumbria appealed to his vanity and he readily agreed to give me his daughter in marriage. I couldn't help but wonder what the poor girl would make of this when she found out. It seemed that that would be sooner rather than later as Styr sent a messenger off to Leeds with orders for his family to join him as soon as possible.

Things were moving at a pace that I was uncomfortable with. My poor Ecgfrida wouldn't even hear that she had been divorced before I was re-married at this rate. Besides, I hadn't yet seen Siga. She might be young but she might also be hideous. I wasn't one of those men who could rut with anything with a hole between her legs. I prayed that she was attractive, but I wouldn't find out until we met at the altar, or so Wulfstan informed me.

He had decided, with Styr, that the wedding ceremony should take place immediately before the war council, and then everyone could go off and get drunk afterwards at our wedding feast.

'You didn't think to consult me?' I stormed at him when he told me.

Wulfstan shrugged, which annoyed me even more.

'It seemed to me that it was an ideal way of getting the Danes on side before we discussed the relief of Durham,' he explained.

'You should have asked me if I agreed.'

'Don't be petulant, Uhtred. It doesn't suit you. What would you have said had I asked you?'

He had a point, it was just that I didn't like being taken for granted.

'Very well. But in future don't make decisions that involve me without discussing them with me first.'

'I've got the message,' he said stiffly.

It was obvious that he liked being told off even less that I liked being ignored.

Early the next day I attended Lauds with the monks and the mass which followed it as preparation for my coming wedding. I ate little to break my fast as I was, I confess, nervous about marrying Sige. I had made a hash of my wedding night with Ecgfrida and I wanted it to go well this time.

It had rained overnight, making the path from the refractory to the cathedral muddy and I cursed as my new leather shoes and scarlet trousers, tied with yellow ribbons up to the knee, became splattered with brown splodges.

My bride wore a dark blue over-dress which only came down to mid-calf and so had escaped the mud. On the other hand the hem of the cream woollen under-dress was stained brown, not that I spent much time looking at Sige's clothing. As an unmarried girl her hair was worn loose; it would be covered during the ceremony, but for now it cascaded around her face in a glorious mass of golden hair.

Her face was oval with a petite nose and a full, rather sensuous mouth. As she drew closer I could see that her eyes were a rather piercing light blue. When she smiled demurely she exposed even white teeth. She was the prettiest girl I'd seen in a long time and any guilt I might have felt at divorcing Ecgfrith disappeared as I grinned back at her like an inane loon.

I don't remember much about the ceremony but I was sorry to see my new wife disappear with her mother when it was over. The realisation that the next item on the agenda was for me to convince the nobles of Northumbria to raise the siege of Durham hit me like a bucketful of cold water.

'Yesterday some of you doubted my commitment to you. You saw me as a Bernician and not as a Northumbrian. Well today I stand before you as someone who has put aside his Bernician wife in order to marry one of you, a Dane from Leeds. My home is now in York.'

A great cheer went up from the Danish jarls and also from the Anglo-Saxon thanes of Deira, though they were in the minority. My own nobles from Bernicia looked less pleased, however.

'That doesn't mean that I have forsaken my countrymen north of the River Tees. I intend to rule all of Northumbria from the Firth of Forth to the Humber with fairness and justice for all. But first we have to rid ourselves of the Scottish scourge.'

I nodded to two of my men at the back of the cathedral who came forward carrying a wooden board which they set up on the altar facing the nave so that everyone could see what was drawn on it.

'This is a map of Durham. The blue line is the River Wear; as you can see it curves around the burh on three sides, making it look like a pouch of coins. The river is deep and fast flowing and the banks on which the burh stands are steep. At the top of the slope there is a tall palisade so it is virtually impossible for the Scots to assault it on those three sides.

'They are camped here, to the north where the land is flat. The burh is defended by a palisade here,' I said, pointing with my sword, 'across the isthmus at the base of the hill on which Durham stands, and another here,'

I pointed again, drawing a line across the board where the distance between two parts of the river was narrowest.

'This protects the steep slope up to the top of the hill where the thane's hall and the monastery are located. So far the Scots haven't even managed to breach the first palisade. My plan is to advance up the east bank of the Tees and trap them between us and the walls of Durham.'

I would still have to cross over the Wear at some point but I could worry about that later.

'Have we enough men to defeat them?' one of the thanes from Lothian called out.

'Our numbers will be evenly matched, if the reports of their strength are at all accurate,' I replied.

'But they will be penned in without being able to manoeuvre. It's where our archers will be able to reap a rich harvest. Few of the Scots own byrnies, or even helmets, and many use small shields called targes. That leaves them vulnerable to our archers firing over the heads of our warriors to strike at their rear ranks.'

'Pah,' one of the Danish ealdormen said in derision. 'I've never found your bowmen much good against a shield wall.'

'That may be so, I said trying hard not to lose my temper. 'But the Scots don't use the shield wall. They charge en masse and rely on the fight turning into a melee, where their superior numbers and energy can overwhelm their enemies.'

'I doubt you will need all of us if what you say is true,' he said doggedly.

'Have you ever seen the Scots in battle? No? Well I have. I was fourteen the first time I witnessed how they fight and they destroyed a Norse army. I don't want just to defeat them, I want to make sure that they never come south of the Forth for a generation, and that means annihilating them. To do that I need every single man.'

There were still a few more questions but, from the atmosphere in the cathedral from that moment on, I knew I had won them over.

~~~

The first time I got to speak to Sige was at the feast afterwards. She was shy and demure at first but

194

after she had drunk a tankard of mead or two she lost her inhibitions and began to talk quite animatedly. She was not only beautiful, she had a fine sense of humour and a gift for imitating people. I'd feared that, at fifteen, I would find her gauche and immature with limited conversation, but she entranced me.

Oh, she didn't have the incisive mind that Ecgfrida had, nor was she as knowledgeable about the kind of things that interest men, but she was good at banter and she had an insightful mind as far as people were concerned. For that reason she evidently didn't like her younger brother, who sat next to her, very much.

He had just turned fourteen and his name was Thurbrand, which meant bear. He would have been better named Slange – snake. I quickly realised that he had a high opinion of himself. Whereas his sister could imitate several of the nobles present in an amusing, but not derogatory, way, Thurbrand expressed opinions of his elders that were snide and demeaning.

His mother sat on the other side of him and seemed to find her son funny. I didn't and eventually tired of hearing him deride people, some of whom were my friends.

'If you can't keep a civil tongue in your head, Thurbrand, then I suggest you keep it still before I tear it out.'

I had spoken in Danish so many of the Anglo-Saxons sitting nearby didn't understand what I'd said. However, from my tone and the way that the boy glowered at me afterwards, no one could be in any doubt that my new brother-in-law had displeased me more than a little.

Sige grasped my hand and squeezed it.

'Well said,' she whispered. 'He's a spoilt brat.'

His mother looked offended and glared at me whilst his father, sitting on my other side, continued to talk to his neighbour, the archbishop, without a pause. I guessed that his wife spoiled the little shite and Styr let her get on with it for the sake of domestic harmony. My new father-in-law might lack moral fibre if that were the case. I hoped I was wrong because I needed the man.

Thurbrand spent the rest of feast sulking, not uttering a word, despite his mother's attempts to cajole him into a better humour. His silence suited me fine. If I'd known the trouble he was going to cause in a decade's time I'd have had the nasty little prick quietly murdered, but hindsight is a wonderful thing.

~~~

At last Sige and I could leave the feast and be alone together for the first time. I was anticipating the moment like a love struck sixteen year old, but I was determined not to make the same mistake as I had with Ecgfrida. Sige was even younger than my first bride had been and I was no longer a young man. She must be dreading what was to come. I didn't think what her mother had told her would have prepared her at all well either.

By the time I entered my bedchamber in the earl's hall Sige had been undressed by her maid and lay in bed waiting for me. I started to undress myself but Sige got up and came to me naked. She undressed me in a way I can only describe as sensual. If I wasn't excited before, I was now.

I contained my urges as she led me to the bed and I forced myself to take my time, caressing and kissing her all over. By the time I had finished she was moaning with desire and I was also in a heightened state of excitement. Nevertheless I took things slowly to ensure that Sige got as much pleasure from our lovemaking as I did. If anything, I think she may have got more, to judge by the scratches on my back the next morning.

We made love twice more that night and again in the morning. Of course, I had no way of knowing at the time, but when I left her to lead the army north the next day my second son was already growing inside her.

~~~

If I wanted to kill as many of the invaders as possible to ensure that they couldn't invade again for a generation I needed to secure the old Roman bridge over the River Wear at Chester-le-Street. This was the only crossing point to the east of Durham and the route the Scots had taken on their way south. The only other crossing points were to the south and, if we managed to defeat them, they would hardly be likely to flee in that direction.

Originally built in stone, sections of the triple span bridge had been washed away and other parts had crumbled into the river over the centuries since it was constructed. It had been repaired in timber several times and the central span was now rather narrow. Four men on foot, two horsemen or a cart would take up the full width of it. It was therefore going to be relatively easy to defend it against a routed enemy.

My scouts had reported that both ends of the bridge were guarded. Evidently Malcolm appreciated its strategic value. I needed to take out both sets of guards at the same time and make sure none escaped as my strategy for trapping Malcolm's army depended on taking him by surprise.

I had left Leland on his sick bed and, to tell the truth, I didn't expect to see him alive again. I had appointed a warrior named Osric to replace him. He had been with me since we were both boys and I trusted him implicitly. I now gave Osric the unenviable task of picking thirty men to swim across the river two miles upstream. On my signal they were to surround and kill the guards on the far bank. It had to be coordinated with the attack on the Scots on this bank and so I allowed them four hours to get into position.

They set off just after dark had descended over the land. The sky was cloudless but it was a new moon so there was just enough light to see by without being too bright to give our plans away. My scouts had counted the Scots and their estimate was two score on the east bank, the side we were on, and a dozen on the far bank. I needed to cut off the men this side of the bridge or they would run across and Osric would find it difficult to contain everyone; some would inevitably escape to raise the alarm.

I chose Styr to lead his Danes in the main attack on the Scots on the east bank whilst I led the rest of my household warriors in a race to seize our end of the bridge before any of the enemy could cross.

The signal was to be a fire arrow fired at low trajectory over the river so it couldn't be seen from the main Scots encampment outside Durham. When I judged it to be around three o'clock in the morning I prayed that Osric and his men were in position and gave the signal for the archer to light and fire his arrow.

As it sped across the river I ran silently from the trees fifty yards from the end of the bridge with forty of my men close behind me. Styr launched his attack with his fifty Danes simultaneously. Of course many more trained warriors were available but I knew that if I took too many with me chaos would result and we'd either end up killing each other in the darkness, or some of the Scots would manage to slip away in the confusion.

I reached the bridge just as two Scots came haring towards me. I could hear the sound of combat coming from the area of their tents and prayed that Styr would quickly deal with the rest. I pulled my shield close to my body just as the first of the Scots thrust his spear at me. It glanced harmlessly away to one side and I brought my sword up, piercing his chest just below the sternum.

Before I could pull it out the second man thrust his own spear at my throat and I had to jerk my head to one side to avoid it. Nevertheless I felt a searing pain in my neck and knew that he had sliced into it at the side. Blood started to flow down onto my shoulder and chest just as Kenric reached my side and chopped my assailant's head from his body with an axe. The head bounced away into the gloom and the body collapsed at my feet.

He examined my neck and said that it looked worse than it was. Nevertheless I was losing a lot of blood. Just at that moment Uuen reached me and unceremoniously pushed Kenric out of the way.

'Lie down so I can sew it up before you bleed to death,' he told me, taking charge as if I was the servant and he the master.

I grinned at him. 'Yes, lord. At once, lord!'

He looked at me impatiently and I did as I was bid.

'Someone get me some river water and I need a clean cloth.'

A minute later someone handed him both and he proceeded to wash the blood away and press the cloth to the gash to slow the bleeding.

'Can you hold the cloth in place please, and press hard,' he asked Kenrick whilst he got catgut and needle ready.

Just at that moment Styr arrived, blood gleaming blackly in the moonlight on his arms and byrnie.

'It's not mine,' he said grimly. 'They're all dead.'

'Thank you,' I replied faintly.

Everything around me was growing darker and I began to lose a grip on reality. I saw Eadwulf coming at me with a sword and behind him Thurbrand was grinning slyly as he took coins from a man dressed as a Dane, but who I didn't recognise. Then everything went black.

When I awoke my neck hurt like fury and I felt extremely weak. I was still lying where I'd fallen and I became aware that Uuen was wrapping a bandage around my neck.

'Will he live?' I heard Osric ask someone.

'Yes, the spear missed the carotid artery on that side by a whisker, but the earl has lost a lot of blood. He'll be weak for a day or two until he recovers,' Uuen replied.

'Osric, did you get them all?' I asked, trying to sit up, but being pressed back into the prone position by Uuen.

'Yes, lord. No-one escaped. I took the precaution of putting four men a few hundred yards along the road to Durham and they caught the one Scot who managed to evade us.'

'Well done. Uuen, do stop fussing,' I told him impatiently. 'I feel fine.'

I felt far from fine but I needed the army to see me on my feet.

'Help me up, and get someone to bring me my horse.'

I knew I couldn't walk the six miles to Durham but I should be able to cling onto the pommel of my saddle for long enough.

'Lord, there is no point in exerting yourself until the army is ready to march, and I assume that won't be until dawn? Just lie there for now,' Uuen said, speaking to me as if I was a small child.

'And have rumours that I am seriously wounded start to circulate? What effect would that have on morale do you think? Now move and do as you're told!'

Uuen shrugged as if to say 'on your own head be it' and went to fetch my stallion.

'Oh, and Uuen,' I called after him. 'Thank you,' I said as he turned back to look at me.

He smiled, nodded and ran off towards our camp.

Chapter Thirteen – The Battle of Durham

Late July 1006

I suppose I could have left the main bulk of the army further south whilst we secured the bridge, but I didn't want to split my forces. Now, leaving two hundred of the fyrd under Osric's command to erect defences to hold the bridge, the rest of us turned about and headed south again along the east bank of the Wear.

When the Wear turned south west towards Durham we turned off the old Roman road that we had followed on our way north. Now we were making slower progress along little more than a track. I was worried about sending up a dust cloud which would alert the Scots to our approach but, thankfully, most of the track ran through a wood, which meant that the track was hard but not dry enough to turn to dust. Anything we did throw up would be hidden by the trees.

Two scouts came back to say that the Scots were camped in the open between the end of the wood and the palisade defending the approach to Durham. Like the palisade, the camp lay between the two sections of the river, Durham itself sitting on a hill around which the river flowed in a curve. I rode forward with the scouts to see for myself.

As I had hoped, we had them trapped, but it was late in the day and I didn't want to risk allowing too many of them to escape as night fell. We withdrew further into the woods and spent an uncomfortable night sleeping in the open. I still felt weak from loss of blood but, despite waking stiff and cold, I felt stronger than I had the previous evening. My neck hurt like hell though.

Uuen bathed the wound again and changed the dressing, muttering that it didn't seem to have got infected.

'Make sure you stay well away from the fighting,' he admonished me.

'I'm not a child, and you forget your place.'

'Please yourself. I just don't want to have to find a new master,' he said sourly.

It was only then that I remembered that he was a Pict by birth, a Scot in other words. He could have run off during the night and re-joined his own people. Not only that, he could have warned Malcolm of our presence and no doubt the king would have rewarded him, and not just with his freedom. The fact that he hadn't said a lot about his loyalty to me.

'And I couldn't have wished for a better body servant,' I told him. 'Thank you for looking after me so well. I owe you your freedom and, if you wish, I'll give you a farm after this is all over.'

'Thank you, lord. My freedom means a lot to me, but I have no wish to work the land. If you will have me, I'd like to stay as your servant.'

'I couldn't be more pleased. Now help me get this damned byrnie on without opening up the wound again.'

~~~

I was honest enough to admit that I'd be more of a liability than a help as a warrior that day, but it was difficult for me to stay safely in the background and watch others do the fighting for me.

As dawn was breaking the army of Northumbria formed up at the edge of the wood. We were as quiet as possible but there was the inevitable clang of spear point against helmet and the crunching of twigs underfoot. However, the Scots camp was quiet until one or two men appeared to make their way over to the west hand branch of the river to collect water whilst others used the east side to piss in and crouch in the water near the bank to defecate.

No one noticed us until the armoured warriors in the first three ranks advanced into the open meadow, shoulder to shoulder and carrying their shields before them. They were followed by everyone who could use a bow and then came the fyrd. I brought up the rear with fifty of my household warriors, all mounted. Their role wasn't so much to guard me; hopefully that wouldn't be necessary; but to hunt down any who managed to get past our shield wall.

When the cry of alarm went up, the Scots rushed out of their tents to gawp at us before frantically scrambling for their armour and weapons. The first flight of arrows was in the air, aimed at high trajectory, as soon as the warning cry was sounded. The wicked points came down to hit unarmoured bodies, killing and wounding scores. Almost immediately a second volley landed and then a third.

By the time that the Scots had thought to raise their shields, called targes, above their heads there must have been a couple of hundred who'd been hit. Even after they had the targes raised the barbed points stuck fast in legs and other parts of the body unprotected by the small shields. A few even penetrated the targe itself, pinning it to the hand holding it.

Then someone managed to instil some sort of order to the chaos in front of us and the whole mass of men ran towards us, howling their rage. They were in no particular formation, just a wild horde.

'Brace,' I ordered and my warriors halted. The front rank lowered their large circular shields to cover their legs and the row behind used theirs to protect the torsos of their comrades. Finally the third rank held their shields at forty five degrees above the other two to protect everyone's heads and shoulders. The archers withdrew and the first ranks of the fryd came forward to push against the rear row of warriors to help them maintain their position. The rest of the fyrd waited behind. I had trained them how to fight the Scots otherwise we could well have been overwhelmed.

The screaming wave of Scots hit the shield wall, many dying on the spears and swords poking between the narrow openings between shields like the spikes of a hedgehog. Others leaped in the air and landed on the upper shields before jumping down into the space behind the formation. This was where the fyrd came into their own. They were ready for them and killed them as they landed, before they had a chance to defend themselves. Those with daggers were particularly effective at slitting the throats of the Scots as they hit the ground.

Within ten minutes the attack was over and the survivors were running back to their camp to regroup. They left behind many hundreds of dead and wounded. As we advanced once more my men killed the wounded with a quick thrust into their necks.

The Scots had lost much of their bravado and they milled about at the edge of their rows of tents, unsure what to do. Then Malcolm appeared and urged them to form up ready to make one last attempt to break our shield wall. However, there were not so many now and we had suffered no more than fifty casualties.

'Archers to the fore' I ordered and this time the warriors parted to let them through.

Now they sent arrow after arrow at low trajectory at individual targets, concentrating on the leaders and those who had now managed to don their byrnies and vests of chain mail. The Scots roared again and started to charge. There was less than a hundred yards between the two armies and the archers only just made it to the rear in time before the shield wall reformed.

This time the attack was more measured. The Scots used their shields to protect themselves as they thrust through the gaps between our shields and they killed and wounded many more of us. But they were dying in droves all the same.

Men of the fyrd helped the wounded to the rear as the Scots finally gave up the attack and withdrew to reform once more. Now there weren't enough of our armoured warriors to make a shield wall three deep and so I gave the order to concentrate our strength in the middle. The wings would only be two deep. Furthermore our archers had nearly run out of arrows. I prayed that the next attack would be the last. It was, but not in the way I imagined.

This time the Scots formed up in one massive wedge with their warriors who had chainmail and the larger shields at the point. They would try and split our shield wall in half. I glanced to their rear where Malcolm and his mormaers, thanes and chieftains sat on their horses with his personal bodyguard on ponies. There were perhaps eighty of them in total. I had expected to see Owain with Malcolm but I didn't spot him.

As the Scots howled their war cries once more and charged forward the gates in the palisade behind Malcolm and his horsemen opened and the garrison came running out. There were only about fifty of them, all in chain mail with helmets, but behind them came about two or three hundred of the ordinary inhabitants of Durham.

They consisted of men and boys, even a few women, armed with butchers' cleavers, knives, pitchforks and wood axes. The Scottish king's bodyguard wheeled around to intercept them but they were stationary and didn't stand a chance. I saw one brave boy, who couldn't have been more than ten, dart under the belly of one of the ponies and stab upwards. The pony disappeared and his rider was quickly killed. Others were pulled from their mounts and dispatched in seconds.

Within a minute or so the people of Durham had destroyed the king's bodyguard and had started to dish out the same treatment to the chieftains and nobles. I even saw Malcolm's Royal Standard fall into the maelstrom of killing.

My attention then reverted to the main battle. The wedge hadn't headed for the centre of our line, but off to the right where there were only two lines of warriors, mainly Danes. They did their best to hold back the wedge, and many of the Scots at the front of the wedge fell, but the line buckled and then it split.

Our warriors fought hard against the Scots at the side of the wedge as it forced its way ever deeper into the fyrd behind the shield wall, but eventually a significant number of the enemy managed to force their way through.

I rode over and ordered the fyrd behind our centre and left wing to charge into their flank. The main fight had descended into a disorganised melee and when the fyrd joined in the fray the Scots were pushed towards the river. Seeing many of their comrades forced into the water, where they were swept away by the current, quite a few of the Scots renewed their efforts to fight their way clear and, having done so, fled north along the bank of the river.

We had won but I was desperate to make sure that as few as possible survived to reach Scotland again.

I sent my horsemen to chase them down and they pursued them all the way to the bridge at Chester-le-Street, where the routed Scots found it held against them by Osric. In flight most had thrown away their weapons and so, being trapped, a massacre followed. Some inevitably managed to get away but the border was well over a hundred miles away and comparatively few made it back safely. I heard later that only around eight hundred returned, and precious few of those were their nobles. Northumbria was safe from the Scots for a generation.

Unfortunately Malcolm wasn't amongst the dead, nor was Owain. The former had apparently fled upstream along the Wear until he reached a ford. I heard much later that it took two months for Malcolm to reach Stirling where he faced a furious reception and a challenge for his throne. It was rumoured that he had put down the revolt ruthlessly, killing every one of his male relatives so that there was no-one left to threaten his rule.

Chapter Fourteen - Thurbrand

Autumn 1006

I walked into the bishop's hall in Durham uncertain as to my reception. My exertions in the concluding stages of the battle had re-opened my wound and I had to suffer Uuen's admonishments as he replaced the broken stiches and re-bandaged my neck. Consequently I hadn't seen Aldhun in the immediate aftermath of our victory. The next day he sent a monk to my camp to ask that I come and see him to discuss *matters of mutual interest*, as he put it.

'Thank you for coming, Uhtred. I thought it would be better to meet here in the privacy of my hall rather than in the middle of your camp.'

'I understand. I'm sorry that I didn't have a chance to talk to you yesterday, after the battle, but my wound needed attention.'

It sounded like a feeble excuse but it was the truth.

'Yes, I hope it heals well,' he said insincerely. 'Look, I understand why you have put aside my daughter in favour of a Danish girl. At least I assume you did it to win the fickle Danes over?'

I nodded, not feeling inclined to explain myself further.

'You can't expect me to be happy about it though. She is my only child and I worry about the future of her and her son.'

'Aldred is now of an age to start his education and Archbishop Wulfstan has arranged for him to be taught with the novices at York until he is old enough to start his training as a warrior. Don't worry that I will favour any sons I might have with Sige; I assure you that Aldred will be remain my heir.'

'I would expect no less of you, but I'm relieved to hear you confirm it. But what of my daughter? I know that she doesn't particularly desire to become a nun so sending her to a monastery isn't an option.'

'One of my thanes, Kilvert of Thirsk, has offered to take her as his wife in return for a sizeable dowry,' I told him. 'Naturally I will provide the dowry.'

I had expended a great deal of my wealth recently and, although my share of the loot from the dead Scots would fill my coffers again to some extent, I had promised Kilvert to give Ecgfrida the vill adjoining Thirsk, which had been owned by the previous Earl of York, rather than gold and silver. In practice he would add it to his lands, of course.

'Very well, I will say no more, except to thank you for delivering us from the hands of Malcolm and his Scots.'

'I hope that we can part, at least if not as friends, as colleagues in the governance and spiritual welfare of Northumbria?'

'Of course; you and the archbishop will always have my support,' he said a trifle stiffly.

I kissed his bishop's ring and left. I must confess to being a little relieved. The meeting had gone as well as it could have done. However, Aldhun appeared to shun my company after that and I saw little of him in the following decade.

~~~

It took a little time to bury the dead and distribute the spoils. Our men were buried in individual graves in a newly concentrated cemetery a little away from the town, whilst the Scots were put in a series of common graves on the battlefield. Once the grass grew over them no one would know that the pits full of corpses were there.

I delayed my return to York until my neck wound had fully healed. As I gradually got better I started to exercise with sword and shield and to ride further and further afield. It was therefore the middle of August before I got to grips with the administration of my new earldom.

By then Sige had given me the glad tidings that she was pregnant and said that the midwife expected the baby to be born in March the following year. I was elated, of course, and quickly calculated when it must have been conceived. I had been away for nearly three months and I had a natural suspicion that the baby might not be mine. I was therefore relieved when I worked out that it was most likely to date from our wedding night.

I felt my suspicions had been unworthy when Sige showed me how much she had missed me on the night of my return, and every night after that, until I felt that we should refrain until after the birth. Even then she found ways to give me pleasure. The same couldn't be said for her family.

Styr had finally tired of his wife. Perhaps my putting aside Ecgfrida had motivated him, but he sent her to a monastery to become a nun, which left him free to marry another. I wasn't surprised to hear that the woman he'd chosen had been his secret mistress for a year or more. All this wouldn't have been a problem in itself but Thurbrand took his mother's side and accused his father of adultery. Furthermore he lodged a claim on her behalf for half his father's lands.

Although a sin condemned by the Church, in practice little was done to punish the adultery of a husband. On the other hand, wives who committed such a sin were harshly treated. Thurbrand's claims would not therefore have mattered very much had it not been for his mother's assets. She owned property and, as a divorced woman, she was entitled to a share of Styr's land as well, just as I had given a vill to Ecgfrida on our divorce.

As she was to become a nun, any property she owned would become the Church's, so Thurbrand wasn't acting to protect his mother's rights so much as to spite his father. As Styr was an ealdorman the case would have to be heard by me as his earl.

I was puzzled as to the boy's motives. As his father's only son he would be his heir and all his property would be his in due course. He was not only trying to reduce his inheritance, it seemed to me, but

214

also risking being cut out of his father's will entirely. Either the lad was an idiot or had very strong principles. From the little I'd seen of him, I didn't think it was the latter.

I decided to consult Wulfstan and see if he could shed any further light on the situation.

'Styr has never got on with his son, from what I've managed to glean. There are rumours that the boy isn't his but I have no idea whether that's true or not. They certainly don't look alike; he favours his mother in that regard,' the archbishop began.

'I don't have to tell you that the matter is sensitive. Styr is very influential amongst the Danes of Deira. If you find against him, as you should do strictly speaking, you will lose some of the support you gained by beating Malcolm at Durham. Of course, I should really encourage you to find against him because then, as a nun, his wife's property will come to the Church.'

'I'm not sure that you have been much help to me, archbishop.' I said with a grim smile.

'Perhaps not, but if I were you I would act justly and find against Styr but then fine him a paltry sum.'

'Thank you; that is much more helpful. Of course such fines are divided between the king and myself as earl but I suppose you would appreciate a small donation as well, as you could have expected at lot more?'

'You assume correctly, lord Uhtred.'

I remained talking to Wulfstan over a tankard of mead for some time and then returned to my hall in a much better frame of mind.

215

My hall was packed for the hearing. Styr arrived first with a number of Danish supporters and then his former wife came in with Thurbrand. They both scowled at Styr and went and sat on the bench set aside for them.

'It is customary for those attending my court with a petition to acknowledge me properly before taking their seats,' I pointed out with a frown.

Thurbrand got up and made the most perfunctory of bows towards me and sat down again, scowling at me.

'I suppose that will have to do, but you don't do yourself any favours, boy.'

Secretly I was pleased. His lack of respect to me in my own hall would make it easier for me to award his mother a paltry sum in compensation.

'Who brings the complaint against Ealdorman Styr?'

'I do,' Thurbrand said getting to his feet.

'I understand that you are fifteen and therefore legally a man?'

'Yes, of course.'

'I suggest that you show me a little more deference, boy, or I will dismiss this petition forthwith,' I barked at him.

Nothing would have given me greater pleasure but I didn't want to be seen as an unfair judge in front of the people who had packed the hall.

'I apologise Earl Uhtred,' he said glowering at me.

'However, if I have understood your written petition correctly, it is your mother who is the wronged party, not you, or so it is claimed?'

'That is correct; I speak on her behalf.'

'A woman has as much right to justice, as laid down in the law, as a man. I don't see why you need to represent her.'

'She has asked me to.'

'Very well, outline your mother's case.'

'The Ealdorman Styr committed adultery with a servant girl and then put aside my mother, his wife, so that he could marry the strumpet. We, that is my mother, claims her dowry and half of his lands in recompense, as laid down by law. He must also be punished for the sin of adultery.'

'I gather that your mother has now taken her vows as a nun, is that correct?'

I could see that it was so because she sat on the bench next to her son wearing the habit and head covering of a nun.

'Yes, that is true, but she wishes to give the lands and property to which she is entitled to me.'

'But as a nun she had taken vows of chastity, poverty and obedience. Monks and nuns do not own property of any kind. They have to surrender all that they own to the Church. You must be aware of this?'

'Yes, but she would have given me her property before she took her vows had my father not refused to give my mother what was hers.'

'Then she should have held off taking her vows until this matter came before me for judgement. As it is, any property she previously owned now belongs to the Church,' I explained. 'Is Archbishop Wulfstan here?'

'I am, lord earl,' he said, getting to his feet.

217

'Have the Church lodged a petition against Ealdorman Styr for half his lands and this nun's dowry?'

'No, lord Uhtred. Nor do we intend to do so. We waive our right to it.'

'Thank you, archbishop.'

'So it seems that the only matter remaining is the matter of adultery. Styr, do you admit the charge?'

'I do, lord.'

'In that case I fine you the sum of ten silver pence. Steward, what is the next petition?'

Thurbrand got to his feet, his hands clenched in fury.

'You have not heard the last of this, Uhtred, I will have my revenge for this travesty of justice,' he railed against me.

His hand went to where he normally wore his dagger but he, like everyone attending, had to surrender all weapons before entering the court. I had thought it a formality but it now seemed a sensible precaution.

'I fine you ten silver pence for disturbing the peace. Now get out before I have you arrested.'

Thurbrand never did pay his fine. A little later his father told me that he had left Northumbria but he didn't know where he'd gone. It wasn't until three years later that I heard that he was now in Denmark and was one of the companions of the fourteen year old son of the Danish King, a boy called Cnut.

Chapter Fifteen – Eadwulf Cudel

1009

My second son, Eadulf, was born in March 1007 and fifteen months later Sige gave birth to a daughter, but she arrived early and only lived for a few days. I was sad, naturally, but Sige was heartbroken and nothing I said seemed to help. She seemed to lose interest in everything, including our son. When I told her to pull herself together and look after the one child we did have we had a blazing row. I was probably tactless and I suppose I could have been more sympathetic, but it wasn't in my nature to mope and I couldn't stand it when others did.

In the spring of 1009 I set off on my annual tour of the earldom, holding court and delivering judgements, making sure that the fyrd were being trained and collecting the taxes due to me. I had hoped that Sige would come with me but she refused and so I took Aldred, who was now coming up to twelve, with me. It was, of course, my intention that he would succeed me as earl when the time came, so this would be a valuable learning experience for him.

Unfortunately Sige didn't see it that way. She was secretly hoping that I would cast Aldred aside in favour of Eadulf as my heir. Of course, I was still only in my late thirties and could expect to live for another couple of decades if I died of natural causes. Unfortunately there was always the possibility of dying in battle or of being killed in some other manner. Besides, it wasn't just my choice. The fact that Aldred was my eldest son would make him my natural successor, but it was ultimately a matter for the king.

I had watched Aldred grow up, of course, but I realised quite quickly after we set out that I didn't know my son as a person. I therefore took the opportunity to answer all his questions, and he had a lot – he was an inquisitive boy, and to find out what his ambitions and interests were. I was also interested in discovering his strengths and weaknesses.

I was pleased to find out that he was as unlike my brother as it was possible to be. He appeared to have high moral standards and, although he seemed to respect me, he couldn't hide the fact that he blamed me for casting aside his mother.

'Do you expect to succeed me, Aldred?' I asked him on the third day as we approached Bebbanburg.

'Isn't that up to the king to decide, father?'

'Theoretically, yes, but I'd be very surprised if he appointed someone outside the family. I like to think that I have the loyalty of most of my nobles and freemen and I don't suppose that they would take kindly to a stranger being made their earl.'

'Yes, I can see that, but you aren't at death's door yet and so Eadulf may well be a man before you are. Then there is Uncle Eadwulf, of course.'

'Eadwulf? He's lazy, incompetent and a fornicator. The ealdormen and the thanes don't respect him and the Church disapproves of his morals.'

'Nevertheless I've heard rumours that he's trying to gather men to his side.'

'Rumours? What rumours?'

'Well, the talk amongst the monks at York monastery is that he has a base in the Cheviot Hills and he is recruiting men.'

'Hmm, monks do love to gossip like old women so I suppose there may be some truth in that, but where is he getting the money to pay them?'

I hadn't really given much thought to Eadwulf since I had kicked him out of Bebbanburg. Perhaps I should have taken more interest in what he was up to, but I had more important things on my mind at the time.

'The theory is that he is raiding the Britons who have settled in the land to the west of Lothian.'

It seemed plausible. Although the Scots and the Strathclyde Britons had lost too many men to raise another large army until their young boys grew to manhood, raids on them were likely to result in retaliation, especially the theft of cattle and the burning of outlying farmsteads. I needed to put a stop to this before it got serious.

'Have you heard anything about the activities of my brother, Horsa?' I asked the man I'd left in charge of Bebbanburg.

'It's said that he had killed the family who owned land in Ettrickdale and established a stronghold there. He's gathered some hundred outlaws and leaderless warriors to his side.'

'Why hasn't Gosric done something about him, if he's murdered this poor family?'

'I suspect that Gosric supports him, lord,' Horsa said, looking uncomfortable. 'The family were Strathclyde Britons and he is worried about them encroaching into the west of his shire.'

It made sense. Gosric was the local ealdorman and he had raised his concerns about the expansion of Strathclyde with me before. But Gosric was being short-sighted. Stirring up trouble on his western border was likely to cause him more problems, not solve existing ones.

'Select twenty of your best warriors, they can join mine when we leave tomorrow.'

'Where are we going, lord?'

'To see Gosric first and then on to see my troublesome brother.'

~~~

It may have been early April but it was bitterly cold when I walked out of my hall at Bebbanburg just after dawn, made worse by the biting wind whistling in off the North Sea. I wrapped my thick woollen cloak with the wolf skin collar tight about me as I made for the stables. Most of the escort I had brought with me and the warriors from the fortress were already there and each was similarly dressed in a warm cloak, except for my son.

'Where's your thick cloak, Aldred? You'll freeze to death in that one.'

'Thought it would be warmer, father. I only have this one with me. It is impregnated with lanolin so it's good at keeping out the rain.'

'It's more likely to snow than rain today,' I told him severely, then relented when I saw how miserable he was.

'Wait here,'

I walked back up to the hall and searched through one of the coffers that contained clothes that I had worn as a boy. They had been kept for Waltheof's future grandchildren but, of course, I had never lived there after my first marriage and my brother had never sired children as far as I knew, which was surprising seeing how many slaves and drabs he'd managed to bed. I found what I sought and retraced my steps to the stables.

'Tie the cloak you're wearing behind your saddle and put this one on.'

Aldred staggered under the weight of the one I threw him. It was made from the pelt of two bears and it had been given to me when I'd been twelve. It had been my father's before me when he was just coming up to manhood. In the days when it had been made bears were becoming rare in this part of England, but were not unknown; now I didn't think any were left.

'Thank you father!' my son exclaimed, beaming at me with pleasure.

'Have you got gloves?'

223

He pulled out a pair of leather gauntlets and showed me.

'Put them on, and wear your arming cap to keep your head warm too.'

We didn't normally wear helmets when travelling, unless we were expecting trouble. They were uncomfortable and they made it difficult to see and hear properly. However, the leather or padded linen caps worn under them were useful for keeping one's head and ears warm.

We rode out of the fortress just over sixty strong. I wasn't expecting trouble, but at least I had the men to enforce my orders should it become necessary.

~~~

It was still unseasonably cold and we had just ridden through a light snow shower when the burh of Selkirk came into sight. Gosric came out of his hall with his wife and two daughters as we dismounted. The two girls were eleven and twelve and both of them seemed very interested in my son in his bearskin cloak. I glanced at Aldred and noted that he was studying them, albeit rather shyly. I tried to remember if I was interested in girls at his age and suspected that I was just becoming aware of them. I smiled to myself. My son was growing up.

'Welcome, Earl Uhtred, this is unexpected. We thought you were visiting us in a month's time.'

Selkirk, like all the seats of my ealdormen, was on the list of places to visit but I had changed the itinerary in order to deal with the problem of Eadwulf first.

'My apologies, Gosric. I have come early because of disturbing tidings which have reached me, but that can wait until we are inside, away from this cursed snow.'

'Of course, forgive me. Come into the hall.'

Once inside I greeted his wife, who I'd met before, and he introduced his daughters, Æðelhild and Hereswið. I in turn introduced Aldred and the two girls looked down demurely, simpering, before looking up at him coyly through lowered lids. I had a feeling that Gosric was going to have problems with those two. They seemed rather too practiced in the art of attracting boys, given their ages. Certainly Aldred couldn't take his eyes off them, especially the elder of the two. I decided that it was time that I had a talk with my son.

However, that would have to wait. When we ate Æðelhild and Hereswið sat either side of Aldred and they vied for his attention. I could see that he was lapping it up until their mother scolded them for being brazen. I could tell from my son's expression that he didn't know what the word meant but he too curbed his high spirits when the two girls started to behave more demurely.

As soon as they and the women had left I leaned close to Gosric, hoping that he was still sober enough for us to have a sensible conversation.

'I understand that my brother has been raiding the Britons who have settled to the west of here,' I began in a conversational tone.

Gosric shifted uncomfortably in his seat before replying.

'So I understand.'

'What have you done about it?' I said, keeping my tone neutral.

'Done? Nothing, it's outside my shire.'

'You do realise the likely consequences of Eadwulf's raids?'

'It dissuades more settlers from encroaching into the disputed land between Lothian and Strathclyde,' he said defensively.

'Perhaps, but it is also likely to persuade Owain to take action to defend his people, and that could prove serious for you and your shire.'

'But, like Malcolm, Owain lost many of his men of fighting age at Durham.'

'Except that Owain himself and half of his army were away foraging at the time of the battle, so he can probably still raise the best part of a thousand fighters if he had to.'

'Oh, I wasn't aware of that.'

'Nor was I until recently. A party of monks visited York from Iona and they told the archbishop.'

Like Lindisfarne, Iona had been abandoned in the ninth century when the monks who survived its destruction by Vikings moved to Kells in Ireland but, unlike the community of Lindisfarne, the monks had returned a few decades ago under the protection of Amlaíb Cuarán, the Norse King of Dublin. He was now buried there but the protection of the monastery had continued under the present king, Sigtrygg Silkbeard, who was said to a very devout Christian.

'So you see it is very much in your interest, and mine, that the activities of my brother cease immediately. It might help if you sent wergeld to Owain.'

Wergeld was the payment made to the family of a murdered or injured man to stop a blood feud between the perpetrator's and the victim's family developing.

'Wergeld, why me? It's your brother who is the culprit.'

'And you expect me to believe that he hasn't been paying you part of the proceeds to turn a blind eye?'

Gosric refused to meet my eye and muttered something about any payment being part of his due as taxes.

'Oh, and have these taxes been declared to my steward?' I asked, knowing full well that they hadn't been.

He sighed and scowled at me.

'Very well, how much wergeld must I send?'

'Everything that Eadwulf has given you. My brother will add the rest from what he has stolen.'

'He has gathered a sizeable band of desperate men around him. The men you have brought with you won't be enough to overcome them, not without significant losses.'

'In that case you had better summon your nearest thanes and their household warriors and muster as many of the fyrd as you can in the next two days.'

~~~

When I saw him at mass the next morning Gosric had evidently decided to cooperate fully with me and by dawn on the third day some thirty thanes and warriors had arrived, together with a hundred and twenty members of the fyrd. Added to Gosric's own warband, I now had well over two hundred men with which to confront my brother.

We travelled slowly as most of my little force were on foot. It was obvious that word of our coming would reach Eadwulf and so I sent all those on horseback, some fifty five men in all, to circle around my brother's camp on the Yarrow Water and stop him escaping into the vastness of Ettrick Forest.

We could see the hall built of wattle and daub with a turf roof half a mile away as we approached along the valley. There were a few outbuildings, constructed in the same manner, but no other dwellings. Presumably my brother's men lived in the hall with him. When we got there, advancing in shield wall formation just in case of attack, we found the place deserted apart from a dozen slave girls and a few boys.

When Horsa arrived with the horsemen half an hour later we knew that Eadwulf had escaped my clutches.

'Do you know where Eadwulf and his men have gone?' I asked the slaves, who clustered in front of me like a flock of sheep penned in by a pack of wolves; that is all except one. She had fiery red hair and, as I soon discovered, a temperament to match. She glared at me defiantly and I addressed my remarks to her.

'I'm not going to harm you. If you tell me the truth I'll set you free.'

'How do we know we can trust you? One of your men said that you were Eadwulf's brother.'

'I am and we couldn't be more dissimilar. I'm Uhtred, Earl of Northumbria, and I've come to stop Eadwulf's raids in the wild lands to the west. Am I correct in assuming that you are a Briton from Strathclyde?'

It wasn't much of a guess. That had to be where these slaves had all come from and, although the redhead spoke good English, it was with an accent that indicated that her mother tongue was Brythonic, the Celtic language spoken by the northern Britons and similar to the tongue of the Picts.

'That bastard Eadwulf killed my family and burnt our farm to the ground after pillaging it and taking our livestock. Then the turd forced me to share his bed.'

'I take it you didn't do so willingly?'

She spat a globule of phlegm onto the ground.

'He raped me, not once but repeatedly, and he enjoyed it. If you find him give him to me and the other women. We'll castrate him and laugh whilst he bleeds to death.'

I suddenly realised that Aldred was listening to this with a look of fascinated horror on his face. For a moment I considered telling Horsa to take him out of earshot, but then I reasoned he would be twelve next month and the whole point of taking him with me was to broaden his education. Well, this was certainly doing that.

'Do you know where he is?'

'No, they left yesterday morning to go raiding again. There is little left within a dozen miles to the west and the north-west so my guess is that he had headed south into the Craik Forest.'

'Thank you. One further question. Why didn't you run as soon as he left you?'

'For the same reason we stayed when you appeared. The forest is full of wolves and we are a long way from our people. Two women did take their chances six months ago. Some of Eadwulf's men found them a week later. They had been partially eaten and they brought their corpses back to show us. We decided it was better to stay here alive rather than run and die.'

I nodded and let the slaves go so that they could get on with their normal tasks of preparing food for us and looking after the camp.

'What will you do? Gosric asked me when he, Horsa and the thanes were seated in Eadwulf's hovel of a hall drinking possibly the worst ale I'd ever tasted.

'Send out scouts to give warning of his return. Then we'll ambush him and his men as soon as they enter this hall. I want him alive but the rest can die.'

The interior of the hall was lit only by the open door, two shuttered windows and the hole in the roof that allowed most of the smoke to escape. When they entered the gloomy hall from broad daylight it would take time for their eyes to adjust. All my warriors had to do was to stand still against the walls and then attack whilst the enemy was still blind. Those still outside could be dealt with by archers up in the roof and the fyrd concealed in the outbuildings.

Had it been a sunny day the plan might have worked perfectly, but the day they returned was gloomy and rain sheeted down out of the black sky. That meant that the contrast between outside and the interior was not as great as I'd hoped and the archers couldn't use their bows to good effect. Wet bowstrings reduce their range and power significantly.

As soon as the first dozen men entered the hall, shaking the water off their cloaks and yelling at the slaves to get the fires lit so that they could dry out, they spotted my men and drew their swords. We outnumbered them four to one so they were quickly disposed of, the sole survivor being my brother, but there were far more still outside than I'd thought and they were all experienced fighters, unlike the fyrd.

The thirty five outlaws and mercenaries were heavily outnumbered by the fyrd but they started to cut them down with ease and Gosric's men backed off. Unfortunately the rest of my warriors were lying in wait outside the settlement to cut off any who escaped. Therefore it wasn't until I stepped outside the hall that I saw the raiders re-mounting their horses unhindered by the cowed men of the fyrd, a dozen of whom already lay dead, that I realised that we were in danger of allowing most of the murdering swine to escape.

True, ten of my men now barred the track to the west but they were there to kill the odd escapee.

They wouldn't be able to stop over three times their number mounted on horses.

'To me,' I yelled back into the hall and launched myself from the top of the steps outside the doorway onto the back of the horse nearest me. I punched my dagger into the rider's neck and toppled him out of the saddle, then I used the sword in my other hand to cut at the head of the next man. It was difficult because the horse had panicked at the sudden change of rider and was being skittish. It wasn't a good blow and it glanced off his helmet but it struck his shoulder, breaking it. He fell from his horse screaming in pain. Suddenly a boy darted forward and cut his throat with a dagger – a boy wearing a bearskin cloak.

Aldred's valiant action gave the fyrd renewed courage and they rushed forward with a roar and started to drag Eadwulf's men from their horses and butcher them. By the time that the rest of my warriors had rushed out from the hall there was little for them to do except kill the last few. Two managed to ride away but they would run into my cut-off group.

It had been a little perilous for a time, but in the end the outcome was all that I could have hoped for, apart from the losses amongst the fyrd. We put our dead in a store shed out of the rain for now and piled the outlaws a little away from the settlement for the animals to feast on. We now had nearly fifty more horses which I decided to give to Gosric so that he could train his household warriors to fight on horseback. The plunder that Eadwulf had amassed was divided, half amongst our men in the usual way, and half to go to King Owain, together with the released slaves, in recompense for the raids.

'What did you think you were doing, Eadwulf?' I asked my brother when he was dragged before me. 'Trying to start a war?'

'You left me with nothing. What did you expect me to do, become a sell sword?'

'Hardly, no one would employ a mercenary who couldn't win a fight with a ten year old boy,' I scoffed. 'No, I gave you a farm. I expected you to settle down and work the land for a living.'

'I was born the son of an earl; an earl who left me his earldom until you stole it from me. I'm not scratching a living in the dirt,' he replied contemptuously.

'I didn't steal it from you,' I replied patiently. 'The king made me earl over all of Northumbria.'

I studied him for some time whilst he glared back at me.

'I should send you to hell to join your companions. However, you are my brother and, much I might regret that fact, I won't see you killed. I hereby declare you formally to be outside the law. I would advise you to go into exile. Give him a horse and let him go.'

To make someone an outlaw was the harshest punishment I could legally impose. No one was allowed to give Eadwulf food, shelter, or any other sort of support. To do so was to commit the crime of aiding and abetting, and the culprit would himself be subjected to the same punishment. Because Eadwulf

233

was denied the protection of the law, anyone could now kill him with impunity.

'Do you think it was wise to let him go?' Horsa asked me quietly when we were seated around the fire pit drinking more of Eadwulf's appalling ale. The only people within earshot were Uuen, who was drying my clothes, and Aldred, who was examining the sword I'd given him from my share of the plunder in recognition of his act of bravery.

'Probably not. Let's hope that he has the sense to stay out of England from now on.'

He did, for a while, but the next time I saw him I had cause to regret my decision not to kill him when I had the chance.

Chapter Sixteen – Sweyn Forkbeard

1013

In the four years after my brother went into exile we were left in peace in Northumbria. Owain accepted the restitution I made to him for Eadwulf's depredations against his people and there was another positive outcome. Because of the fate he and his men had meted out to the settlers in the forested hills between Strathclyde and Stirlingshire, no one else seemed willing to risk taking their place and the borderlands to the west remained largely uninhabited.

The rest of England was not so fortunate. Thorkell the Tall had raided the south coast in 1009 and had returned to pillage all over East Anglia and Wessex during the following three years. Each time Æthelred paid danegeld to Thorkell to make him go away and each year he returned. Finally in the spring of 1013 the king gave Thorkell and his Danes land and allowed them to settle near London.

Evidently Thorkell had been paying his king, Sweyn Forkbeard, a proportion of the danegeld he'd extracted from Æthelred. Now that this source of income had dried up the King of Denmark decided to invade England himself. However, his aim was not merely to extract a further bribe from the English king. He had gathered a vast host on the promise of granting them land in England. His aim was conquest and he landed at Sandwich in August 1013.

Initially this didn't affect us in the north. Æthelred had asked me to bring the army of Northumbria south but I was conscious that the Battle of Durham had occurred seven years ago and many in Scotland and Strathclyde who had been boys at that time had grown up and were now young warriors. Malcolm had started to make threatening moves again and so I explained to the king that I needed to stay to defend the north of his kingdom. Perhaps he thought I was dissembling but it was the truth.

Having to prepare for war again came as something of a shock after so many years of peace. My argument with Sige had long since faded into a distant memory. Oh, she still had ambitions for Eadulf, who was now six years old, but Aldred had passed his sixteenth birthday and was held in high regard by my warriors. The ealdormen and thanes had also accepted him as my heir, which pleased me greatly.

She had maintained a frosty silence for a while after my return from Selkirkshire, but she couldn't keep it up and we quickly returned to our previous intimacy. No children resulted, however, and our relationship wasn't quite as close as it had been before.

Gradually news filtered north to York. Sweyn had laid siege to London, trapping Æthelred inside. Surprisingly, Thorkell the Tall, who had been made an ealdorman, had proved loyal to Æthelred and was helping him defend London.

The burh had strong stone walls and Sweyn had no siege engines, nor did the Danes have the engineers to construct them. At the end of September he had given up the siege and rampaged his way through Wessex. By the time he'd reached Bath the ealdormen had had enough and Wessex capitulated. Sweyn returned to London and, realising that the odds were stacked against him, Æthelred fled with his family to Normandy. London capitulated and Sweyn sailed up the east coast and into the Humber, before travelling down the River Trent to Gainsborough.

At the beginning of November a delegation of my Danish ealdormen and jarls came to see me. I could tell from their sombre mood that they didn't bring good news.

'Lord, you will have heard that Sweyn's son, Cnut, has received the submission of Mercia?'

My heart sank. I had heard that he had taken Bedford and Oxford but not that the whole of Mercia had submitted to him. That meant that Sweyn and Cnut controlled all of England apart from Northumbria.

'So it seems that we are alone,' I replied glumly.

The men before me looked at each other uncomfortably.

'Earl Uhtred, Sweyn Forkbeard has announced that he is now the King of England and anyone who continues to resist will be branded a traitor; their lives will be forfeit and their families exiled.'

This was worse than I'd supposed. Northumbria would now have difficulty in remaining outside Sweyn's rule; few of my men would be willing to risk execution and the casting out of their families if I decided to resist. I doubted that I could have raised more than a handful to fight the Danes, and that would serve no useful purpose whatsoever. I might be many things but I was not a fool.

'There is more, Uhtred.'

This time it was my father-in-law who spoke. He handed me a sealed leather cylinder sealed with a wax impression I didn't recognise.

'It's from King Sweyn himself,' he muttered, not meeting my eye.

It was written in Danish and although I could speak both Danish and Norse after a fashion, I had trouble reading either language. Nevertheless I managed to gather the gist of what it said.

'My ealdormen and I are summoned to Gainsborough for Sweyn's coronation on Christmas Day and to swear fealty to him. He will also make announcements as to the future administration of his kingdom,' I told them, paraphrasing what I'd read.

I had resigned myself to transferring my loyalty to the Danish king; indeed I could see no other practical alternative. However, I didn't like the sound of the last part. Was I about to be deprived of my earldom? If so, I would fight after all, I decided.

'We will travel to Gainsborough together,' I announced. 'Each of us will bring five warriors, no more. That will be an appropriate escort without appearing to be threatening. We will meet at Selby three days before Christmas, then cross the Ouse at Howden. That will mean we can arrive at Gainsborough the day before the coronation.'

When they had taken their leave I sat morosely waving away any who approached me. I couldn't believe that my comfortable little world had been turned on its head in such a short time. What made it even worse was the fact that Thurbrand, Sige's brother who had sworn to have revenge on me, was now one of Cnut's closest companions.

~~~

In addition to the fifteen ealdormen of Northumbria, I had invited the bishops and abbots to accompany me. Only Aldhun pleaded sickness and didn't join us at Selby. Evidently he still hadn't forgiven me for divorcing Ecgfrida. I don't suppose it helped that her second husband, Kilvert, had also repudiated her after a while and she had been forced to become a nun after all. No doubt Kilvert had found her as cold in bed as I had.

As we approached the small town of Gainsborough we must have made an imposing sight. With my banner, that of the archbishop and those of the Bishop of Hexham and the fifteen shires flying over our heads, there were nearly a hundred churchmen, nobles and warriors, all mounted, followed by a long baggage train with our servants, tents and provisions strung out behind us.

Most of the forty ealdormen of Wessex, Mercia and East Anglia had already arrived, as had all the various bishops and abbots but Lyfing, Archbishop of Canterbury, was noticeable by his absence. He had only recently been appointed and had yet to receive his pallium from the Pope. That meant he was unable to officiate as archbishop and so that honour fell to Wulfstan of York. It had been something of an own goal by the Danes as they had killed Lyfing's predecessor, Archbishop Ælfheah, for refusing to cooperate with them.

Gainsborough seemed a strange place for Sweyn to have chosen as his administrative capital. It was one of the main towns of Mercia and had been the capital of the ancient Anglo-Saxon Kingdom of Lindsey for a time, but it was small compared to Winchester, London and York. It was close to Torksey, where the Great Heathen Army had overwintered a century and a half previously, so it may have had some emotional attachment for the Danes.

Sweyn had built a large new hall there for himself and his army of clerks and priests who were to manage his new kingdom. His army was based at Thonock, some two miles north of Gainsborough and only his personal guards, called housecarls, actually lived in Gainsborough.

We were met at the outskirts of the town by one of these housecarls, a large man dressed in chainmail that covered more of his body than a byrnie would have. Whereas a byrnie covered the top of the arms and the torso from collar to half way down the thighs, this man's coat of iron links included a coif which left only his face exposed and it was longer, covering all of his arms and coming down to the knees. It was split up to the groin so that it wearer could ride a horse. I was impressed by the extra protection it offered but I wondered how much heavier it was.

He wore a segmented helmet with a nasal similar to the ones we wore, rather than the Viking helmets of old. In his hands he carried a double handed battle axe and he had a shield on his back painted yellow with a crude depiction of a blue lion. There was a flag of the same design flying beside the hall and I later learned that this was the emblem of the kings of Denmark.

'Who are you?' he asked in heavily accented English.

'Earl Uhtred of Northumbria and this is the Archbishop of York,' I replied in Danish.

He seemed unimpressed.

'You go camp with others,' he said, again in his atrocious English.

'No, tell Sweyn Forkbeard that Uhtred of Northumbria is here with the archbishop who will place the crown upon his head. Without this man,' I said, indicating Wulfstan, 'he doesn't get to become king.'

At last I seemed to be getting through to him.

'Wait here,' he said reverting to Danish at last.

He told another two housecarls standing close by to keep any eye on us, though what he thought they were going to do faced with so many armed nobles and warriors I have no idea.

Gainsborough didn't even have a palisade around it, though there was one around the king's hall, so it obviously wasn't a site chosen for its defensive possibilities. I didn't know how many housecarls there were in total but I suspected not many more than a hundred. If we and the other ealdormen and their warriors camped down by the river had decided to attack they wouldn't have stood much of a chance.

But that wasn't likely to happen. I remained surprised how quickly England had capitulated when one considered the mighty struggle that Alfred of Wessex put up to defeat the last Danish invasion. It said much about the poor calibre of Æthelred as a king compared to his renowned ancestor.

'You and the archbishop may stay in the hall and bring one servant each,' the housecarl told them when he returned. 'The rest of you camp over there with the others.'

I looked at Wulfstan. He wasn't a man to have servants as such. His needs were taken care of by one of the novices each day in York and he certainly hadn't brought any novices on this journey.

'I'll bring my chaplain,' he said turning to beckon one of the more elderly priests forward.

He and I rode past the scowling housecarl followed by the priest and Uuen whilst Styr and the rest turned and made their way across to a campsite beyond the others beside the Trent. It might be further away but at least it was upstream of whatever filth the other contingents might deposit in the water.

The hall was evidently new; the ceiling hadn't been darkened by smoke from the fires below that both heated the place and cooked the food, nor did its acrid smell pervade everywhere yet. There were bays down each side which housed tables and benches for eating and drinking and which were used as sleeping platforms at night. The centre of hall housed three separate fire pits with more tables and benches between them.

At the far end there was a raised platform with one long table, more benches and a large chair in the middle – presumably Sweyn's throne. Behind that there was a wooden partition six foot high with a door behind the chair. That had to be the king's private chambers. The space was illuminated by a number of candles but the only natural light came from the door when it was open.

It was primitive to my eye; something from an earlier age. My own hall at York was built of stone with windows to let in light and wooden floors covered in rushes which were changed regularly. Here the floor was of beaten earth with everything from discarded animal bones, vomit and dog faeces trodden into it.

A harassed looking man I took to be Sweyn's steward came forward to ask who we were. When I told him he gestured to the side bays.

'Grab one of those for yourselves if you can find one without someone else's kit in it; mind you, you may have to share if this place gets any fuller.'

I was beginning to think that we should have gone with the others. I would have been much more comfortable in my own tent. When I caught sight of Thurbrand talking to another young man further down the hall I sensed trouble brewing. He hadn't seen me yet and I didn't want to cause a scene so I told Uuen to go and retrieve our horses.

'It may be best if I don't stay here,' I told Wulfstan, nodding towards Thurbrand.

'That may be wise. I believe the other man is Cnut.'

I didn't like slinking out of the hall like a whipped cur but I felt my position was parlous enough without Thurbrand attacking me or calling for my head.

I didn't see the archbishop or Thurbrand again until the day of the coronation. The ceremony itself was unremarkable and then it came time for each English noble, whether Dane, Angle or Saxon, to kneel before Sweyn Forkbeard and take his hands in theirs and pledge him fealty.

As the only earl present it fell to me to be the first and it was then that I caught Thurbrand looking at me with hate filled eyes as he stood beside Cnut. He made a move towards me but Cnut grabbed his sleeve and held him back, whispering urgently in his ear. I breathed a sigh of relief, but then I saw someone else in the crowd around Cnut and the sight shocked me. It was my brother Eadwulf. Unlike Thurbrand he made no move to attack me; he just stood there with a self-satisfied smirk on his face.

I knelt and swore my oath but instead of releasing my hands Sweyn kept hold of them.

'I know you have a reputation as a fighter and I want you to keep my northern borders safe, but at my son's request you are to reinstate Eadwulf as your heir. Do you understand?'

'I do, but my second son is half Dane. Wouldn't he be a better choice?'

'And how old is he?'

'Seven as yet, but I am far from an old man.'

'None of us can count on living long in these uncertain times, Uhtred. Certainly not for the decade needed for Eadulf to reach maturity. No, Eadwulf is my choice.'

His words chilled me and proved strangely prophetic, but for him, not me.

~~~

After the coronation and the oath taking we stayed in the hall to celebrate mass. It seemed that Sweyn was as devout as people said. Finally he got to his feet to explain his plans for the future governance of England. Certain ealdormen hadn't been invited to Gainsborough, it seemed. They were to be replaced by Danes. Some of the vills which had belonged to Æthelred, his family and those nobles who had gone with him into exile were confiscated and, whilst Sweyn retained some, he distributed the rest amongst his supporters.

Finally he explained that I wasn't to be the only earl. Whilst Æthelred had kept Wessex, Kent and Mercia in his own hand, he now created earls to govern these regions, all of whom were, of course, Danes. He also made Thorkell the Tall the Earl of East Anglia, replacing Leofsige who had been killed by Thorkell the previous year. It seemed that the man's temporary lapse in helping Æthelred to hold London had been forgiven; or perhaps it was just that Thorkell was too powerful to have as an enemy.

After Sweyn had finished we all sat down for the feast. To my surprise I was invited to join the king on the high table with the other newly created earls. I was given the place of honour on Sweyn's right handside with Cnut next to me. Thorkell sat on the king's other side.

'Tell me, Uhtred, is it true you defeated Olaf Tryggvason when you were only fourteen?' Cnut asked me whilst chewing on a leg of venison.

'You speak very good English, prince. I played a part in his defeat but the leaders on the day were my father and Malcolm, now King of Scots.'

'The same Malcolm you annihilated at Durham?'

'Indeed, although sadly he himself escaped.'

'You are a man to be watched it seems. I'm told that Northumbria is the largest earldom in England, is that true,'

'In terms of land area, yes, but it is sparsely populated, especially in the northern half, compared the fertile lands further south.'

'How many men can you muster then?'

'We had just over three thousand at Durham, why do you ask?'

'Malcolm is quiet for now but who knows how long that will last. The Forth is a long way north, I wanted to be certain that you could continue to hold the area without help from elsewhere.'

I didn't believe that was the whole truth. Yes, he might worry about Scotland, but I had a feeling he also wanted to know how strong I was in case I broke my oath of fealty.

We left early the next morning and were lucky enough to reach York whilst the weather was still fine. The day after that a cold wind blew in from the north-east and brought with it the first snow of the winter.

Chapter Seventeen – The Return of Æthelred

Winter 1014

That winter was another fierce one. By the start of January the snow covered the ground to a depth of several inches and there were few travellers about. News was therefore slow to reach us in York. It was milder at the end of the month and the snow melted, making many routes impassable due to flooding.

York had stockpiled food for the winter, of course, but it relied on buying more at the weekly markets. However, they were sparsely attended due to the difficulty in getting wagons through the thick mud which covered the roads and tracks. Those who did make it through didn't bring in nearly enough.

It wasn't anyone's fault, of course, but people had to have someone to blame and Sweyn became very unpopular. I did my best to help by sending my men out with packhorses to buy any surplus supplies that they could find. Naturally the inhabitants of York were grateful but I couldn't help worrying how the other towns in my earldom were managing.

The weather gradually improved and by the middle of February travel had returned to normal for the time of year. It was then that the news reached us. Sweyn Forkbeard had been killed on the third of February. He had been riding from Gainsborough to his army's camp at Thonock to see how they were faring when his horse had slipped in the mud and he'd been thrown. He wasn't wearing a helmet and his head was crushed when it hit a rock.

His death sent shockwaves through Scandinavia as well as England. He had been King of Denmark and Norway as well as England.

'You've heard that Cnut has returned to Denmark with his army to contest the throne which his younger brother Harald has seized. Apparently Sweyn had left him as regent whilst he was away and so it was easy for him to take the crown,' Wulfstan said as we sat in his private chamber drinking mead and discussing the implications.

'Have you heard who Cnut has left in charge here whilst he is back in Denmark?' I asked.

'Thorkell the Tall, or so I hear. He'd have been wiser to secure his position here and wait until after his coronation before tackling his brother. What will you do?'

I thought for a while.

'My oath was given to Sweyn, not Cnut and certainly not to Thorkell. It all depends on whether Æthelred has the guts to return and re-take his kingdom.'

In March he did return but it was Edmund, his eldest son, who took England back for him, ousting the earls imposed by Sweyn and the jarls who'd been given his father's lands. The Danes of Deira hadn't profited from Sweyn's conquest; indeed they were rather looked down upon by Sweyn's nobles, and so I had little problem in persuading them to accept Æthelred again.

By the summer Æthelred was back in charge of England and Wulfstan had been summoned south to crown Æthelred. It was unnecessary as he'd remained a king in exile in the eyes of nearly all his subjects, but it was done to mark his return to power.

I was at Bebbanburg in the middle of July when two letters reached me. When I had left York Sige had been fit and well. It therefore came as a great shock when I read that one of her maids had found her dead when she went to wake her two days after I had left. It was sudden and unexplained. All the infirmarian at the abbey could say was that her heart must have suddenly stopped beating.

I was devastated and immediately made plans for Aldred and I to return to York. My other son, Eadulf, would need me and there was the funeral to arrange.

I didn't open the second letter until we were just about to leave. Indeed I had forgotten about it until Aldred reminded me. It was a summons to London from Æthelred. He didn't say why he wanted to see me and I assumed that I would be required to re-affirm my oath to him. Of course, it could be because I had submitted to Sweyn and was to be punished. I cursed. Whatever the reason, it was the last thing I needed right now.

I reached York late on the third day, saddle sore and stiff having covered fifty miles every day. As Wulfstan was still in London with the king I asked the abbot to perform the service and we buried my wife in the monastery cemetery. Eadulf did his best not to cry but, at barely seven years old, it was natural for him to miss his mother.

London was a long way away, some two hundred miles or more, but I decided that I would have to take him with me. I couldn't leave him to be looked after by servants just after losing his mother. However, spending a lot more time in the saddle didn't appeal to me and it was too far for Eadulf to ride his pony; I therefore decided to go by sea.

I would have preferred to travel down from Bebbanburg by ship, but all our vessels were away trading at the moment. So I bought passage for myself, my sons, Uuen, Tonbert and seven other household warriors, or housecarls as they were now being called in imitation of the Danish bodyguards. It was a merchant ship called a knarr and, as we had a cabin, we were comfortable enough. However, I was a little concerned about pirates. Thankfully we were travelling in convoy and had a birlinn as escort.

Eadulf suffered from seasickness a little, but otherwise we had a good journey until we were level with a place in Essex the captain said was called Harwich. Suddenly three craft emerged from the estuary of the Orwell and the Stour and headed towards us on an interception course. Two of the pirates were Viking longships and the other was a smaller boat that the captain said was called a karve. The two bigger ships had thirty oars a side or more but the karve only had eight, indicating a crew of no more than twenty including the steersman, ships boys and so on.

We had eight seamen in addition to me and my men, making a total of nineteen, including Uuen. Numbers were therefore even and I was willing to bet that my warriors were more than a match for a few Vikings.

They may have been Danes who had been left behind by Cnut but it was more likely that they were Norse or Danish raiders who had crossed the North Sea and then lain in wait for unsuspecting merchantmen. The birlinn escorting us had twenty five oars a side and was therefore slightly smaller than the two longships. Nevertheless it headed for one of the Viking ships which turned to meet it. The other longship headed for the rest of fleet, which scattered in panic. All except for our knarr.

We headed for the karve, which turned to meet us. They must have thought us brave or stupid; they had no way of knowing that there were ten experienced mailed warriors on board.

We hid in the aft cabin until the Vikings grappled us and started to climb aboard. I admonished Eadulf to stay hidden and led the rest of us in a charge which drove half a dozen of the boarders back onto their own ship, leaving a few for the crew to deal with. I leaped down onto the smaller ship with Aldred on one side of me and Tonbert on the other. Vikings don't like to fight at sea wearing mail in case they fall overboard so our opponents only wore leather jerkins as protection.

A large man with a huge paunch faced me. He lifted his axe intending to split my head in two but I thrust the point of my dagger into his arm pit, forcing him to let go with that hand. The axe missed me and, before he could recover, I thrust my sword into his neck. He fell to the deck leaving me facing a Viking who couldn't have been more than twelve; no doubt one of the ships' boys who looked after the sail and acted as servants to the warriors who rowed her.

He wore no more than a tunic and trousers but he had a sword in one hand and a dagger in the other. I didn't want to kill a boy but he would have spitted me if I'd given him half a chance. He thrust his sword at me and I batted it away. The boy was quick and, before I realised it, he stabbed me with his dagger. Thankfully the blow lacked the power a man could have put behind it and it failed to part the links of my chain mail byrnie.

I saw my chance and brought the pommel of my sword down on the boy's head. He dropped like a stone. The blow might have killed him but I hoped that he was just unconscious.

I turned to look for my next opponent but it was all over. The Vikings were either dead or too incapacitated to be of any further danger. I went to check on the brave lad who'd stood up to me and I was pleased to find out that he was still breathing.

'Throw them overboard, I ordered, 'except for this boy. He's just unconscious. Tie him up.'

'The wounded too, lord?' Tonbert asked, unsure whether I really wanted to put the wounded over the side to drown.

'Yes, cut their throats first though.' I was in a hurry but there was no need to make them suffer.

'Then let's get this ship underway so we can go to the aid of the others.'

There were two other ships boys, both a little older than my assailant, but they'd both been killed in the fight. Leaving the knarr behind we headed for the second of the longships which had grappled the largest of the merchant knarrs. By the time we got there the fight for her was over and the Vikings were throwing the dead sailors over the side. We tied our craft to the other side of the long ship and no doubt the few warriors left behind on her thought that we were their fellow Vikings come to help; until they saw our armour.

By that time it was too late. Leaving the karve to drift clear, we swarmed aboard the longship and made short work of the six men and four boys left aboard. We cut the longship free and left the rest of the Vikings in possession of the knarr. Having only eight oars for manoeuvring in harbour, it relied on its sail for progress out at sea and thus it was much slower than the sleek longships. Aboard her the fifty or so Vikings were a danger to no one.

Now we headed for the fierce battle that was taking place between the birlinn and the other longship. Once more we came alongside the longship and poured over the gunwale. The longship was deserted except for five ships' boys.

'Surrender and you'll live,' I told them in Danish.

They looked a little puzzled so I tried again in Norse. This time they understood and reluctantly dropped their weapons. Leaving Uuen and one of my housecarls to watch them the rest of us jumped onto the deck of the birlinn. The deck was slippery with blood and faeces where wounded and dying men had lost control of their bowels and I very nearly fell over as I landed. The crew of the birlinn were giving a good account of themselves and, from a quick glance around, I estimated that an equal number from each ship were out of the fight.

Our arrival changed all that. We now outnumbered the Vikings and we set about trapping them between us and the birlinn's warriors and then cutting them down. When there were barely a dozen of the pirates left they surrendered. We had lost men, of course. Two of my housecarls had been killed and another three had flesh wounds, but we had saved the fleet, all apart from the knarr the Vikings had captured, which was now sailing away, tacking to and fro as it headed for Norway.

I gave the five ships' boys a choice: they could be sold as slaves in London or they could join the birlinn's crew to make up for some of our lost numbers. Wisely they chose the latter.

The boy I'd knocked out didn't join them. My sons needed a servant to look after them and so I gave him that option rather than the slave market in London. He gave me a murderous look but accepted. I made him swear an oath of loyalty on the Bible, once I'd confirmed that he was a Christian, and so Eirik entered my sons' service.

~~~

The captured Viking ships were designed for speed when rowed. The sail they carried could add to that speed when the wind was in the right direction, or it could propel the ship at a much slower pace when the rowers needed a rest. We didn't have the manpower to row them but relying solely on the wind didn't matter as the merchant ships moved at the same speed as a longship under sail.

We arrived in London without further incident and the captain of the knarr on which we had set out volunteered to sell the three Viking vessels in return for a ten per cent cut of the proceeds. Meanwhile we made our way into the city in search of the king's hall.

Centuries ago the first Saxon settlers had shunned the old Roman city within its stone walls, believing it to be full of ghosts. They had established a Saxon settlement called Lundenwic to the west. However, when the Great Heathen Army had captured the place they had occupied the walled city, which became known as Lundenburgh. When they were driven out Lundenburgh developed into an important government and trading centre and Lundenwic was gradually abandoned.

However, we weren't bound for the city. Fifty years ago Saint Dunstan and Æthelred's father, King Edgar, had established a monastery for Benedictine monks on the site of Lundenwic to the west of the city. Properly called the Monastery of Saint Peter, the locals called its church the West Minster to distinguish it from the cathedral church of Saint Paul in the city.

We sought lodgings for the night as guests of the monastery. It suited my purpose to stay there rather than in a tavern in the city. Monks were great gossips and I wanted to pick up any rumours which might explain why I had been summoned.

It seemed that Æthelred had been re-instated as king by the nobles of Wessex and Mercia subject to one condition: that the laws he had passed in previous years were repealed and a new code of laws instituted. This was why Wulfstan had been absent. He was charged with leading the team who were writing the new laws.

Æthelred's rule had not affected us much in Northumbria but it seemed that in the south the king had ruled haphazardly, to put it mildly. He enforced those laws which suited him, often harshly, and ignored those which might be detrimental to his interests. In other words he had ruled as a despot. It certainly explained why the nobles of England had submitted to Sweyn without much of a fight. They were glad to be rid of Æthelred, but then regretted it when the Danish king had placed his Danes in all the major positions of power.

However, much as that enlightened me about the background to what had happened, it didn't explain why I was here.

~~~

The king's hall had been a Roman basilica at some stage. It had fallen into ruin, like all the old stone buildings in the city, but Æthelred had employed masons to repair the walls with stone taken from elsewhere and had roofed it in timber overlaid with red tiles recovered from other buildings. It wasn't overly large but it was impressive.

What had been the nave many centuries ago was now the main hall and the three other sections of the basilica had been divided off to provide separate living accommodation for the king and his family plus a large room where those who administered the kingdom worked.

Like all halls, there was a fire pit in the middle of the hall with a simple hole left in the tiled roof for the smoke to escape through. The floor consisted of small mosaic tiles. It had broken up in a lot of places, exposing the concrete floor beneath. It looked as if it had depicted people, perhaps saints, at some stage but now it was difficult to be certain.

A lot of people stood around the hall waiting for an audience with either the king or his son, Edmund. Æthelred had sired eight sons and four daughters by two wives, the second being Emma of Normandy. The two eldest boys, Æthelstan and Ecgberht were dead, the former quite recently, and so Edmund found himself as the heir to the throne, something he hadn't anticipated.

To my surprise I wasn't kept waiting; the chamberlain took me through one of the side doors into a small room as soon as I had made myself known to him.

'Earl Uhtred of Northumbria,' the man announced as he opened the door and stood aside for me to enter.

'Uhtred, welcome. Thank you for coming,' Æthelred said standing behind a small table covered in scrolls.

There were three other people in the room. The Lady Emma of Normandy sat on a chair in one corner of the room and the other two people stood between her and the desk. I recognised Edmund but the girl who stood by his side was unknown to me. She appeared to be about fourteen or fifteen and looked so like Emma that she had to be her daughter. Like her mother she was very pretty.

'You will know that Sweyn's son, Cnut is gathering men in Denmark and Norway for another invasion,' the king said without preamble. 'As he is the elder brother, I had hoped that he would contest the throne of Denmark seized by his younger sibling, Harald. Instead it seems that Harald is assisting him to raise an army whilst Cnut's brother-in-law, Eric of Hlathir, who rules Norway on behalf of Harald, is apparently helping him to fund this new invasion.'

'We need your help to resist Cnut and drive him back into the sea,' Edmund put in. 'You rule all of England north of the Humber and your Danes seem loyal to you. Unfortunately the same cannot be said of the ones in the former Danelaw area of Mercia.'

I didn't hesitate. With my wretched brother and Thurbrand close to Cnut, I didn't imagine that he would hold me in high regard.

'Of course. What do you require of me?'

'Just be ready with your nobles, warriors and fyrd to come to my aid when I send for you,' Æthelred told me.

'On another matter,' he continued. 'I was sorry to hear about the death of your wife. I understand that you only have two sons and no daughters?'

I wondered where this was going. He can have only just heard about Sige's death and I was surprised that the news had reached London so quickly, unless one of my men had been talking in the taverns.

'I want to both reward you and bind you to me more closely, Uhtred. I therefore propose to give you my daughter, Ælfgifu, in marriage.'

To say that I was stunned would be an understatement. It was the last thing I expected him to say. So much for thinking that I might be out of favour. Then it occurred to me that he must have decided on this before he heard about Sige. He'd presumably expected me to put her aside in order to marry Ælfgifu. I was extremely glad that I hadn't been put in that position. Quite apart from my personal feelings, the Danes of Deira would never have forgiven me for casting Styr's daughter aside, especially if it was so that I could marry the daughter of the unpopular Æthelred. It illustrated once again how thoughtless Æthelred was. He should have realised that, instead of making the north more secure, it could have made the situation far worse.

'I don't know what to say, lord king. I am overwhelmed by your generous offer,' I temporised whilst I gathered my thoughts.

I snuck a glance at the girl, wondering how she felt to be given like a prize heifer to a man in his mid-forties. Perhaps I expected her to look horrified at the idea, or to be looking demurely at the ground, but she wasn't. She was looking at me quite boldly with half a smile playing around her lips. Perhaps she wasn't as averse to the idea as I had supposed. Certainly the thought of bedding her created a feeling of pleasurable anticipation in my loins.

However, the king seemed to have assumed my reply meant that I had accepted.

'Good. Well, you won't want to come back all this way again so soon, and I don't have the time to escort my daughter to York, so I suggest we arrange the ceremony for the day after tomorrow. I presume you'd like Archbishop Wulfstan to officiate?'

I had a feeling that things were getting a little out of control. Before the silence got embarrassing I nodded and confirmed that I would.

'I'll ask my son, Aldred, to be my groomsman,' I added. 'Where will the service be held?'

'Not in Saint Paul's; that damned man, Bishop Ælfwig, will insist on conducting the ceremony. No, in the church of Saint Peter in the monastery.'

Ælfwig had been appointed by Sweyn and had been confirmed in post by the Pope in February that year, just before news of Sweyn's death had reached London. Æthelred hated him for no other reason than Sweyn had selected him but there was nothing he could do about it.

'As to groomsman, I think that my son Edmund would be more appropriate, don't you?'

I bit back an angry retort and nodded curtly instead. I had nothing against Edmund; in fact what I'd heard about him had all been positive, but I didn't know him personally.

261

'In that case,' Edmund said with a smile, 'we had better explore the taverns of the city tonight so that we can get to know one another. Bring Aldred along too.'

Edmund was in his early twenties and I had a feeling that his idea of a good time would involve a visit to a brothel or two. I wasn't averse to the idea but I didn't want my son along for the ride. Besides we would make an odd trio as I was old enough to be Edmund's father.

'Perhaps that's not such a good idea,' the king interposed. 'It might embarrass the earl for his son to see him enjoying the delights of the city.'

Judging by the looks on the faces of Emma and her daughter he wasn't the only one opposed to Edmund's proposal, but I suspected that they didn't want me to go along either. Perhaps Edmund had a reputation as something of a rake. I had heard little about him so I didn't know.

'Don't worry, father. I'll behave myself. In fact why doesn't Edwy come along as well? He must be about the same age as Aldred.'

Edwy was the eldest of Edmund's surviving brothers and the last to be born to Æthelred's first wife.

'You might as well take my brother Edward along too,' Ælfgifu said with a giggle.

Edmund emitted a laugh, immediately stifled when his father glared at him.

'Don't be infantile, Ælfgifu,' her father said with some asperity. 'Well, I don't think we need to detain you any longer, Uhtred. I'm sure there are things you should be doing.'

I bowed and took my leave. I learned later that the twelve year old Edward was a scholarly boy renowned for his piety. I could see then why the idea of him frequenting taverns was amusing.

~~~

For a day in late July my wedding day proved unseasonable. It was raining and cold enough to make me shiver when I got out of bed. I had planned on wearing a new linen over tunic but changed my mind and pulled on a dark green woollen one embroidered with silver leaves instead. I wore light green trousers, tied below the knee with yellow ribbons, and brown leather shoes. The belt and the sheath holding my dagger were both studded in gold and my scarlet cloak was fastened in place with a gold broach with a large ruby in the centre. I hoped that I didn't look too much like a popinjay but I needed to look the part if I was to marry into the royal house of Wessex.

The evening in London with Edmund had not proved the ordeal I'd feared. Had I been twenty years younger and not accompanied by my son I would have relished all that the city had to offer but perhaps I had grown staid over the decades. Thankfully Edmund had used good judgement in picking our watering holes and, I suspect to my son's disappointment, a visit to a brothel wasn't suggested.

Aldred and Edwy had got on well together and were soon whispering to one another like conspirators; I could only guess what they were discussing but it seemed to cause them great hilarity at times. I found Edmund good company and he had a fund of amusing stories. I only hoped that I would get on just as well with his sister.

I splashed through the puddles to the church where Edmund and my sons were waiting. I was pleased to see that Edwy was also there. Although Edwy wasn't likely to become king you never knew these days and having friends in the right places could be helpful to Aldred later on.

Ælfgifu looked even prettier than I'd remembered from our one brief meeting a couple of days ago. I could tell that Aldred was smitten too; that wasn't a something I'd thought about. I still thought of him as a child but, of course he was a couple of years older than his new step-mother. I hoped that it wasn't going to develop into a problem.

The ceremony and Wulfstan's homily were both mercifully brief; the feast afterwards less so. I thought that the king was never going to leave so that Ælfgifu and I could be alone.

At last he got up and, wishing us an enjoyable night with a sly grin in his face, he left. Her maids took my new wife away to a guest cell, which was all the monastery could offer for our nuptials, and I remained trying to curb my impatience whilst I talked to Edmund and some of the other guests. After a decent interval, which was probably no more than ten minutes, I left and ran across the courtyard to the guesthouse, feeling like a boy who'd never made love before.

The cell was tiny and the bed was narrow and hard but it didn't matter. Ælfgifu seemed as keen to bed me as I was her. She was actually a little disappointed when I said that I was tired out. I slept soundly for some time but, if I imagined that I could sleep until dawn, I was mistaken. By the time we had to get up to attend mass I was exhausted. Exhausted but deliriously happy. I am certain that our first child was conceived that night.

~~~

'How was it, father?' Aldred whispered to me during mass.

'That's an improper question for a son to ask his father,' I replied primly, earning a reproachful look from the abbot, who was the celebrant that morning. 'But let's say I have rarely been as happy, or as shattered.'

Aldred looked at me in astonishment. Evidently it wasn't the answer he was expecting.

'I didn't mean that,' he whispered fiercely. 'I meant will you get on well together?'

'No idea, we didn't...' I stopped speaking; not because the abbot looked pointedly at me again for whispering during the service, but because I was about to say that we didn't get to talk much.

'Yes, I think we'll get along just fine.'

'Good,' my son said with a finality that meant he wished he had never asked.

Chapter Eighteen – Cnut's Invasion

1015

It took some time for us to reach York. Travelling with a covered cart for my new wife and her maids slowed us down to a walking pace, but at least it meant that I didn't have to worry about seven year old Eadulf having to ride all that way, not that he liked having to ride with the women.

It took me a little while to deal with the usual problems that came with governing the earldom but, as soon as I was free, we travelled on to Bebbanburg. Ælfgifu loved the rugged coastline and the stronghold on its vast lump of basalt rock so I decided to stay there for a while. It was whilst we were there that she told me that she was pregnant.

I suggested that she remain there whilst I conducted my annual, if rather belated, tour of the shires that made up Bernicia, but she would have none of it. She also insisted that Eadulf came with us which earned her the boy's undying affection. I realised that I wouldn't have time to tour Deira as well that year and so I sent Aldred on his own.

He thanked me for the opportunity to demonstrate that he was worthy of the trust I placed in him and I decided that I could use him more and more as my deputy, making life easier for myself as I grew older.

We were staying at the monastery at Melrose in early September when the message from Edmund reached me. I read it with disbelief, my cosy little world being shattered once more. I gave her brother's letter to Ælfgifu for her to read.

> *To Earl Uhtred greetings,*
>
> *I need your help. Earl Eadric of Mercia has put to death Siferth and Morcar, two wealthy thanes in Cheshire, for treason. They were in secret communication with Cnut it appears. I have been sent with a small escort to arrest Siferth's widow, who abetted them in this, and to seize their lands.*
>
> *However, upon arriving in Chester I found the Danes of Cheshire, Shropshire and Staffordshire in revolt, accusing my father of fabricating the charges against the two thanes.*
>
> *I am trapped in Chester, fearing for my life if I leave here. I have no idea where Eadric is; he certainly hasn't come to my aid. I need you to raise the army of Northumbria and come to Chester so that together we can put down this revolt.*
>
> *Your brother in Christ,*
> *Edmund Ætheling*

'You must go to him,' she said as soon as she had finished reading the brief missive.

'Of course, but I'll need to send you and Eadulf back to Bebbanburg and send out messengers to summon the men of Bernicia to my side and I don't have enough mounted warriors with us for both.'

'Then we'll stay here until an escort can come to take us to Bebbanburg. Don't worry about us. Send out your riders.'

She suddenly stopped what she was saying and frowned.

'Why just the men of Bernicia? Surely Deira is much closer to Chester?'

'Yes, but it's the Danes of northern Mercia who are in revolt. The two thanes who were executed were Angles, judging from their names. I think that this is all a pretext to distract us whilst Cnut invades; if so, I don't think I can rely on the Danes of Deira.'

'Oh, I see. What about Aldred? Will he be safe?'

'I hope so, but I'll send a messenger to warn him as well.'

Five days later I set off from Hexham with a force of a thousand men. It took us over a week to reach Chester, another old Roman walled town, where we found several hundred Danes camped before the walls.

When we appeared in battle formation they hastily formed up to oppose us, but they must have realised that their cause was lost, even before the gates opened and Edmund rode out at the head of fifty mounted housecarls and the town watch.

Three men rode out from their ranks and waited whilst Edmund cantered around their flank and came to join me. We greeted each other briefly and then we rode forward with my ealdormen to meet the rebel leaders.

'Why have you risen in revolt,' Edmund asked angrily as soon as we halted fifty yards away from them.

'Because your father acted unjustly, as ever, in killing two of our nobles and confiscating their land. You must pay wergeld to Edith, Siferth's widow as she is the only surviving member of the family.'

'I agree,' Edmund said with a broad smile.

I didn't understand why he had capitulated when we now outnumbered them.

'What? Why? You are meant to arrest her, not pay her compensation,' I said, looking at him in amazement.

'Because Siferth's widow is now my wife and so I would be paying wergeld to myself.'

The Danish leaders were as dumbfounded as I was and everyone began talking at once. Edmund held up his hand for silence, grinning like a loon.

'It's quite simple. We fell in love as soon as we met and were married a week ago.'

It all sounded very unlikely to me, but why would he lie I asked myself. It had to be true.

'You will all pay a fine for rebellion against your king and disperse,' he said, his face hardening. 'Whatever your grievance taking up arms against me was not the way to resolve matters.'

However, the Danes sat there, not moving.

'You haven't heard then?' the one in the centre asked with a grim smile. 'Cnut landed two weeks ago and is now laying waste the south coast. I hear that your father, instead of meeting him in battle, has scuttled off to London to hide behind its walls whilst

Wessex burns. Æthelred isn't likely to be our king for much longer.'

Edmund's face grew puce with rage but he managed to control himself.

'This changes nothing. You will be escorted back to your homes where you will pay the fines I impose. Do as I say or you will all be killed where you stand. Do you understand?'

Reluctantly the three Danes agreed and rode back to their men.

'I need you to stay here and see that they do as I ordered, Uhtred. I also want you to seek out Eadric and find out why he didn't come to my aid. If necessary you have my authority to arrest him. I must return to London and organise the defence against Cnut as it doesn't sound as if my father is doing so.'

I felt that I needed to get back to my own earldom and prepare its defence but I had little option but to agree.

~~~

Edmund hadn't specified how much each of the Danish nobles had to pay. One was an ealdorman and there were a dozen thanes. It seemed that in Mercia they had stopped using the Scandinavian term jarl some time ago but it meant the same thing: a landowner who owned at least one hundred and fifty acres and who led a band of warriors. I therefore decided that each should pay one silver penny for each acre they owned. It wasn't popular but neither was it excessively punitive. They reluctantly agreed.

It took time for me to visit each hall to collect the money and my own men were grumbling about being away from home for so long. My solution was to pay them a proportion of the fines; it hadn't been sanctioned by Edmund, but then he hadn't told me what the fines were to be so he would never know.

It was November before we were able to return to Northumbria. I never did find Earl Eadric and I later heard that he had defected to join Cnut. No doubt he felt he had little option. His own nobles were unlikely to forgive him for killing the two thanes and so flight was a sensible choice if he wanted to live.

I arrived back at Bebbenburg just as the weather broke. The rain turned to hail as we rode the last few miles, stinging our faces and making the horses skittish. It was with some relief that I entered the hall to be greeted by my heavily pregnant wife and both my sons. Aldred's tour of Deira had gone without a problem and he had returned to Bebbanburg safely before news of Cnut's invasion became common knowledge.

We were safe in the fortress but my conscience nagged at me. My place wasn't here, skulking in Bernicia; it was in York organising the defence of my earldom against the inevitable attack by Cnut. Nevertheless I decided to wait until the baby was safely delivered.

The winter started mild and wet and it continued like that until after the Christmas celebrations. My daughter, who we christened Ealdgyth, was born on the twenty eighth of December. Surprisingly, considering that Ælfgifu was only just fifteen, the birth had been quite easy, or so I was told. The baby was quite small, which had obviously helped, but cried lustily from the moment she emerged and seemed healthy.

In early January my wife insisted that she was fit to travel and so we set off for York immediately after the baby's baptism. This was conducted, not in the small church inside the fortress of Bebbenburg, but in the ruins of the old monastic church on the Holy Island of Lindisfarne. Many of my predecessors as lords of Bebbanburg had engaged a personal chaplain but I had never seen the need. The local priest from the village below the stronghold officiated and, if he objected to standing freezing to death in the windswept remains of the old stone church which had been destroyed by the Vikings decades ago, he never gave any indication. In fact I think he was pleased to be standing on ground under which Saint Aidan, the very first Bishop of Lindisfarne, and Saint Cuthbert, until his removal to Durham, had been laid to rest.

Ealdgyth was far too young to join us and she remained at Bebbanburg with her wet nurse. I had thought of sailing down to York, but there seemed to be storms every few days and so I decided we would have to travel by road. These had been turned into quagmires by the incessant rain and sleet, but the day before we were due to set out the weather changed.

If it had been cold on Lindisfarne for the baptism, made worse by the bitter wind, it was as nothing compared to the conditions when we woke on the morning of our departure. The bitingly cold wind blowing in from the north east now cut through the warmest furs, making us all shiver. The skies were blue without even a hint of a cloud and there had been a severe frost overnight. This was good news in one way as it meant that the deep mud was frozen but it made frostbite a very real possibility.

As the day wore on it got even colder but at midday the weather changed. White clouds scudded overhead at first but they got darker and darker as the day wore on. It became a little warmer, but that wasn't saying much. Thankfully the snow, when it came, was light and barely covered the ground.

We rode as far as Durham in some discomfort but without mishap. Aldhun greeted us politely enough but the atmosphere was as icy as the weather, especially when I introduced Ælfgifu to him. I was glad when we left the next day, despite the heavier snow that was now falling.

We were all soaked and very cold when we reached the hall of the Ealdorman of Catterick in the late afternoon and morale was at a low ebb. By now we were in Deira and my spirits sank even further when I heard what he had to tell me.

'The rift between the Danes and the Anglo-Saxons is worse than it has ever been,' he said as soon as we had changed into dry clothing.

Ælfgifu and I went and sat with him in front of the fire and gratefully accepted goblets of heated mead from a servant as he continued.

'The Danes support Cnut to a man; the rest of us are still loyal to Æthelred, much as he is disliked, due to the fear that we will be replaced by Cnut's followers if he wins.'

'I see. It sounds as if I've been away from York for too long.'

My comment earned me a glare from my wife; presumably she thought I was blaming her.

'Not that I could really have returned any earlier,' I added to placate her.

'With the archbishop still in London it has fallen on Styr's shoulders to try and hold Deira together.'

'Do you know where Cnut is now?'

'The last I heard he'd abandoned the siege of London and is overwintering in Gloucestershire.'

Ælfgifu and I went to bed with a heavy hearts that night. I tried to reassure her but I don't think she believed me when I said that ultimately her father and Edmund would triumph. To be honest, I found it difficult to be positive when the future seemed so bleak.

Chapter Nineteen – The Conquest of England

Winter 1015-1016

Surprisingly Ælfgifu seemed in a much better mood in the morning and we made love for the first time since the birth of Ealdgyth. Afterwards she became morose again and said how worried she was about the fate of her family, meaning her father and siblings. I resisted the temptation to point out to her that her new family was in the just as much peril if Cnut prevailed, perhaps even more so as my wretched brother and Thurbrand, both of whom hated my guts, were amongst his companions. It concerned me more than the fate of Æthelred, whose foolish decisions in the past were to blame for our present danger.

It was just over forty miles to York and normally we would have stayed overnight at the monastery at Ripon en route, but I was anxious to reach the town and find out the current situation for myself.

We were tired and saddle sore by the time we arrived. Thankfully there had only been the odd flurry of snow during the journey that day, so at least we were dry. Within an hour of my arrival I had two visitors, the Abbot of York and Jarl Styr.

The abbot came first and handed me a letter he had received two days previously from Archbishop Wulfstan. I ignored the flowery greeting and polite preamble and cast my eyes down to the meat of the matter.

The king and Edmund Ætheling have both returned to London and I fear that Æthelred is not in the best of health. He is, of course, now forty eight and showing his age.

That gave me pause for thought. I was only three years younger but, apart from the odd ache and pain, I certainly didn't feel at all old. I went back to reading.

Cnut and his army are in Gloucester. Edmund says that it makes sense as it is a good base for him. I'm told that from there he can strike south into Wessex or north east into Mercia once the better weather comes.

Cnut is a Christian, as are most of his men I believe, but it doesn't stop them from pillaging monasteries and churches, raping nuns and killing priests and monks. I fear for what is going to happen to England until this struggle for the throne is over. I have pleaded with Æthelred to come to some compromise with Cnut for the good of the people, but he won't listen. Edmund is, I believe, more flexible in his approach but, of course, he is not king.

Now I come to the point of my letter. Edmund has entered into negotiations with Earl Eadric to raise the

Mercians to join him and I understand that Eadric has agreed.

I read that with some surprise. I had thought that Eadric was out of favour with his Mercian nobles, both Danes and Angles, and had joined Cnut. From what Wulfstan had written it sounded as if he had managed to wheedle himself back into power, though I was at a loss to understand how he'd managed that. I hoped that Edmund had more sense than to trust him. The man was more slippery than a viper.

If Edmund is going to succeed he will need the assistance of the Northumbrians. I've heard that Earl Uhtred is still at Bebbanburg in the north, but hopefully he will have returned to York by the time you receive this. Either way you need to prevail upon him to join forces with Edmund; send a messenger to find him if necessary. Time is of the essence as I expect Cnut to recommence his attempt to conquer England in March.

I handed the letter back to the abbot with my thanks and asked him to show me any further missives he received from Wulfstan.

He hadn't been gone for more than a few minutes and I was still trying to collect my thoughts when Styr arrived.

'You've heard the latest tidings, I assume?' he said, getting straight to the point.

'The abbot showed me the archbishop's letter; I assume you know what it says?'

'Yes, I haven't read it but he told me the gist of it. I'm afraid that there is no hope of mustering the men of Deira to join Edmund. Nearly all of the jarls now openly support Cnut and, if you try to call a muster, it would just drive them into open revolt.'

'I suppose that I could call out the fyrd of Bernicia but it's been ten years since Durham and many a Scots boy will have grown to manhood in that time.'

'You fear an invasion of Lothian if you take away its fyrd to fight in Mercia?'

'Yes, in fact I'm certain of it. In any case, Cnut may decide to try and subdue Wessex first.'

'I doubt it. Wessex is recovering from the mauling he gave it last autumn. He can be reasonably confident that it will remain quiescent whilst he deals with Mercia and Northumbria, especially as Wessex has no one to lead it at the moment.'

'Æthelred?' I suggested.

'I doubt it. He's too old and sick; in any case he's no military leader.'

'Sick?'

'The rumour is that he's returned to London to die.'

'That could be a good thing. People will follow Edmund whereas their support for his father is lukewarm, at best.'

'That's true, but he really should have died last year, before Cnut invaded. Edmund might have been able to unite the kingdom then. It's too late now.'

I was going to argue but I knew deep down that he was right. I felt impotent but all I could do was wait and see what transpired when campaigning started in the spring.

~~~

To Uhtred, my son in Christ, greetings, the letter from Wulfstan which arrived in the middle of March began.

As you may have heard, Edmund Ætheling was betrayed by Earl Eadric and he has been forced to retreat to London.

I hadn't heard but it didn't surprise me. Eadric was a weasel who would betray his own mother for a pouch of coppers. Edmund was a fool to have trusted him. Once Cnut had finished subduing Mercia I doubted very much that he would turn south to tackle London or Wessex and it seemed that Wulfstan thought the same.

The rumours here are that he will wish to finish conquering everywhere north of the River Thames before he tackles the much more difficult nut to crack that is London. I hear that the Danes of your earldom aren't to be trusted so you have an impossible task if you wish to oppose Cnut.
I would tell you my own thoughts but I'm unwilling to commit them to paper. You can probably guess what my advice would be in any case.

I sighed. Wulfstan was a scholar and a law giver, not a soldier and he was against war on principle. However, he was no coward and, if he thought that there was a good chance that we would prevail against Cnut he would be in favour of resisting him. I knew in my heart that Cnut would be crowned King of England, if not soon, then eventually. The only way of stopping him was for him to die.

However, it wasn't Cnut who died but Æthelred.

The news reached York two days after it had happened. A ship arrived from London and no sooner had the captain told the port reeve than it became common knowledge. It appeared that Edmund had been proclaimed king by the Witan, or by those members of it present in London, and he'd been hastily crowned.

My initial reaction was one of optimism. With Edmund now in charge at last we might have a chance of uniting the kingdom against the invaders, but it was a vain hope and it changed nothing.

By the end of April Cnut had finished subduing both Mercia and East Anglia. By then he was back at Gainsborough, where his father had died. Instead of taking his whole army north into Deira, he split in it two, sending Thorkell south to continue to siege of London whilst he embarked the rest of his fleet and sailed north up the east coast to land at Whitby. By so doing he had divided my earldom in two.

'What do you think he'll do?' Ælfgifu asked me as the family sat gloomily eating a meal that none of us really had much appetite for.

Aldred was all for fighting, however hopeless our position whilst Eadulf just looked confused and frightened. Even the news that Ælfgifu was fairly certain that she was pregnant again did little to lift my spirits.

I had a stark choice. I could surrender to Cnut and rely on him being fair minded enough to protect me and my family from Eadwulf and Thurbrand, or we could flee into exile. Ælfgifu was the niece of Duke Richard of Normandy as her mother was the duke's sister. However, grubbing out an existence dependent on the largesse of another held little appeal for me. I was also conscious that I had a duty to act in the best interests of my people.

In the end I decided that I would have to submit to Cnut and hope for the best.

Chapter Twenty –

Treachery

Early May 1016

'You can't do it, Uhtred,' Ælfgifu stormed at me. 'You'll be betraying my brother if you do!'

'I'll be betraying my people if I don't,' I said wearily. 'Look, if I thought I had chance of defeating Cnut I'd summon every man who'd be willing to follow me and fight him, but he's got over three thousand hardened warriors with him and I'd be lucky to muster anything approaching that number. Besides, many of my men would be members of the fyrd and they would be no match for battle hardened warriors; and that assumes that the Danes in Deira remain neutral and don't join Cnut.'

'They would never openly oppose you.'

'I'd like to think that you're right, but it's a risk. Then there's Malcolm and the Scots to consider, not to mention Owain of Strathclyde. I daren't take men from Lothian, or Bernicia come to that. The Abbot of Melrose wrote to me yesterday to warn me that Malcolm is almost ready to launch another invasion.'

'You'd have thought he'd learned his lesson the last time.'

'All our victory at Durham gained us was time. Malcolm has made no secret of the fact that he intends to conquer Lothian.'

We sat in glum silence for a while before she spoke again.

'Do you think Cnut will accept your surrender and allow you to stay as Earl of Northumbria?'

I shrugged. 'He's allowed that traitorous rat Eadric Streona to remain Earl of Mercia,' I pointed out.

'That's true, though I don't understand why.'

'Probably because Mercia is far from accepting Cnut as king and Streona has been charged to wage war on those of his own people who have remained loyal to Edmund. I could never do that.'

'Your mind is made up then?'

'Yes, I'll send a message to Cnut at Gainsborough saying that I will remain neutral in the struggle for the throne between him and Edmund on condition that he doesn't pillage Northumbria. I'll point out the threat from Scotland and say that we need to keep the earldom strong to resist Malcolm and Owain.'

'I understand why you need to do this, but my heart is heavy with worry for Edmund. I can only pray that he prevails in the end, as King Alfred did.'

Everyone credited Alfred with beating the Danes and laying the foundations for a united England. In fact I believed that his only achievement was in preventing Danish conquest at that time by partitioning England between the Danes in the north and the Saxons in the south. It was his son, Edward, who united all of England, except for Northumbria, and it was Edward's son Æthelstan who finally defeated the Danes of Deira. My great-grandfather, Aldred, was Earl of Bernicia at the time and he'd acknowledged Æthelstan as King of the English, thus extending the latter's realm from the Channel to the Firth of Forth.

'We can certainly pray for his success,' I agreed, though I was far from sanguine.

I sent my messenger the next day.

~~~

'I've had a reply from Cnut,' I told my wife ten days later. 'I'm to travel to Gainsborough to submit to him personally. He says that I am to travel to the confluence of the Humber and the Trent where a longship will be waiting to convey me down the Trent to Gainsborough.'

'A longship? But there won't be room on board for you and your housecarls as well as the crew will there?'

'No, he must assume that I will come alone.'

'You can't go; you mustn't. It's a trap.'

'Perhaps. So I'll travel down the coast in my own birlinn, crewed by my housecarls. That way, if he does intend to ensnare me, we stand a chance of fighting our way clear.'

'Why risk it?'

'Because, having given me safe conduct, if Cnut breaks his word he will lose support amongst the Deiran Danes, to whom honour is more important than anything else.'

'I still don't like it.'

'I'll be careful, I promise.'

We made love that night, gently because of the baby growing inside her, and in the morning I, Uuen, Osric and forty housecarls set out in my largest birlinn. At the same time Ælfgifu rode away in the opposite direction, albeit reluctantly. I wanted her back in the safety of Bebbanburg, promising I would come and join her after my meeting with Cnut. I needed to return there in any case to coordinate our defence against the threatened invasion by Malcolm and his Scots.

~~~

The voyage down to the mouth of the Humber passed without incident. There was a stiff breeze most of the way and only one shower of rain so we arrived feeling fresh and ready for trouble. There was no longship waiting for us but I did spot a warrior on a horse on the south bank of the Humber who rode away as soon as we arrived inside the estuary.

We turned into the River Trent intending to sail all the way down to Gainsborough, some twenty miles away, but there was a chain across the river half way there manned by half a dozen surly looking Danes.

'You'll have to moor here and walk to wherever you are going,' one of them called across to us.

'I'm Uhtred, Earl of Northumbria, come to see Jarl Cnut, let us past,' I shouted back in Danish.

'It's King Cnut, Saxon scum, and I don't care who you are. No one goes further upriver without a pass from the king.'

I was surprised that Cnut was now calling himself king, but I supposed he could call himself whatever he liked; it didn't mean anything. The only consecrated and anointed king in England was Edmund.

We found a suitable spot on the opposite bank to the Danish guard on the chain boom and moored the birlinn. Leaving the shipmaster, the three ships' boys and two warriors to guard her, the rest of us set off on foot down the track that ran parallel to the river. It was now late in the afternoon and it would take us three or four hours to walk the rest of the way, crossing over to the east bank at Owston where there was a ferry.

I'd decided to go as far as I could down the west bank – the opposite side of the river from Gainsborough – just in case someone was waiting to ambush us. I had no intention of arriving at Cnut's camp during the night and so I decided to head for a farmstead and spend the night in a barn.

When we got there we found that the Danes had been there before us. The bodies of three men, two women and six children lay in the open. The women and the girls, even the youngest, had obviously been raped and every corpse had been horribly mutilated. My blood boiled and I was on the point of turning around and heading for York to muster everyone to my banner who would fight against men who could do such a thing. However, Osric brought me to my senses when he said that this was what awaited our people if I didn't submit.

We didn't leave until mid-morning having dug graves for the dead family and buried them with due ceremony. It took us a long time to cross on the ferry as it could only hold half a dozen at a time, so it was well into the afternoon before we reached an extensive wooded area a couple of miles north of Gainsborough.

By then I had begun to relax. I reasoned that, it Cnut meant me harm, he would have arranged for me to be attacked well away from his location. My logic was probably sound and perhaps Cnut was acting in good faith, but a few hundred yards into the trees I became aware of movement on either side of the track. I know that we were in for a fight when Thurbrand, Styr's estranged son, stepped out of the trees a hundred yards ahead of us.

~~~

He wasn't alone. Men emerged to form a shield wall in front of him and then I heard the unmistakeable sound of shields banging together behind us. I looked to the sides and I could see several Danes in the trees as well. We were surrounded.

'What do you want Thurbrand? I have a safe conduct from Cnut. Do you intend to dishonour him?'

'He may have granted you safe passage but I haven't, nor have I forgotten the way you humiliated me.'

'I count thirty ahead of us and presumably there are the same number behind us,' Osric whispered in my ear. 'I've no idea how many there are in the trees but we'd stand more chance against them I think.'

'I agree. Signal the men to break left, away from the river. Now!'

Our sudden move surprised the ambushers and for a moment I thought that we might be able to fight our way clear. I found myself up against a large Dane holding a two-handed double-bladed axe who brought it down towards my head. I sidestepped and held up my shield. The axe glanced off it, cutting into the leather covering and gouging a chunk out of the lime wood of which it was made. My arm went numb and I struggled to keep a grip on my damaged shield.

My opponent had expected his blow to meet solid resistance and, when it didn't, he overbalanced, staggering slightly before he recovered. It gave me the opportunity I needed and I thrust the point of my sword deep into his thigh, turning the blade to and fro to worsen the damage before I pulled it clear. He howled in fury and pain and, as I stepped around him, he tried to follow me, but his leg gave way. Before he could get up I chopped down onto his neck, cutting the spinal cord and he fell to the ground.

I took the opportunity for a swift look around and saw a number of things. Uuen climbing a tree, a rider on a horse watching the fight but making no attempt to take part and the furious hand to hand battles, many of which my men seemed to be winning. As a Dane came running at me from my right hand side I turned to meet him. It was at that moment that I realised that I knew the watching horseman. It was my brother Eadwulf. I might have known that he'd be involved in trying to kill me and I wondered whether Cnut would make him earl instead of my son Aldred. The thought depressed me but I pushed it away. I needed to concentrate on staying alive.

My attacker was young and inexperienced. I thrust at his groin and he lowered his shield to protect the area by instinct. It was feint and at the last moment I brought my sword up and thrust the point into the soft flesh behind his beardless jaw. It met no resistance and travelled up into the soft tissue of his brain. He dropped like a stone, dead before he hit the ground and I pulled my sword free, not without a little difficulty.

Initially we had gained the upper hand as we were more numerous than the men in the trees, but now the groups who had blocked the track ahead and behind us entered the fray and we found ourselves outnumbered by two to one.

Out of the corner of my eye I saw one of my men, a youngster called Wictred, kill his opponent and then run deep into the wood. The next moment I found myself confronted by two Danes. I blocked the blow from one sword with my shield and parried the other with my sword. I was hard pressed but I was holding my own against them. However, just as I had wounded one and the other was tiring, I felt a blow to my back. I was aware of the links of my chain mail parting and of something striking by backbone; I fell to the ground. I tried to get up but I couldn't move, and then the pain hit me. It was so great that I screamed in agony but then, mercifully, the pain receded and I felt everything becoming dim and distant.

After that there was only blackness.

Epilogue

Late March 1016 to Spring 1017

Uuen watched in horror from his vantage point in the tree as Uhtred was stabbed in the back by Thurbrand. As he collapsed to the ground the Dane thrust his blade into his master's back again and again until one of his own men pulled him away. Uuen watched in despair as one by one Uhtred's housecarls were killed until eventually there wasn't one left alive. However, he'd seen Wictred fight his way clear and then pause to look back before disappearing further into the wood.

He couldn't make his mind up whether the boy, at sixteen the youngest of Uhtred's household warriors, was a coward or had decided his duty was to survive to tell the tale. He knew Wictred a little and, after thinking about it, Uuen concluded that Wictred hadn't run because he was afraid. He too was determined to find his way back to Northumbria to let everyone know of the treacherous ambush, but he would have to wait until it was safe to descend from the tree.

It didn't take long for the Danes to strip the bodies of everything of value, including their byrnies, drag the bodies to the river and throw them in, to be carried downstream towards the Humber and thence out to sea. Half an hour after Uhtred had been killed Uuen was running north back the way they'd come that day. He reached the ferry just as it was about to depart to take a solitary passenger across. He recognised Wictred and the two embraced, both happy the other had survived. Neither spoke of what had happened as they were rowed to the other side; it was all too raw. The slaying of Earl Uhtred had seemed unreal to both of them at first, but by the time they reached the place where they'd left the birlinn the next day his death had sunk in.

The ship was still there and it took a while for them to relate their tale to those who had remained with it. Everyone looked over at the Danes on the far bank but they sat around laughing and joking, seemingly having no interest in the ship and what was left of its crew.

The four men managed to turn the craft around using the oars and, with a wind from the south east, the boys hoisted the mainsail to take them upriver. Uuen prayed that the wind would stay in that direction so that they could continue up the east coast under sail; there weren't nearly enough of them to propel the heavy ship by rowing.

'Should we return to York?' Wictred asked the shipmaster.

'We should get back to Bebbanburg and tell the Lady Ælfgifu what has happened,' Uuen cut in before the man could reply.

The shipmaster nodded.

'Yes, that would be best.'

~~~

At the end of March the following year Eadwulf rode up to the gates of Bebbanburg. Cnut had been furious when he found out the reason for Uhtred's failure to appear and submit to him. Consequently he hadn't appointed Eadwulf to succeed his brother but instead had made Eric Håkonsson Earl of Northumbria.

Thurbrand too was in disfavour but he'd been allowed to succeed his father, Styr, when he died in the winter of 1016. Eventually Cnut had relented and allowed Eadwulf to become Earl of Bernicia, but he would be subservient to Eric. He felt cheated but he had to accept Cnut's decision.

As Eadwulf neared the mighty fortress his scouts returned to tell him that a birlinn had just set sail from Budle Bay. He cursed. He had no doubt that it contained the nephews he'd sworn to kill, along with Ælfgifu and her baby daughters. Uhtred's death had done much to assuage the black rage that had consumed him ever since his enforced exile but he wouldn't be happy until he'd exterminated all of his brother's brood.

Much to his annoyance the gates remained firmly shut in his face; moreover Uhtred's banner of the black wolf's head on a blood red field still flew over the stronghold. Eadwulf used the same device but on a yellow background, as had his father and countless lords of Bebbanburg before him.

'Open in the name of King Cnut and Eadwulf, Earl of Bernicia,' the new earl's captain of housecarls called out.

Edmund Ironside had fought on after his father's death but with little success. Eventually he and Cnut had signed a treaty whereby Edmund was allowed to keep Wessex but Cnut became ruler of Mercia, East Anglia and Northumbria. When Edmund had died the previous November in mysterious circumstances Cnut was acknowledged as King of the English and had just been crowned as such in London.

'Greetings Earl Eadwulf, we welcome you as the brother of Earl Uhtred,' a voice called back.

'It's not much of a welcome when you keep the gates of my fortress shut against me. Now, open them immediately or face the consequences.'

'We will, of course, just as soon as we have your assurance that no harm will befall any who are inside Bebbanburg.'

'Who has the temerity to impose conditions on me,' Eadwulf shouted back, now getting furious at the delay.

'My name is Horsa. I am the captain of the fortress's garrison,' the voice replied.

'Not for much longer,' Eadwulf muttered to himself.

'Very well, Horsa. Open the gates. I swear I mean no harm to those who reside within. Those who are content to swear an oath of loyalty to me may stay; the rest may depart in peace.'

'Thank you, lord Eadwulf.'

The gates creaked open and the earl and his housecarls rode through the gates and up to the area in front of the hall. There they dismounted and stable boys came running to take their horses away.

Eadwulf stood in front of Horsa as the latter bent the knee to him.

'You may rise, Horsa. Get your men to surrender their weapons to my housecarls please.'

'Why lord?' Horsa asked looking puzzled.

'Because I say so. Are you questioning my orders?'

Eadwulf's eyes narrowed dangerously.

'No, of course not. Do as the earl says,' he said, turning to his men.

Once the last weapons had been collected Eadwulf grunted in relief. His men and Horsa's were roughly equal in number and he had been worried about a fight where the outcome was uncertain.

'Good, now kneel again and bend your neck.'

Horsa did as he was bid, thinking that the earl was about to ask for his oath. Instead Eadwulf drew his sword and brought it down on Horsa's neck. It was meant to be a killing blow and he'd expected to see the man's head bounce away, but it lacked power and his aim was poor. Instead of striking his head from his torso, the sword cut part way into the junction of head and neck and was halted by Horsa's collar bone.

He cried out in pain and then staggered to his feet, blood spurting spasmodically from the wound. His men were horrified and stood there stunned for a moment, but then they uttered a howl of rage and, despite the fact that they had no weapons, they attacked Eadwulf's housecarls, tearing swords and spears from the surprised men's grasp. The fight that Eadwulf had been desperate to avoid was happening all the same.

Realising that he was the target of Horsa's warriors' fury, he hastily ran into the hall and told the servants to bar the doors. He cowered inside until one of his housecarls told him that it was safe to come out, not without a trace of derision in his voice.

Horsa and half of his men lay dead and the rest had been subdued and were being tied up. Eadwulf had also lost over a third of his housecarls.

'Execute them,' he screamed at the captain of his men.

'No, lord. You promised them that they could depart unharmed,' the housecarl replied firmly.

'But they attacked you and tried to kill me!'

'Only because you broke your word and tried to kill Horsa.'

Eadwulf looked around at his housecarls and quailed at the mixture of derision, distaste and outright defiance that he saw there.

'Very well. The man is dead anyway. Take their byrnies and helmets and escort them out of the fortress.'

He knew he was being weak but he didn't know what else to do. He turned on his heel and stomped back into the hall in a furious mood, striking an unfortunate boy who happened to be within reach as he did so. The boy was thrown back and his head collided with the edge of a table, killing him instantly.

The female servants ran and cowered in a corner. They knew of his reputation and wondered which of them the new earl would take to his bed that night. Whoever it was wouldn't be in for a session of pleasant lovemaking.

Eadwulf slumped down into what had been his father's chair. This was not the homecoming that he'd dreamt of.

~~~

Aldred stood in the stern of the birlinn with his hand around Eadulf's shoulder as they watched the distant shoreline fade into the distance. The stronghold of Bebbanburg stood high above the sea below, dominating the coast. Below them under a makeshift awning made of a piece of sailcloth Ælfgifu tried to comfort Ealdgyth who, at eighteen months didn't understand what was happening, but was old enough to pick up on the sombre mood surrounding her. Baby Ælfthryth, Uhtred's posthumous daughter, had no such concerns. All she was bothered about was sleeping and being fed.

'Will we ever return, Aldred,' the younger boy asked sadly.

'Of course we will. And when I do, I'll kill Thurbrand myself. That I swear on our father's unburied corpse.'

He grew incandescent with rage every time he thought of his father's body, along with those of his warriors, being thrown into the water for the fish to feed on.

'What about uncle Eadwulf?'

'Oh, yes. Uncle Eadwulf.'

The emphasis he put on the word uncle made it sound as if it was something nasty he'd stepped in.

'His treachery was the greater because he was family, but killing him is not enough. He must be made to suffer first.'

The look of fierce determination in his brother's eyes made Eadulf frightened. However, even at the age of ten he realised that desperately wanting something and achieving it were two entirely different things.

To be continued in

THE BATTLE OF CARHAM 1018

Book II of the Earls of Northumbria Series

Historical Note

The end of the tenth century and the beginning of the eleventh was a time of change and uncertainty for the newly created Kingdom of England. The union of Angles, Saxons and Danes under one ruler was a fragile one, not helped by the growing power of the emerging Kingdom of Alba (Scotland) to the north and raids and incursions by the Norse and by Danes from across the North Sea.

Æthelred, whose nickname *unræd* means *poorly advised* but which has been mistranslated as *unready*, had succeeded to the throne after the assassination of his older half-brother, Edward the Martyr. His brother's murder was carried out by supporters of Æthelred's claim to the throne, although he must have been too young at the time to have had any personal involvement. Nevertheless, the manner of his accession got him off to a poor start.

The chief problems during Æthelred's reign were conflict with the Danes and unrest at home due to his corrupt and ineffective rule. After several decades of relative peace, Danish raids on English territory began again in earnest in the 980s. Following the Battle of Maldon in 991, Æthelred paid tribute to Olaf Tryggvason, a Norwegian who I have portrayed in this story as an invader of Northumbria, though there is no evidence that he did so.

In 1002, Æthelred is said to have ordered the St. Brice's Day massacre of Danish settlers. Whether he actually instigated the slaughter remains a question;

however, he doesn't seem to have done anything to prevent it or to punish those responsible. This xenophobic attack followed a succession of raids on Wessex by Danes from their homeland of Denmark. Any involvement by English Danes is questionable.

In 1013, King Sweyn Forkbeard of Denmark invaded England, whether this was to revenge the death of his sister and her husband eleven years previously or not, it does seem to have been a serious attempt at conquest. Æthelred fled to Normandy and on Christmas Day in 1013 Sweyn was enthroned as king in his place. However, Sweyn died five weeks later and Æthelred was invited to return in early 1014 after he'd promised to rule more justly. He seems to have defeated Sweyn's son, Cnut, quickly and he retreated to Denmark to recruit a new invasion force. It isn't clear what happened to Sweyn's army but perhaps they returned home rather than follow an inexperienced young man.

Cnut returned to England in August 1015. Over the next few months, he pillaged most of England. In early 1016 Uhtred campaigned with Edmund Ironside in Cheshire and the surrounding shires. When he heard that Cnut was about to invade Northumbria Uhtred returned and quickly realised that further opposition was futile and submitted.

Cnut summoned Uhtred to a meeting, possibly to get him to swear an oath in person. On his way there Uhtred and his escort of forty warriors were ambushed and killed by Thurbrand. It's unclear whether he was acting on instructions from Cnut or not.

When Æthelred died on 23 April 1016 his son, Edmund Ironside, succeeded him. It was not until the summer of 1016 that any serious fighting took place. Edmund fought five battles against the Danes, culminating in his defeat on 18 October 1016 at the Battle of Assandun. Edmund and Cnut agreed to divide the kingdom, Edmund taking Wessex and Cnut the rest of the country, but Edmund died shortly afterwards. The cause of death may have been due to wounds received in battle or disease, but it is certainly a possibility that he was murdered.

Intent on keeping his succession secure, Cnut sent Edmund Ironside's two infant sons to his brother in Sweden with orders that they were to be quietly murdered. Instead, the princes were spared and sent to safety to the Kingdom of Hungary. Other members of Æthelred's family, including his son Edward, later to become King Edward the Confessor, fled to Normandy. With the last of the House of Wessex in exile Cnut was now the undisputed ruler of all England and set about ruthlessly subduing any remaining pockets of opposition.

Uhtred was succeeded in Bernicia by his brother Eadwulf Cudel. Cnut made the Norwegian, Eric of Hlathir, Earl of York, thus balancing power in the north. By so doing he might have negated any opposition to his rule amongst the traditionally independently minded Northumbrians, but lack of cohesive government did make the North much more vulnerable to attack from the Scots.

He also killed the treacherous Eadric Streona and no replacement was appointed until Leofric, the husband of Lady Godiva, famed for riding through the streets of Coventry naked, became Earl of Mercia in 1030.

The story of Earl Eadwulf, the Battle of Carham and the loss of Lothian, the blood feud between Uhtred's sons and Thurbrand's family and the last of the Earls of Northumbria will be told in subsequent novels in this series.

NOVELS IN THE KINGS OF NORTHUMBRIA SERIES

Whiteblade
616 to 634 AD

Warriors of the North
634 to 642 AD

Bretwalda
642 to 656 AD

The Power and the Glory
656 to 670 AD

The Fall of the House of Æthelfrith
670 to 730 AD

Treasons, Stratagems and Spoils
737 to 796 AD

The Wolf and the Raven
821 to 862 AD

The Sons of the Raven
865 to 927 AD

Made in the USA
San Bernardino, CA
06 July 2020

74880345R00188